Dear QPB Member,

I'm delighted that you have a chance to take an early look at my book, *Knick Knack Paddy Whack*. As you will shortly discover it is either a greyish cautionary coming-of-age tale set in rural Ireland in the eighties written for the most part in the form of a deadpan monologue *or* it's projectile drivel.

I set out to write a funny, tender, and, I suppose, horrifying story covering all the usual hackneyed themes you'd associate with scaldy-faced adolescence but for me, the book, as well as life, is sort of about overcoming inarticulacy. Does that make any sense?

Ardal O'Hanlon

KNICK KNACK PADDY WHACK

A NOVEL

ARDAL O'HANLON

HENRY HOLT AND COMPANY ◆ NEW YORK

Henry Holt and Company, LLC
Publishers since 1866
115 West 18th Street
New York, New York 10011

Henry Holt® is a registered trademark
of Henry Holt and Company, LLC.

Library of Congress Cataloging-in-Publication Data
O'Hanlon, Ardal
[Talk of the town]
Knick knack paddy whack : a novel / Ardal O'Hanlon.
p.   cm.
Originally published as : The talk of the town. London :
Hodder and Stoughton, 1998.
ISBN 0-8050-6330-7
I. Title.
PR6065.H236T35   2000
823'.914—dc21   99-40754
                                                      CIP

Henry Holt books are available for special promotions and
premiums. For details contact: Director, Special Markets.

Originally published in the United Kingdom under the title
The Talk of the Town in 1998 by Hodder and Stoughton,
a division of Hodder Headline

First American Edition 2000

Printed in the United States of America

10   9   8   7   6   5   4   3   2   1

For Melanie,
for everything

Acknowledgements

I would like to thank lots of people but especially the following:

my wife, parents and family, you know who you are;

all my friends, you don't but I do;

Kevin Deehan and Gemma Hill who took the time and trouble to read the bloody book at an early stage;

the computer department of H & K (Ireland) who salvaged the thing after I pressed the wrong button;

Bernard and Mary Loughlin and all at the Tyrone Guthrie Centre for the Inept for helping me to break the back of the book;

my agent and scourge Dawn Sedgwick for her constant harassment;

my late auntie Maura Ward who kept me in literature and wine during the terrible twenties;

my editor at Hodder, Angela Herlihy, who has the patience and good heart and probably the wings of an angel;

all the authors I've ever read whose efforts shaped the way I think and live;

and most of all Baby M who arrived too late to offset the cynicism so rampant in this story.

PART I

I met Plunkett McKenna on Parnell Square when I was waiting for the bus home to Castlecock. A skinny useless fella with buck teeth. He was in my class at school.

'Hey Scully boy!'

He shouts at the top of his voice even though he was right beside me. I hated the way he put 'boy' at the end of every sentence. His father did the same when he was alive, God rest his soul, a miserable hunchback who read the electricity meters in the town until he died after falling off a chair. He was doubled over by then like a camp-bed, the poor man, and had to climb up on the chair to get a pot of jam out of the cupboard when he lost his balance. Plunkett himself, who by the way was a well-known squealer at school, found him surrounded by broken glass and home-made gooseberry jam. At least that's what my brother Joe told me and there's nothing he doesn't know.

And he had no business calling me 'Scully' either. I mean it was my name, my surname, but only the best of friends or old men, their trousers held up by lengths of rope, were entitled to be so familiar. If he had said 'Well Patrick!' and then shut up that would have suited me just fine.

'Are you going home for the weekend boy?'

Where the fuck did he think I was going? And me waiting for the bus!

'Yeah.'

'And where are you for tonight boy?'

'Dunno. I'll probably be meeting some of the lads above in Dolans.'

That was one thing for certain. I wouldn't be going anywhere near Dolans tonight or any other night for that matter. I hate Dolans. I wouldn't spit in it if it was on fire. And I hate McKenna too. I've always hated McKenna. And him hopping from foot to foot to keep warm like some sort of badly-nourished dancing bear. Curly black hair and curly teeth too, coming out of his mouth at all angles. Sucking spittle up the inside of his molars. The nosey fuckin' knowall bastard. Knows what you're thinking too so he does. I have no idea what the fuck he was doing up in Dublin. It wasn't for work anyway, that's for sure. Never worked a day in his life, the cunt.

'I was just up for a few tests, boy, at the hospital.'

I nodded. I remembered hearing all right that he had something wrong with him, a kidney condition or something. Plunkett McKenna, the first person I meet, and he's got hardly anything to do with my story. Imagine that.

'Is there anyone sitting beside you on the bus boy?'

'Yeah, I'm waiting for Balls O'Reilly.'

It was true, thank God. Now Balls O'Reilly, by contrast, he's got an awful lot to do with everything I have to say. Mind you, I knew he'd be late. Balls was always late. Two buses had come and gone already. But O'Reilly'd have an excuse. He always did.

'Bangers, five for fifty. Get your bangers, sparklers and stinkbombs. Five for fifty, the bangers, love!'

A crowd of oul' toothless women hawking in harmony. Selling contraband fireworks from deep inside their knickers for Bonfire Night.

The rain was bucketing down at this stage. Some chance

of those bangers going off, love, I thought to myself. Damp squibs. It was torrential altogether. McKenna and myself were standing in the doorway of some art gallery not saying a word. Hands in the pockets, fingering a couple of rings, my rucksack on the ground. He only had a plastic VG bag. That was all he had to his name, no coat or nothing, no family, no friends. Soaked to the skin, shivering, sleeves of his jumper pulled down over his hands. There were about twenty others waiting for the last bus to Castlecock. Some of them looked vaguely familiar, to be avoided like the plague.

I had a few days off for Hallowe'en so I decided to go home. As a matter of fact, from now on I'll be going home every weekend because I fuckin' hate Dublin. It can be a very unfriendly place, so it can. A couple of weeks ago, I was coming out of a chip shop with a bag of chips and this fella comes along and karate kicks the chips out of my hand for absolutely no reason, and then he says to me 'Are you startin'?' and I says to him, 'No, I'm not startin'!' and off he went.

Francesca, my girlfriend, was on her way to her mother's below in Wicklow for a few days. Her mother wasn't at all well and depended on Francesca. Personally, I think she should have been in a home. However, the old lady ran a pub in this wee village there on her own ever since the father died. As far as I know he had been his own best customer for years but Francesca never talks about him. She just says 'oh him' and throws her eyes up to Heaven. The pub had been for sale this good while but unfortunately there were no takers. And I'm not surprised either because to be perfectly frank it's a kip. I was down there myself on New Year's Eve when the mother was away visiting her sister in England. I went down to help Francesca behind the bar. Balls came too and between us we drank the place dry. Jaysus, it was deadly crack. By the way, in case you're wondering about her name, Francesca has no Italian blood in her whatsoever or indeed no exotic connections although she does look sort of Oriental. Her surname is Kelly and she was called after a great horse in the sixties. I think that's one of the reasons why she won't talk about her father. She hasn't forgiven him for that. There's a faded photo of that horse crossing the finishing line at the Curragh hanging above the bar to this very day. And I'll tell you one thing, old man Kelly must have won a lot of money on 'Francesca', that's all I can say, enough to buy the pub anyway.

We've being going out with each other on and off for just over a year now but lately we haven't been getting on too well. In fact, we had a fierce argument during the week. She was annoying me so much, I could have killed her. I mean, don't get me wrong, I do love her, I do, even though she's tiny and unco-operative. She's very cute altogether. I have never seen facial skin as silky and pure as Francesca's, not even on a baby or a china doll or a bowl of Angel Delight touched up by a child's spoon. I could safely say that she'd have absolutely no need whatsoever for Nivea Cream or any of those top-class lotions. I'm not saying she's the best-looking girl in the whole world but she certainly has the smoothest, most unsullied face. No spots, no moles, no broken veins, no colour, no make-up, no warts, no hair, not so much as a trace of down, not a blemish apart from the tiny indentations on either side of her nose where her glasses rest. It is a lovely wee face framed by straight black hair parted in the middle a bit like Sabrina's from *Charlie's Angels*. But I've had enough of her. I can't explain it, it's just, I don't know.

I was trying my best to ignore McKenna when a well-organised shower of tramps swooped down among us and started pestering us for money. The dirty bastards. Most of the bystanders escaped by back-backing into the gallery behind them. It was probably the first time in their lives they ever saw a painting, the fucking culchies. I stood my ground and stared straight ahead like a guard outside the courthouse during a terrorist trial. My father was in the guards before he died. So I know what I'm talking about. I applied, myself, for Templemore last year but they said I was too small, a quarter of an inch too small. Some friends of the oul' fella were going to see what they could do, apart from stretching me, but I haven't heard anything in a while. In the meantime, I left home and moved to Dublin, and last December I got a job as a security man in a jewellery shop. I've been there ever since. I'm plainclothes.

Anyway these winos were trying to wind me up with threats and abuse but they were only wasting their time. It was just as well for them that Geoghegan wasn't here or, God forbid, Shovels. They'd have put manners on them. McKenna of course the little cowardly cunt ended up giving them a pound.

Just then a pair of guards on the beat came into view. The tramps scarpered, the street-traders pushing prams scarpered, half of Dublin scarpered as if they all had something to hide. And you can be sure most of them did too, the ignorant fuckin' Jackeen cunts. Every last one of them. They'd rob you blind, poke the eye out of your head, take the shirt off your back, blow their noses in it, and then probably rape you in a van. And they think they're fuckin' hilarious, 'how's your snowballs?' and that type of thing. I fuckin' scarpered too, just in case, into the Hugh Lane Municipal Gallery behind me. The staff in there, most of them as old and motionless as the exhibits themselves, in their wee green blazers, must have thought there was a sudden but short-lived upsurge in interest in portraits of poncey squires in breeches. I'd like to take this opportunity to assure them that there wasn't.

Bangers went off as darkness collapsed like dodgy scaffolding over the rush hour. Loud cracks everywhere, like pistol shots on TV. Thousands of people, heads down, hurrying on the wet footpath towards the bank holiday weekend, half anticipating a bomb. I wouldn't have been surprised if one of the sellers exploded like a Calamity Jane or whatever you call those rockets – Catherine wheels I think it is. I wouldn't care either, the oul' disease-ridden hags. There'd be a drop in crime levels on the morning of the funeral if her bastard offspring took time off to mourn.

Eventually O'Reilly turned up carrying a step-ladder but by then the next bus had arrived and I was on it and the bus was full. You weren't allowed to keep seats and O'Reilly was furious.

'Why didn't you keep me a seat, Scully, you cunt ya?'

If there is one thing I hate it's people talking loudly on a bus. The whole bus craning for a gawk. The woman beside me was very embarrassed, very.

'Fuck off, wouldya?' I hissed, 'I was waiting for over three-quarters of an hour.'

'It's not my fault I'm late. I had to go back to the flat to pick up this. I was supposed to bring it home months ago.'

He had borrowed the step-ladder from his father a good while ago so as he could paint the flat, well our room anyway. It had been extremely drab and stained with damp and fungus and the evidence of a food fight. But what did the bastard do to make up for that? Only paint it black, I swear to God, ceiling and all. There was no window in the room so Balls sketched a window-frame in the same silver paint he'd recently done his bicycle with and filled in the four imaginary panes with yet more black paint. 'Sure we're only ever here at night,' he explained. We had no heat either. There was an old superser all right that had no gas tank within. The only heater in the whole house was hollow that is to say except for a few blankets that Balls had left inside it. And whenever anyone called around and said, 'I'm fuckin' freezin' hi!' Balls would open the back of the superser as if to turn it on and throw a smelly blanket at the visitor. He thought that was hilarious, he was an awful messer. One night when we were all shivering like mice, he painted orange flames on to a sheet of paper and placed it in the fireplace. And I know it's a stupid thing to say but we did actually feel a bit warmer.

We shared a ground-floor flat in the middle of a Georgian house in Rathmines that had been converted into about a hundred flats with a fella from Wexford, a courier by the name of Dermot Geoghegan whom I mentioned earlier. He was a serious man, always looking for trouble. It was a dingy enough place but cheap. Unfortunately there were only two bedrooms, one for Geoghegan and one for the pair of us. Mind you, O'Reilly was out with his college crowd half the time so it wasn't too bad. I had the room to myself. His real name is Xavier and I think he was studying Media Studies or some shite. He is called Balls on account of his nerve. There was nothing he wouldn't do, especially if he had a few pints on him. For example, he was always taking his lad out in the pub, anything for a laugh. Always acting the maggot. By the way, it's not as if his parents were in a hurry for the ladder. They own a fuckin' hardware shop.

Seeing as there were no seats left, O'Reilly had to stand in the aisle the whole way home. It served him right although it was a pity in a way because we could have had a bit of crack. The bus was very damp and thick with cigarette smoke. I would say that everybody on the bus was smoking except me. I hate smokers. Francesca takes the odd one knowing my attitude full well. My father promised me a hundred pounds if I didn't drink or smoke before I was eighteen. I was only about five or six when he made the promise and a hundred pounds sounded like a lot of money back then. It is fuck all now that I'm nineteen. Daddy if you can hear me you owe me fifty quid, I don't smoke.

The bus was cramped. It was irresponsible in my opinion and probably illegal to transport that amount of people at the same time. We were squashed in like pigs. And I couldn't believe the amount of luggage some people take with them. I mean I've seen pictures in books of Third World transportation and I know the way they carry on over there. People hanging off the sides and goats and hens on board as well as the contents of entire homes. But this is Ireland in the latter half of the twentieth century and economic circumstances are different. To the best of my knowledge there was no livestock on the bus apart from a goldfish in a plastic bag some fella was bringing home as a present. But there were rucksacks and step-ladders as I have already mentioned, suitcases and hold-alls, cardboard boxes and plastic bags, ironing boards, pots and pans, a television set, a metal dustbin, wickerwork, sleeping bags full of dirty clothes, tons and tons of personal possessions, presents, household goods. There was no room to move or even breathe, wedged in as we were by the damp bric-à-brac of these temporary migrants. Every space was occupied, overhead and underfoot. They were like a bunch of ants humping scraps back to the hill for inspection and I know all about ants. The flat is infested with them.

Anyway, I fell asleep on the bus despite the fact that I was very agitated as it bumped and lurched out of the city. I nearly always did. It was the driver's Charlie Pride tape that put me to sleep, not that I mind Charlie Pride. In fact I think he's very good. Balls called it dreary old country shite and put on his Walkman to listen to some fuckin' noise he picked up in college, Simple Minds or some shower of cunts like that. That was Balls, always trying to be up-to-date.

The driver was a great character, a wee oul' fella who shouldn't have been allowed to drive a Ford Anglia never mind a bus, forever laughing and joking. He has one of the filthiest, dirtiest tongues I ever heard in my whole life.

Sometimes if the bus wasn't too full I'd sit up beside him for the crack, seeing as how he was a neighbour of mine. In every single town we went through on the way home, he'd point out a road or a street or a tree where he said he'd rode some woman in the past. Or he'd indicate a spot on the side of the road where he'd picked up a hitch-hiker who later sucked him off when he used to be a lorry-driver. He was full of shite. I used to collect the money from the passengers for him now and again in exchange for free transport, but not today. No, I was going to enjoy a good snooze if the woman beside me would ever shut up.

She'd been trying to start up a conversation ever since we left the city. Every time she caught my eye she'd smile shyly, a wee dumpy woman in a pink jumper she'd knitted herself, big daisies on the front. It looked like something she'd got off the wall of a children's classroom. A librarian I'd say. An intellectual of some sort anyway. She was reading a Maeve Binchy blockbuster. But unfortunately for me she wasn't buried in it. She'd read a few paragraphs and then look dreamily out of the window or sigh to herself. Before long she put the book down and started to make those preliminary noises people make before deciding what they're going to say. Composing her thoughts.

'Would you like a sweet, Patrick?'

'No thanks!'

How the fuck did she know my name? I looked down to see if I was still wearing my name tag on my breast pocket but I wasn't. However I was going red, red as a beetroot, a cluster of needles under each armpit.

'How come you know my name?'

'I went to school with your sister Valerie. Deirdre Freeman's my name. Are you sure you won't have one?'

'I will so.' Anything to keep you quiet, I thought to myself. They weren't sweets either, Zubes, they were, cough sweets from a tin that'd make you choke.

'How come Francesca's not with you?' That took me by surprise. She knew all about me and Francesca, where I worked, the guards, Balls, the whole lot. She must have been studying for an exam on me: The Life and Times of Patrick Scully. That's just typical. People you've never met before know everything, well nearly everything. I worked it out in my head that one sweet would get her five minutes of chat and five minutes only but she was far too clever for that. Deirdre Freeman had a big bag of sweets, a sackful between her legs which contained every type of chocolate bar and can of soft drink and enough crisps to power a playground. The Zubes, I suppose, she'd explain to herself were some sort of medicine, not really sweets at all, an antidote to the sweets. Lozenges to reduce the guilt.

'They're for my nieces and nephews,' she said. 'For Hallowe'en,' she added unnecessarily.

It turned out she wasn't a librarian at all but was in the civil service. Worked in the dole office on Thomas Street. In fact she told me she'd seen Plunkett McKenna in there that morning making a claim, the sly pointy-eared little bollocks. If there is one thing I can't stand it's people ripping off the State. She lived about fifteen miles the far side of Castlecock, in Dooshatt, and was engaged to be married. That, I have to say, came as a bit of a surprise. I had put her down as shelf material without a doubt.

'Would you like a fag?'

Fuck sake. She must have known I didn't smoke.

'No thanks, Deirdre!'

'Do you mind if I smoke?'

'No.' I could hardly fuckin' breathe. After a while, she put the fag out and stopped talking too. Wonders will never cease. I thought, good, a bit of peace and quiet. But no, she starts to hum. It was driving me insane. The humming went on until she fell asleep just as we were coming into Slane. By then the chatter on the bus as a whole had quietened down to a murmur but visibility remained low due to the smoke. The Charlie Pride tape was obviously damaged because it sounded as if a monster was singing in slow motion. Nobody noticed the difference. It seemed to me that the majority of passengers were still smoking in their sleep. I looked around to see Balls fast asleep standing up with his head resting against the overhead rack, a fag dangling from his mouth too. It wouldn't have surprised me to find the driver sleeping too. I eventually fell asleep myself, only to wake up about five minutes later to find Deirdre's head in my lap dribbling on to my good trousers. I was mortified in case anybody thought she was my girlfriend. So I lifted her head up in my hands and pushed it against the window. With a bit of luck, her syrupy spittle would glue her to the window-pane.

About ten miles from home the bus came to a juddering halt behind a line of traffic. We couldn't see what was going on because all the windows were steamed up but Balls said it was probably an accident. I thought it might be roadworks but Balls insisted it was a crash. He could be very stubborn. Mind you I thought I could make out a flashing blue light in the distance. So anyway myself and Balls and a few other passengers got off the bus to investigate. It was an accident all right, as Balls very quickly pointed out. What happened was, about a half a mile further on, another bus had veered off the road and plunged into a field. There were a couple of ambulances in attendance, a fire brigade and a few squad cars.

'That's a serious amount of blood boy.'

It was McKenna of course, the nosey bastard, first on the scene. He must have sprinted ahead of us.

'Howarya Spock, what happened?' says O'Reilly. For some reason, he always called McKenna, Spock. And to this day I have no idea why.

'The bus was overtaking a car on the corner, it looks like she skidded, went right over the ditch boy.'

'Anyone killed?'

'Aye there was, a woman. A woman was killed boy.'

'Was she local?'

Somebody butted in and said she was one of the butcher's daughters, Carolan. I knew the Carolans well, neighbours of mine. Our dog stole a cooked chicken from their shop once. We discussed it for a while on the side of the road in the rain and came to the conclusion that it must have been Mary. She was the only one of the Carolans who worked in Dublin. A secretary I think in a dental practice. Very sad altogether.

'I used to go out with her,' says Balls.

Of course he did. There wasn't a woman in the town he hadn't been with at one time or another. I don't know if he got the ride or not. I doubt it. In fact I don't think he ever got the ride off anyone. If he did I don't think I would have heard the end of it.

'Ten badly injured, a lot of them in shock boy.'

Thanks for the update you cunt.

A reporter for the *Dundalk Democrat* came over to us just as the ambulance was pulling away. People were jumping into their cars as fast as they could, slamming the doors shut and speeding away, not to make up for lost time as you might think. No, it was so as they could follow the ambulance in a convoy to its final destination. That was the thing to do in our part of the country. As soon as a fire engine or an ambulance or a police car or even an ice-cream van made an appearance, people stopped whatever they were doing to follow it. It was very important you see to know what was going on, to be first with the news. In an impoverished town where fuck-all happened, gossip was gold dust.

'Any witnesses?' the reporter says.

'I was on the bus,' pipes up McKenna. Typical. Always

wanting to be the centre of attention. He didn't tell him it was a different bus he was on that arrived about three-quarters of an hour after the accident.

Myself and Balls left him there to enjoy his moment of glory and went back to our own bus. I thought to myself, I could just as easily have been on the bus that crashed. I was in time for it and all only I waited for Balls. Just as well I waited for Balls. They might be all talking about me now in hushed tones. 'Scully, from the town.' 'Not Patrick Scully, the guard's son.' 'Aye, the same.' 'Oh no.' 'Oh yes. The poor mother, her nerves are bad enough as it is.' 'She'll be destroyed.' 'And he was such a good footballer too.' 'He was.' 'The Lord works in mysterious ways.'

By the time I got back to the bus, everyone was talking about the crash.

'Anyone hurt?'

'One of the Carolans from the Hill was killed.'

'Oh God!'

'That's terrible!'

'Lovely girls, the Carolans.'

And so on. The mood was quite different for the remainder of the journey, a mixture of shock and excitement. People couldn't wait to get home to tell their families the news.

2

The bus dropped us off on the main street, outside Fraser's the newsagent's. McKenna scurried off to his rat hole without saying a word. I said goodbye to O'Reilly, 'I'll see you in a couple of hours above in the Lock Inn.'

'Right so.'

Off he went with his step-ladder on his shoulder, very pleased with himself altogether on account of the looks he was getting from the locals and the ignorant culchies in town to do a last bit of shopping for the weekend. O'Reilly was a big show-off like that. Always looking for attention. One time he came home sporting a pair of purple Doc Martens boots and another time he got off the bus wearing a nun's headdress, pretending there was nothing out of the ordinary about that. No respect for anything. I'm on for a bit of crack but taking the mickey out of the nuns is going too far. Sometimes you'd be embarrassed to be seen with him.

'Well Scully!'

'Well!'

The shops were still full, even though it was about seven o'clock. The men sat in cars and tractors smoking cigarettes like a crowd of private detectives gathering information as they waited for their wives to give them the nod to start the engine while they carried the twenty bags of weekend groceries from the shops.

'Jaysus, young Scully, I haven't seen you in a while. To what do we owe the pleasure?'

I was delighted to be home. It was my town. Unlike Dublin, people would actually say hello to you. I felt like I'd arrived back after many years at sea to claim my inheritance, older, wiser, having mastered the world, my deeds and my crimes, the stuff of distant rumour, my savage heart finally at rest. 'Yes Mr Scully, the estate is exactly as you left it.' The sweat was pumping off me at this stage even though it was quite cold outside, the sudden change in atmosphere I suppose. It was drizzling too so I stopped for a second under an awning.

It was great to get away from Francesca. To be honest she was sickening my arse lately. She'd come down to Castlecock a few times, three times in total, but I was never very comfortable when she was around. She's not bad-looking but she's very quiet, too quiet in my opinion. I never know what she's thinking. I suppose I never really knew where I stood with her. It's very hard to have any crack with the lads when you have the responsibility of looking after your girlfriend, specially when she makes no effort whatsoever. The thing I hate most about Francesca is the way she speaks so slowly when she's had a few drinks. Don't get me wrong, I'm used to people around here speaking slowly, choosing each word with careful consideration for maximum offensiveness. But with her it's just slow and stupid and to be honest embarrassing for me. She can't really hold her drink.

Of course when Francesca was down, the mother went into a big sulk for the whole weekend, she hardly spoke, even though Francesca always sleeps in Valerie's old room. So that doesn't help the situation either.

'Well Scully!' It was Shovels Malone, on his way home from work.

'Well Shovels!' He persuaded me to go for a quick pint

below in Devlins. A man of very few words, he didn't actually ask me in plain language to accompany him to the pub. No, no, he simply nodded in the general direction of that particular hostelry. And when Shovels suggested something, whether it was with his eyebrows or a tilt of his head, you didn't refuse if you knew what was good for you.

Shovels was a builder by trade and one of the hardest men in the town, I swear he wouldn't take shit from anyone. He was only my age and roughly my height, about five feet ten inches, but built like a tank. When he wasn't camouflaged with paint and mortar and dust, he wore denim from head to toe and had a shock of hair that was both lank and fair.

I remember well the day he arrived in the National school from England at the age of eight. He got in a fight with some older lads over a game of marbles and I offered him sweets so as he'd be my friend. Shovels was called Shovels after his father Shovels Malone, who in turn was called after his father on account of the latter's huge hands. In fact large mitts ran in the family. I'd often seen Shovels pick up a ball off the ground with one hand which is a very hard thing to do. For years after they returned to Ireland he was a neighbour of mine but recently he'd had a disagreement with his family and was now living in the back of an old bread van, in a field out in the country, surrounded by piles of bricks he took from whatever site he happened to be working on at the time with the permission of his boss who was also his cousin. He asked me if I'd help him to build a house in place of the old van. That was about two years ago and we haven't started yet.

Anyway, I told him the crack about the Carolan girl, we sank the pints and arranged to meet up later on in the Lock Inn. This was in my opinion shaping up to be a good night. Me, Balls and Shovels. No women. No trouble.

This was what I loved about the town. Bumping into

people you know. Putting a name to a face. You knew where you stood. When I was younger, I used to draw maps of the town, with a list attached of who lived in what house. I took down the registration number of every vehicle in a little green notebook and matched it with its owner. I found a reg plate down by the courthouse one day, NZV 782, and I knew immediately that it was from the post office van. Must have fallen off. No reward.

Balls was always telling his friends in college about the great characters who provided the town with amusement. 'So and so (I'll not mention his name), rode a cow. I swear to God. He stuck its hind legs in his wellies. I'm telling you and when the judge asked him why did he ride the cow, he said, the cow backed into him. That's true. And then he shot her through the head with a bolt. Isn't that right, Scully?' And I'd go along with it. Most of the time he was exaggerating but I'll give him this, there was a grain of truth in everything he said. He had a great imagination. His listeners were eager and swallowed the whole lot, me adding the odd detail here and there for the crack. Although it wasn't right, mocking the afflicted. Not that Balls cared a damn as long as it was getting the laugh.

There was the man who thought he was a vampire, wore the long black cape and only came out at night. He used to eat cats. One night, and this is definitely true, we were giving him guff up the town. He stopped, gave us the evil eye and tried to cast a spell on us with his ring. An awful creep, mad in the head.

Everywhere you looked, figures from your childhood, lads you played football with, lads you mitched school with, there's a fella used to eat tadpoles, and look it's the Cosgraves, won a television on a television quiz show, the talk of the town for weeks after. You knew where you stood all right, you knew what football teams they supported, the political parties their parents supported with a passion bordering on insanity, where their allegiances lay. You knew their histories, their medical records, the layout of their homes, what they had for breakfast.

See that car there with the passenger door missing? That door has been missing for well over a year. But during the summer, we were coming out of Devlins and we saw the fella who owns that car, Coyle from Lisdaw, actually locking the other doors. Fuckin' eejit. We had a great laugh. Balls says to him, 'You should get an alarm.' You knew their skeletons. Speculation became evidence if the details were lacking. You knew who their friends were, you knew who ruled the roost, wore the trousers, you knew where they worked, how much they earned. Everybody was familiar with the fruit in the orchard of family trees. You weren't just some bogman up from the country. Nobody mocked your accent in public unless you were some mucksavage from outside the town.

I was working in the shop last Tuesday. Following this knacker around. You could tell he was up to no good because he wasn't an American tourist, he had no business whatsoever being in the shop. 'Would you give me some fuckin' room to breathe,' he bellowed at the top of his voice, in a Dublin accent. 'You fuckin' culchie scumbag.' I looked him straight in the eye even though I was shitting myself. 'I'll be waiting for you outside and I'm going to kick your fuckin' head in you fuckin' scumbag. You're a scumbag.'

That was good, him calling *me* a fuckin' scumbag. He wasn't there anyway at the end of my shift, probably in jail or else dead. You didn't have to put up with that sort of thing in Castlecock.

Mind you I didn't mind old people taking things from the shop. Last month, I was watching the monitors and I saw an old lady putting a pewter jug in her handbag. I passed no remarks. Mr Dunn is only an old bollox anyway. Fuckin' slave driver.

Anyway, I arrived home at the house, at about quarter past eight.

'Look what the cat dragged in.' My mother. 'Surprise, surprise!'

It was not a surprise. She knew right well I was coming home. I rang her this afternoon. ('Mammy, I'll be home this evening.' 'Will you now?' 'I will aye.') Anyway she grabbed the rucksack out of my hands. I grabbed it back. 'No.' We had a brief tug of war contest over the bag. She managed to prise it from my grasp. She's strong and stubborn. My nails were very long, I've a phobia about cutting them – I get the shivers – so I let go. She headed for the scullery, to empty the contents into the washing machine before she went any further. I followed her.

'No, Mammy.'

'No what?'

'I've no washing.'

'That's a laugh, since when did you come home without laundry?'

'There's things in the pockets. I'll do it myself later.'

'That's a good one. That's a first. Come Sunday night you'll be looking for clean underpants. I'll throw it in now.'

'No!' I said firmly.

A powerful look of disapproval spread across her face like a rash, as if she didn't trust me, as if she knew I'd done something wrong. Just because, for once, I didn't go along with the routine. And me only doing her a back-saving favour.

She was one of the most animated people alive, you know; she could never hide her feelings. When she was happy, let's say she won a pound in a raffle, she'd shriek with delight, skip and clap her hands. But that hasn't happened for about five years.

To be honest she's gone a bit off the rails. I wish I

could say 'ever since Daddy died' because then that might explain it but she was highly strung and housebound long before that.

For about ten minutes, she didn't say a word, she didn't utter a sound apart from the odd harumph. She kept looking at me in silent dismay. By some miracle, a force of decency prevailed upon her to hold off the hounds until I'd cooled down a bit after my journey. She became preoccupied making sandwich-spread sandwiches for my brother, Joe, and three or four of his friends who were sitting in the kitchen drinking bottles of beer.

'Well Pat, any crack?'

'Well Joe, no crack, I'll be down in a minute.'

I meanwhile, rucksack in tow, went upstairs for the three Ss; a shower, a shite and a shave. Seeing as how we didn't have a shower I jumped into a hot bath, no suds, no matter. Oh man, this was going to be some night indeed. Make no mistake about that. No work to worry about and no Francesca either, just pure unadulterated crack with the lads. I shut my eyes and reclined in the tub. By sheer force of habit, I started scaling the walls of the old lighthouse that emerged in the still waters below. I should have said three Ss and a W, in my case. Lying there, weakened by the heat, I recalled the first time I, let's call a spade a spade, pulled my wire. It happened in the very same bath when I was about fourteen years old. I didn't even know what I was doing but whatever it was I couldn't stop myself. It was terrifying but still I went on, eyes clenched shut, whipping up a storm until suddenly the sands shifted and at least two continental plates collided. In that instant I accidentally caught the plugchain in my toe and jerked it free. I watched helplessly, paralysed from the waist down, like a mermaid in a field, as the thick milky fluid spurted from me and shot through the water like effluent from a chemical plant. Jaysus, and I don't mean to labour the point, but as the tide went out around me, I don't know, it was like . . . like the vile retchings of a sea serpent in his last throes, the creature washed up on dry land. So maybe this is what they mean when they say throwing the baby out with the bathwater except, of course, it wasn't really a baby, only the merest molecule of potential. I was immediately stricken with confusion and remorse and mentally packing my bags for hell when the door opened and who walked in? Only my sister Valerie who smiled and walked straight out again. Already troubled and probably damned, I was caught in the act too to make seriously bad matters even worse. I couldn't look at her ever again after that. I couldn't look at anybody she knew or might have spoken to. The rest of my life was going to be spent in the shadows. It was years later before I realised what I had done (and continued to do sometimes three and four times a day) and that everybody else was doing it too but that was small comfort to me as my soul was already tattered like an old sock by then.

I got out of the bath anyway and shaved for the second time that day, poured a half-bottle of Blue Stratos down my chest, brushed my teeth, put on my brand-new grey pleats, my wine tanktop, white pin-collared shirt and wine tie and of course my new leather jacket. A black one elasticated at the waist. The grey one had cracked. While I was doing all this, the doorbell rang. It was a couple of children from up the road dressed up as witches and ghosts, wearing scary masks made from cereal boxes. Trick or treat, they said, whatever the fuck that means. They must have picked it up from some American television programme, the little fuckers. My mother gave them an apple and a few mandarin oranges. I'd say that pissed them off, they wanted money or sweets. Fruit is something you give to patients above in the hospital. I knew one thing for sure, those mandarin oranges would end up splattered on the windscreen of some van.

When I was ten years old my father lit a bonfire up the hill behind our house on Hallowe'en night. All the boys and girls from our street were there. I was late, detained in the house for some reason. It was pitch-black outside except for the flames in the distance. I was very frightened so I ran as fast as I could towards the festive ghostly conflagration. Running hard and blindly, I tripped over a wheelbarrow and gashed my shin. Almost broke my leg in two. I was lying there on my own for ages, wind whispering in my ear, 'Nobody knows you're here.' I was sure I was going to die. But my father knew there was something wrong. I was supposed to help him with the fireworks so maybe that's why he noticed my absence. Either way he couldn't leave the bonfire unsupervised so he had to shepherd the children down the hill. They leapt shrieking through the long grass like a band of apaches, my father with his torch trying to keep them under control, until they found me prostrate beside the wheelbarrow. 'Is he dead?' asked one of the Mohans, gasping with shock in a circle. This was much more exciting than the bonfire. My father carried me in his arms to the car. And put me in the front seat, my first ever time in the front. I felt very important. He had to put all the neighbours' children in the back, all ten of them because my mother was at mass and there was nobody in the house to mind them. And off we all went to the doctor. He gave me two stitches and I was the talk of the town.

I sat down for a shite then looked in briefly to check for worms, as I always did ever since I had them when I was six – I still have nightmares about that – and noticed something metallic gleaming in the mire. I have to admit I was a bit alarmed at first, I mean, you don't expect to find a gold object concealed in your shite every time you sit down on the toilet seat. I quickly flushed the toilet and glanced in again hoping it would have disappeared like a bad dream, but no, the ring was still there. Fuck. Panicking, I flushed again. Still there, looking at me and what's more from its vantage point beneath the water my face was squeezed tightly within its circumference. I fished the ring from the bowl, rinsed it under the hot tap and swallowed it again. Out of sight out of mind and put the finishing touches to my deportment. That was the end of the ablutions. Full marks. I looked in the mirror expecting to be pleasantly surprised by the attractive gentleman facing me but I wasn't. Something was wrong. I couldn't put my finger on it. Maybe it was the new jacket. Still, no time to waste. When I went downstairs, my mother took the dinner out of the oven and put it on the table and launched straight into me. Once she starts there's no stopping her. I think she just waits until she's decided upon the most effective angle of attack.

'We'll have to do something about that hair, Patrick. Do you hear me? You used to have a lovely head of fair hair. Blondie, I used to call you, do you remember that, Paddy? Grecian 2000, that's supposed to be very good. Run up there to Norman Fraser's and get some.'

'No.' It's true, my hair was going a bit grey and it was very embarrassing. Some would say distinguished.

'Suit yourself. But don't say I didn't warn you. Xavier O'Reilly doesn't have grey hair, does he? No he does not, nor Joe. If you want to walk around like an old man that's none of my business. [*Pause.*] There's a wee lump missing as well, Pat. You're not looking after yourself. What's wrong with you at all. You haven't been home for months.'

One month exactly.

'Paddy I'll ask you straight out, once and once only, you're not involved in drugs are you?'

'No I wouldn't touch them.' (I wouldn't either.)

'Look at me when I'm talking to you. You're not a male prostitute are you?'

'Ah Mammy for fuck's sake?'

'I'm your mother. I have a right to know what my son is

doing above in Dublin, tell me the truth, are you involved in illegal bare-knuckle boxing? Are you, are you Patrick?' 'No I am not. There's nothing the matter with me. Would you ever just leave me alone!' She gets these ideas into her head and that's it, she's off. There's no holding her back. She probably hears about them on Gay Byrne and automatically assumes I'm part of it. A couple of months ago there was a bomb in Orly Airport in Paris. My mother saw the pictures of the dying and the wounded on the television and went into hysterics, hysterics altogether. 'Poor Joe, poor wee Joe, is there any news about Joe?' Joe went to London for the summer to work on the sites after his Leaving Cert. And he went by boat. And she knew that but that didn't stop her worrying all the same.

'Anyway, the good news. I was talking to Sergeant Donegan, we'll have word on Monday.'

'Will we?'

'We will, fingers crossed, he was talking to the minister only last week. We'll definitely have news on Monday. Hopefully that'll be the end of . . .' She put her hands up as if to take a throw-in, turned on her heel without finishing the sentence. Oh no, here she comes again. 'And if, touch wood, the news is not what we were hoping, Xavier's daddy will give you a job if you ask him in the hardware shop until you decide what you want to do.'

'I have a job.'

'They're very busy at the moment, coming up to Christmas.'

Unless Sergeant Donegan and the minister and the garda authorities are complete fools there's no way I'll be recruited. It's not just a question of height you know. What my mother doesn't realise is that I failed the Leaving. No honours, no passes. Straight fails. A royal flush of Fs. I forged the results I showed her, the same set I sent off with my application. Even if I told her I failed she wouldn't believe me seeing as how I did so well in my Inter.

'Is there something wrong with the dinner, Paddy? It's not like you to leave your dinner. They must be feeding you well in Dublin anyway. There was a time you'd lick the plate clean.'

'I'm not that hungry Mammy.' I wasn't a bit hungry after all the sweets on the bus. And I had knots in my stomach.

'Will you have a beetroot sandwich?'

She had me there. She knew I could never resist a beetroot sandwich. I loved beetroot. Daddy used to grow beetroot. I loved rhubarb too. That grew wild in a field behind our house and we'd wipe the spit off it and eat it raw when we were thirsty. You couldn't eat too much of it or you'd get poisoned even though it was supposed to be good for your blood. Nothing was simple.

'I will.'

At least she'd call off the dogs now. She took away the plate of dinner I'd barely touched. The one and only time she ever hit me was a few years ago at teatime after I gave her cheek when she accidentally stained my good white shirt with a slice of beetroot. It must have been a Saturday because I was supposed to be bringing up the gifts at the six o'clock mass. She was spearing slices of beetroot with a fork from the jar to our plates when a bit slipped on to my shirt. Leaving a big birthmark. I was furious. It was my favourite shirt and had been just washed and ironed that day.

'Fuck you,' I said.

'What did you say?'

'You ruined my good shirt. It's like a fucking gunshot wound.'

'Don't you ever speak to me like that again.' And she walloped me across the face and then ran out into the kitchen crying her eyes out. Valerie glared at me and followed her out of the room. Like I said it was the first time she ever hit me. Daddy when he was alive would do any hitting that was called for. Usually it has to be said at my mother's insistence. A mild-mannered man, he'd reluctantly usher the miscreant into the bedroom, me or Joe, close the door behind us, pull down our trousers and put us across his knee and give us a few tepid slaps on the bare backside. If Joe was being trounced I'd be outside listening and when he came out I'd ask him, 'How many did you get?' and vice versa. Anyway I later apologised to my mother for my foul language but didn't bring up the gifts at mass that evening. Joe did. And I never went to mass again.

'One of the Carolans from the Hill was killed.' That stopped her in her tracks.

'Go way.'

'She was,' munching on the cold pickled beetroot. 'She was killed stone dead in a crash.'

'Hold on, wait 'til I call Joe, Joe!' The whole crowd gathered around me and I filled them in on the latest tragedy to blight the town.

3

Francesca's Diary

Friday, 22 October 1982

There's nobody and I mean nobody left in Killeeny. It's like a ghost town. Silent except for the occasional sputtering tractor and a constant rumbling noise that seems to come from just beneath the surface of the earth but is probably just the air-conditioning on Lanigan's chicken shack. Summer's pleasant hymn has given way to autumn's discontented hum, the cooler, heavier air creeping in under the hamlet's closed doors and playing the long grass, a fairy-child practising the violin.

I've only been away for a week but already, from my bedroom window, Killeeny looks imagined, more like a folk-memory than the village I've lived in for eighteen years. I feel like a third-generation Irish-American visiting the ancestral patch or a place that sounds like it to their easily-convinced ears. I've just noticed that there has been no building done here in the last ten years, no extensions, not even a porch. No painting. On the narrow roads staggering away from the village, the Mohawks of grass have grown longer. And there's nobody around, just humble shrines to people along the road where they were killed in a car crash or a hit-and-run in more prosperous dancehall days.

Gráinne is doing medicine in the Royal College of Surgeons. Maeve Quinn got arts in UCD. The rest of my 'friends' are in England. Those who are left (i.e. Breda Meegan in a nutshell) basically turn their noses up at me now that I'm at university. They look at me with contempt, as if I've been sent to prison for stealing eggs. (I think it's possible to make paint from eggs. If so, I'd love to release all of Lanigan's hens, break every last egg, and use the mixture to create a grotesque fresco of squinting villagers on our gable wall.)

Since the moment I got off the bus last night, I could sense them eyeing me up and down. 'Who does Francesca Kelly think she is? And she doesn't have two words to put together? Next she'll be wearing clothes that aren't even brown!' It's not as if she could be jealous. I mean, Breda didn't want to go to uni in the first place. She didn't even apply. She actually informed me before the Leaving that she was going to sit at home until somebody asked her to marry him, preferably a man with a car. She proceeded to describe her ideal car in great detail. It sounded like a ten-year-old Hillman Avenger to me with air-freshener and black furry seats. It didn't matter what he looked like as long as he had a moustache and looked like the guy in *Magnum* or any detective on TV. That just shows you the limits of her imagination. And anyway, all the men within a forty-mile radius of Killeeny look like Frank Cannon.

Marriage is the furthest thing from my mind although it would be nice to meet a clean-shaven man with a brain and soft hands. I close my eyes and dream of such hands, smooth, expert, long-fingered, patient, unfortunately detached. And they don't have fingerprints or sweat. What sort of man is this? I'm afraid I've never seen his face. Where are you? People like Breda Big-Arse seem to think that anybody who tries to broaden their horizons and further their education has some sort of a superiority complex. I don't think I'm better than her, I just don't want to be like her.

Mam's attitude is not much better. What am I saying?

It couldn't be worse. She thinks the course is stupid, a 'Mickey-Mouse' course in her words, not that she knows the first thing about it, and still maintains I should hold out for nursing. Nursing? It doesn't seem to occur to her that I might have absolutely no interest whatsoever in nursing. Blood repels me as does vomit and God knows I've wiped up enough of hers in my time. I've tried to explain to her, I don't know how many times, but she physically turns her substantial back on me, accuses me of lacking compassion, and being oblivious to the suffering of those less fortunate than myself. And she hasn't forgotten how to wound. 'College is all very well for pretty, outgoing girls.'

When she goes on like that, I don't think there is anybody less fortunate than myself. And it almost makes me puke to hear her describing the effects of famine in Ethiopia, while stuffing apple tart into her mouth, as if that's going to change my mind. I mean, pass the bucket. She hardly let me go to Dublin, never mind the Horn of Africa. What she wants of course is her own personal nursemaid to remove bones periodically from her throat and attend to all her needs, needs far greater than those of the entire Third World put together.

When I arrived home from Dublin, she didn't ask me anything about college or my new subjects or the digs I'm in or the people I've met. She told me in passing who had died recently. And once this compulsory observance of smalltown etiquette was out of the way she began to pace the kitchen. Chain-smoking, bare-footed and tipsy she left suggestions hanging in the air and her knitting in a huge heap on an arm-chair. I wouldn't have minded so much only it was easily the most important and exhilarating week of my life. Even a sniffy 'Well Fran, as long as you're happy' would have done.

I'm trying my best to understand her position. I mean I know she's not feeling well, she never has since she had pleurisy at the age of five, she can't really manage the pub on her own and despite her remarks to the contrary I know she's lonely. (Surprise surprise.) But I have to get on with my life. Make that, 'I've got to start my life.' I'd go out of my mind if I stay here any longer.

What is she knitting anyway? I suppose it began as a pair of socks for a neighbour's newborn but ten years and a myriad of colours later, it could be anything. Leggings, a scarf, a jumper, a cape. A garment too big for any living thing, that's for sure, I mean, it would fit a field. A macramé of her moods. A psychiatrist would have some fun trying to unravel that. There really is no point talking to her. I don't know much but I know I'm doing the right thing. I just know it.

As soon as I threatened to leave the house, just to go for a walk, she claimed that she was dizzy and had to lie down and asked me to look after the bar for the night without as much as a by your leave. As usual, I withheld my emotions and obeyed. I convince myself that she loves me, appreciates me, can't live without me, that her current possessiveness is her way of saying it. Who am I fooling? She has more or less told me that I am guilty of neglect without a trace of irony in her quivering voice. Well I've played the part of the dutiful daughter without a murmur of complaint for as long as I can remember. I've been bullied and humiliated in front of my friends. I've been continuously told how useless I am by that selfish alcoholic whore and I'm sick of it. God forgive me but it's the truth. It seems like only last night that she announced to Gráinne in front of me that she would have much preferred her as a daughter. I smiled at Gráinne, my whole being crushed like a grape. She didn't know where to look and tried to laugh it off, 'You don't mean that Mrs Kelly.' Coolly, levelly, soberly, my mother said, 'But I do.' I was only fourteen years old at the time.

And five or six years before that again, I overheard her taunting Dad, my raffish father, about his sexual prowess or lack of and adding almost boastfully that she doubted if I was his. If I had a penny for every time she told me that I was an accident, that she deliberately smoked and drank during her pregnancy to try and harm me, I'd be a rich and independent woman. I owe her nothing and I don't forgive her, sitting up in her bed of self-pity, wearing a scarf on her head and large earrings in a hideous parody of Romany fashion. I suspect she fancied herself as some sort of medium, although the only spirits she ever met were my low ones. As well as the colony of demons that hung upside down in her batcave of a skull.

Thank God there weren't that many in the bar and none at all of my generation. I really didn't want to talk about guttering or the rain-destroyed barley. I found it exhausting all the same having to listen to the smalltalk and wisecracks that came as naturally as phlegm to the regulars. My mind was so far away, being massaged and nuzzled and licked by a man from the West, of Spanish descent. Poor hundred-year-old Enda Keane was the last to leave, raving in a language from the last century. I had to help him out the door and walk him the few yards to his house. He can hardly see at all now thanks to his cataracts. I feel so sorry for him. I mean, he lived for darts. And these days can only listen nostalgically to the thunk of the solitary feathered arrow as it is lodged in the plywood that surrounds the cork board. That's something that really annoys me. There is only one dart in the pub but the locals are either too lazy or too mean to get a new set. Or maybe it helps to stretch out time. Holding on to my arm as he rummaged for the key to his hall door, he mumbled something about me being a credit to my father and, you know, he wasn't joking either. Of course I didn't have the heart to pull him up on his ignorance. The reason he was so fond of my dear, departed dad was on account of the latter's 'generosity'. Dad used to give out free drink on the flimsiest premises. All you had to do was correctly answer a trivia question on the Grand National or beat him at draughts or just be there for long enough and you eventually got on the gravy train. None of them visited him in hospital as he faded without a fight, his hollow laugh but a slightly irritating memory in Kelly's bar. Enda's parting words of wisdom were equally well informed. 'College is no place for a lovely girl like you, you can't eat books!' It's hard to believe that this man was a county councillor!! I wouldn't be surprised to learn that mam had planted that valedictory nugget on his person. God, it's like as if the whole town is conspiring to keep me here.

Saturday, 23 October 1982
I woke up this morning fighting for air. The atmosphere was so thick with hypocrisy and cheap toiletries. I can't wait to get back to Dublin/the rest of my life tomorrow night although college has been daunting so far to say the least. The first day was awful. Each of us had to stand up in turn and introduce ourselves to the class, my worst nightmare since the Alateen meeting last year. It was highly embarrassing. I think I said, 'I'm Francesca Kelly from Killeeny, County Wicklow.' Unlike a lot of the others, I failed to add, 'I chose Media Studies because I hope to work in journalism . . . because I want to get into television . . . because I didn't get the points for law (hahaha) . . . because I want to channel my energies into a radical and relevant area of modern life . . . because I want to get up my mother's nose.'

The confidence of some people is truly intimidating but surely in many cases a front. A fickle and desirable commodity. But of course I wouldn't know its nature because I've never had any. The facilitator, as he called himself, then asked us to repeat what the previous person had just said. Of course most of us were unable to do so as we were so preoccupied with trying to compose our own introductions. This was the big chance to get off the mark, make an impression on our peers, dazzle with our spontaneity and wit. Indeed, since then, I've found myself obsessively thinking of something clever to say in company, not as a contribution to a public debate but simply as an opening to a conversation. And I don't mean clever, in an intellectual 'I have some original thoughts on the origin of the sweet tooth' way. I mean, I wish I could just say something not entirely stupid for a change, some throw-away comment or wry observation that someone might actually notice, to which they might respond with a smile, 'Hey she's not just an insignificant frump, do you want to join our fun party for coffee?', something a bit more meaningful than my usual sequence of grunts. And when I finally do think of something to say that's vaguely relevant to the half-chat that occurs between lectures, I bottle out. I clam up, freeze, forgetting that the others in whatever shifting unformed group I find myself loitering on the edge of are in exactly the same boat. They presumably (hopefully), don't know each other yet either and are just as unsure of themselves. Like passengers on a stalled train waiting for an announcement or a free sandwich, watching everybody else for clues as to what to do next. But I feel like such an inarticulate fool. I can't help thinking that they must see me as some sort of weirdo misfit.

This might seem strange but I actually avoid anybody I've already met, anybody who has already borne witness to my social ineptness. I shrink away, I don't want to give them any more ammunition. In a class of about seventy, that leaves me with very few potential friends. It is a worry. When I leave this college in three years' time, I honestly don't care if I get a degree or a job or a soulmate. As long as I have the ability and the confidence to speak my mind clearly, wherever I am and to whomsoever I want, I'll be happy. That's not too much to ask for. Is it?

The week flew by. Weeks can be very impatient like that. Most of the subjects are exactly what I had hoped for and more, and some are absolute bullshit. Psychology, Sociology and Linguistics for instance are all riveting, new countries full of exotica. I find myself nodding in agreement throughout the classes. I'm sure my fellow students think I've got some sort of uncontrollable neck muscle disorder, that will either frighten them off or attract the deviants. 'I'd say the little freak with the glasses gives great blowjobs.' Whereas Film Studies on the other hand seems to be almost exclusively about Westerns, yawn, and Economics is just so boring. I mean, did any of the great economists in history ever feel even remotely embarrassed when their theories were proved wrong?

The lecturers are all 'cooler-booler' (Gráinne's favourite expression). They encourage debate and sycophantic groups. One of the mature students, I think her name is Maura and she drives a Fiat Bambino, is almost certainly sleeping with Tom Doherty (Psychology). Already. The lucky bitch. He is fortyish, greying, wears a cravat and actually sits on the floor during class. I mean, hey, he's so unconventional.

There are some very flamboyant characters among the student population too. On Wednesday afternoon there was a festival atmosphere in the canteen, as various clubs and societies clamoured for our attention. I joined the Athletics Club, the Third World Society, the Labour Party, the Camera Club and because I was practically forced to by a lad dressed up as a caveman, the Left-handed Bass Players Society. You didn't have to be left-handed or indeed play the bass to belong. According to their wacky spokesman, you just had to be mad, which of course is a euphemism for 'desperately seeking attention'. So, needless to say, I joined.

Sunday, 24 October 1982
During mass this morning, Father Flanagan launched a vicious tirade against the media blaming it for the breakdown of the family, divorce, abortion, river pollution and the rest of society's ills. I could sense Mam looking at me out of the corner of her eye, her thick eyeliner an arrow, more or less accusing me of collusion in undermining all that was good and pure. And now she had her suspicions confirmed by the highest authority imaginable, the parish priest. She doesn't have him in her pocket too. Does she?

After mass, I bumped into Pól O'Neadún. Tall, thin, deadly serious Pól, Pioneer pin and *fainne* displayed proudly on the lapel of his tweed jacket, bicycle clips on his trouser legs. I'm surprised he wasn't wearing his medals for Irish dancing too. That's unfair. Pól needs his emblems to remind himself and others of exactly who he is, 'I don't drink, I speak Irish, I ride a bike. I am constant, I am loyal, dependable and true.'

He approached me shyly outside the church and stooping asked me to go for a walk with him down by Finn McCool's footprint – a shallow indentation in a rock that doesn't remotely resemble the shape of a giant's foot, unless of course Finn McCool had an artificial leg made from the trunk of an oak tree. Pól is an expert on myths and legends, local history and oddly the Laws of Physics. I've heard him described as a 'walking encyclopedia' and that's exactly what he's like, a turkey-necked oracle, without curiosity or ambition, a snorkeller rather than a deep-sea diver. I'd love to give him a good shake and urge him to leave. But despite his light and sickly frame, he's attached umbilically to the area, a mammy's boy who's been around since the beginning of time, well, since the invention of bicycles anyway.

Luckily I had an excuse not to go with him i.e., I had to

prepare dinner for the ogress. The truth is, I couldn't face another Sunday morning trudge, ankle-deep in leaves, the smell of boiled cabbage in the air, insincerely greeting the inscrutable denizens of the town.

I felt so bad. I mean we were never officially 'an item' but Pól is under the impression that we are because we used to go for regular walks together during the summer and held hands once. But we never kissed. And surely that's the litmus test for passion.

I've never been kissed properly by any man. Most of the girls in my class had been going to discos in Arklow for at least the last two years. Some even went the whole way. I stayed at home with my books and my romantic dreams intact. I could have joined them I suppose. Mam, I'm sure, wouldn't have even noticed my absence. But I didn't want to go. I didn't have the willpower or the clothes.

I must have been the only one at school who hadn't tried shoplifting or sex. Deirdre Fay produced a semen-stained skirt in the Teapot at lunchtime to shrieks of hilarity from all present. I didn't belong in these huddles. They fell silent or tittered if I neared, as if I were a parent or a little sister or some sort of asexual being. I caught snatches of their conversations . . . boyfriends, arses, big cocks, little cocks, johnnies . . . I suppose I kidded myself that I didn't care. That my yearnings were nobler. Banished beyond the harem walls, I cultivated my outsider status, by being stroppy and mute. They wanted odd. They got odd. I wore slippers to school. I went running after midnight. I drank whole bottles of cough mixture. But so desperate to belong, I even toyed with the idea of having drunken sex with the next man I met, one of their fathers ideally, in a stolen blouse from Cathy's Fashion. 'Are you happy now? I'm just as tainted as you.' I wanted something badly. The truth is I was afraid. Not of the guilt, which each of the girls wore like a garland around her neck, or the reputation that could become your mangy lapdog for life. I was scared of intimacy, interaction, being physically there at an event involving me. Apart from studious Gráinne and one or two others, my social network comprised entirely of fictitious characters. Wonderfully complex rounded dashing men. As a result I've no doubt that my sex life was sublime compared to theirs. Anyway, all that is going to change during the next few weeks. I'm lowering my expectations and my various metaphorical knickers. I've got the PIN number to the real world. Pól looked really hurt and muttered something under his breath like, 'No time for your friends in Killeeny any more.' Him too. He started to cry and everything. Well his lower lip trembled. I started crying as well in the confusion. Looking into his eyes, I realised that he didn't have long to live.

It was with tremendous relief that I got on the bus to take me back to Dublin. Mam, needless to say, didn't even wave goodbye. The bus dropped us off on O'Connell Street which was very lively even at that time of the night (ten p.m.). There were hundreds of people milling around, subdued couples leaving the cinemas, suddenly conscious of their own shortcomings, gangs of skinheads jostling outside the amusement arcades, and lines of country people of all shapes and sizes clutching their baggage in queues for the local buses to take them to their overpriced lodgings. I joined such a queue and tried to ignore a growling drunk who was the image of Milo O'Shea. My fellow travellers left me to my own devices, grateful that the man wasn't pestering them. The number 19 finally arrived and lumbered off towards Phibsboro where I am staying. The bus was dead quiet as everybody counted the cost of the weekend and dreaded the following morning. And then a peculiar thing happened. The gloom was interrupted, softly at first by an elderly Indian man dressed in a suit singing a calypso version of 'Down by the River'. He stared at a baby in the seat opposite as he tapped his foot and his gentle, lilting voice soothed the hearts of all on board. The baby gazed back enraptured by the odd-looking man, its mother slightly perturbed by the attention her child was receiving. The gaunt, smiling stranger, the only man without baggage, sang louder as if to encourage others to join in, the direction of his glance not wavering from the tiny face of his muse. I didn't want him to ever stop. Our trance-like state was broken when he finally stood up and bowed, doffed his cap and said goodnight, winked at the child and got off the bus. We shifted uncomfortably in our seats, too uptight to burst into the applause his performance deserved, which is what we all wanted to do. I mean what is wrong with this country? We failed to obey the bidding of our souls and our native instincts by harmonising with him, we weren't even able to turn and share the wonder with the person sitting next to us.

At the digs, Mrs Dungan was waiting anxiously for me. She was worried on account of the recent spate of attacks on women in the area. (If Mam only knew about them!) She's so nice. Although I was exhausted, we had a great chat before going to bed. She wanted to know all about Killeeny and college and insisted I treat her home as my own during my stay.

4

At about ten past eleven that night I found myself above in the Lock Inn well on with at least half the town. It was very noisy, the usual combination of a *Take Your Pick* live quiz show, lots of shouting and piped heavy rock music, Rory Gallagher I think it was. 'Messing with the Kid.' It wasn't my cup of tea but fair play to him anyway, he is Irish. It was my round.

I bumped into Linda Carolan at the bar. It definitely wasn't her that was dead. It must have been the sister. Still, though, I was surprised to see her in the pub.

'Sorry for your trouble.'

'What trouble Patrick?'

'Sorry to hear about your wee sister.'

'What are you talking about?'

'Your sister, Mary, the one that was killed in the bus crash. I'm very sorry. Please convey my—'

'Mary's above in the house with the flu. Is this some sort of a joke? Because if it is, I don't think it's very funny.' Off she stormed.

Fuck Plunkett McKenna and his wrong information. 'Sorry Mary, I mean, Linda, sorry. Fuck.'

But she was gone. I suppose she'll be talking about me now and pointing at me. 'That Scully fella must have a screw loose.' Fuck her, I was only trying to be nice.

I went outside for a quick puke. The pints would have to wait. It was a good quick clean job, no after-effects and no witnesses to the best of my knowledge. 'Messin' with the Kid, dedundedundedudun I'm messing with the kid', catchy enough so it is . . . There was a couple arguing across the road at the gates of the church. I didn't recognise them, probably some of the Innisbunion crowd in town for the night. He was dressed as Dracula. She was Cleopatra, I think.

'Just fuck off,' says he, 'fuck off.' Pushing her hand roughly away from his arm. There were tears in his eyes. 'I never want to see you again as long as I live.' That's good coming from Dracula.

The girl was screaming her head off. 'Thomas. Come back. I'm sorry.'

Oh ho! Too late now, Cleo. She grabbed him by the ruff of his shirt. It ripped dramatically but he didn't seem to notice, just kept on storming off, towards the lake, bawling elementally at the stars. I like that word, elementally. 'Fuck off, Bernadette. Fuck off and leave me alone, you're only a bitch.'

'I didn't mean it, I swear, I didn't mean it.'

She ran after him, losing one of her high-heels on the way, and literally threw herself at him. He punched in the passenger-seat window of a red Toyota Corolla (it could have been Larry Gollogly's but I'm not hundred per cent sure) and started to run, blood already flowing from his broken hand in triumph. She followed half-running, half-crawling like an ape-girl.

I don't know what they were fighting over. How would I know? She probably looked at another fella she used to go out with years ago and that and the drink was probably all it took to set him off. People get very jealous around here, you see. And I don't mean she looked at him longingly or winked at him or wanted to ask him a question or reminisce fondly about the time she pushed his hand away when he tried to put it inside her knickers or that sort of thing. I mean he might just have passed through her field of vision by accident and she might not have managed to shut her eyes in time and, of course, Thomas the fuckin' Timelord misread the signal. That's all it takes. Very jealous altogether.

I picked up the shoe anyway, a white shoe, and made a wish. A wish that will never come true. Tears came into my eyes. I couldn't control myself. I was just about to fuck off away from there altogether when Balls stuck his head out the door of the Lock Inn.

'Scully, what the fuck are you doing?'

'I'll be in in a minute.' I pretended to be having a slash and lodged the shoe between a couple of railings. She'd be able to pick it up on her way to mass on Sunday morning if she survives until then. And then I went back into the pub. It was my round after all. The table was covered in drinks though, about twenty full pints of Guinness, so there was no need to go up to the bar. I sat down. Balls introduced me to a teddy bear he'd just won in the *Take Your Pick*.

'Meet my new friend. This is Scully.'

He even bought it a whiskey, can you believe that? Somebody asked him why. 'Bears like whiskey,' he said and everybody laughed. I couldn't see the joke myself. As a matter of fact I never thought Balls was that funny at all. All I ever hear is 'Jaysus that Balls O'Reilly fella is deadly crack.' Francesca thinks he's hilarious too. She's always quoting some of the things he said, in front of me and everything. It drives me mad. Of course, he goes into overdrive whenever there's girls around.

'No, Bears prefer vodka,' I said. Everybody stopped laughing and looked away. Even Rory Gallagher stopped for a split-second. Fuckin' eejits. No sense of humour.

The boys were chatting up these two lovely-looking birds

from England. They were over for the weekend, cousins of Sheila Finlay. A pair of tramps in actual fact, dolled up to the nines and enjoying the attention. Waistcoats. Tits.

I must have fallen asleep for a while because when I woke up Rory had been replaced by some marching band playing the National Anthem. I stood up. The whole pub stood up including the two English girls except one fella who couldn't be bothered. Shovels gave him a dirty look but he passed no remarks. If there was one thing Shovels hated it was people not standing for the National Anthem. He had a thing about anti-social behaviour. You know, for example, that time Balls came home wearing the purple Docs, Shovels wouldn't speak to him for the whole weekend. He didn't like unconventional people like this clown sitting down for the National Anthem, or people who dressed in an extravagant fashion, punks or rockers or mods or new romantics, or people who dressed in uniform, guards, soldiers, the bank porter or the Red Cross. He hated students, queers, people who went to boarding school, people who had CB radios (although our Joe had one), people on crutches, fishermen, anyone in the brass band – mind you, that comes under uniforms – anyone wearing a badge or a hat, people with red hair, in fact he hated everybody. We got on all right but I wouldn't like to get on the wrong side of him. Balls used to get on his wick with his mad antics. Only for him being a friend of mine I think he would have got a hiding by now. It can be very tense when the two of them are around.

One night we went to the Mirage, a great nightclub about five miles from town, to see Johnny Logan, the fella who won the Eurovision. Shovels took an instant dislike to him on account of his white suit and spent the whole evening standing in front of the stage spitting at his legs. After the show, which by the way was very good even if it did cost an arm and a leg, the bold Shovels waited for Logan to come out so as he could batter him. But unfortunately he couldn't get near him. So he satisfied himself a few days later by spray-painting 'Johnny Logan is a Cunt' on the wall of the Parish Hall, a message that is still there to this day. Most people agree with it. Personally I don't. I think he did Ireland proud and he's very popular in Turkey.

Anyway we were outside the pub, milling around after we were all turfed out, and he says to me and O'Reilly and the two girls from England, 'Wait there a minute' and he goes over to the lad who wouldn't stand up for the National Anthem.

'Have you some sort of problem?'

'What?'

'Are you a fuckin' Brit?'

'No. I'm Irish.'

'You are not, you're a Brit bastard.'

And he clocked him with a punch. It was very exciting. Your man looked up at him, totally shocked. I could hear a crowd of people muttering under their breaths, 'That's not right. That's not right.' But they didn't bring up the subject with Shovels on account of his reputation.

'That'll teach you to stand for the National Anthem in future.'

Somebody finally pointed out to Shovels what everybody else already knew, that the lad was a bit mentally handicapped and didn't know any better.

Shovels says, 'Well he should have been trained.' I could tell he was sorry he did it in a way.

The Mirage is a fuckin' deadly spot. I would safely say it is the biggest and best nightclub in the world. No exaggeration. People come on Fridays and Saturdays from as far away as Dublin, Belfast and Armagh. Meat Loaf, the very large singer most famous for his bestselling Bat Out of Hell album, played there one time just after his heyday but he only lasted five minutes before some fella called him a big fat bastard and threw a bottle at him. Meat wasn't standing for any of this carry-on. He leapt down off the stage and throttled the culprit before bounding off into the wings giving the middle finger to the crowd as an encore. There was pandemonium and some of the crowd are still looking for their money back.

Who do you think was the first person we met on the bus to the Mirage? Plunkett McKenna, of course, on his own as usual with a big grin on his face pretending he was having a great time. 'Are yez for the Mirage boys?' What a stupid fuckin' question. 'No we're going to the Holy Well.' He didn't hang around for long when he saw that I was sitting beside Shovels. They had a run-in last Christmas.

The two English girls, Eileen and Brigid, were sitting in the seats in front of us, delighted with themselves. The lads on the bus were like monks, drooling at the sight of them but far too shy to approach them. Balls was working his way up and down the aisle, as usual, laughing and joking, giving a running commentary on everything that was going on. I turned around at one stage to find him doing his elephant impression which involved pulling his trouser pockets inside out and letting his cock hang out. There was a variation of this particular prank that called for a pair of glasses but he mustn't have had them on him tonight. We could all do that only we're not as childish as he is. Everybody loves Balls.

I wouldn't be surprised if the two tramps from England were a bit disgusted with the behaviour of Shovels outside the pub. They must have been because they ignored us completely. I admit it was a bit over the top. Although it has to be said it had nothing to do with them or me or anybody else. He wasn't trying to impress anybody. It was purely for his own benefit. Even though his victim was very small and a bit slow in the head, you couldn't call Shovels a bully. No. It didn't matter who they were, or what size, if they annoyed him they got the works. Anyway, there wasn't much crack out of him at this point in time. Deep in thought he was going through some sort of withdrawal after the row, I suppose. You didn't know with him. He's always quiet.

Balls was getting on quite well with one of the girls, Brigid I think or maybe it was Eileen. Well next time I looked he was sitting on her knee anyway, sucking his thumb pretending to be a baby and calling her Mammy. It wouldn't have surprised me to see him sucking her tits. He'd try anything. Somebody let a stink bomb off on the bus. It must have been one of the young fellas down the back. They were squealing with joy, like gurriers. I personally didn't think it was very funny.

'Hey Scully boy! Was that you boy?' said McKenna. I could have killed him. 'Jesus what did you have for your tea boy?' Everyone was falling around the place laughing.

'You could have wiped your arse Scully.' Somebody else jumping on the bandwagon. I said nothing but I could tell my face was on fire. The girls from England were having a good giggle too at my expense. Even O'Reilly was holding his nose at me. I tried to ignore them all. The only thing I knew for sure was that I was going to batter Plunkett McKenna before the night was out.

The Mirage was black. You couldn't move. There must have been over five thousand people there. It was supposed to be a fancy-dress night but there were only about ten people in costume, students probably down from Dublin for the weekend, looking for attention. Most of the people around here wouldn't be bothered with that sort of shite.

Myself and Shovels went over to the bar and ordered a couple of double whiskeys. A friend of his worked behind the bar, Tommy Burns, so we got them for free. I would say we had drunk at least ten pints each earlier on in the evening so we were well on the way. Shovels wasn't saying a word. He just stood there by the bar lowering whiskeys, and glaring at people. Apart from once when he had to go to the toilet, he didn't move at all. Not a muscle. No way was he going to get out of people's way. They'd say 'excuse me' then walk around him. If he was on a trawler in a storm, the sea itself couldn't make him budge when he was in that sort of mood. Out of the corner my eye I saw Balls snogging the English one on the dance floor to the sound of Duran Duran, and nudged Shovels. He passed no remarks but I could see he was taking it all in.

About an hour later Balls calls me aside, takes a pair of girl's knickers out of his pocket, and says. 'Scully, smell that.' The dirty bastard. He told me he rode her out the back. If it was true, and I doubt it very much, it was a bit ignorant in my opinion. I don't believe in sex outside marriage. No, I'm saving myself for Francesca. Anyway they were probably his sister's knickers, ones that he found in the laundry basket at home. I gave him a filthy look to let him know where I stood on the matter and then the pair of us went to sit down where the English girls were parked, leaving Shovels to his mad thoughts. Balls and his one immediately took up where they left off. I thought for a second he was going to disappear down her throat. She was hoovering him up. Meanwhile, I was left looking at the one with the bleached-blonde hair, her sipping a Bacardi and Coke.

'Well Ursula, what do you think of . . . ?'

'The name's Brigid,' she snapped. Very frosty.

'Oh right. Yeah. Eh what do you think of the Mirage?'

'What?' Leaning in, pulling her hair back over her ear. Mmm sexy.

'The Mirage, this place, deadly isn't it?' I shouted over Ram Jam and Black Betty.

'Yeah, it's great.'

I actually felt a surge of pride when she said that. It was great. Compared to all the places she'd been to in London and God knows where else, the Mirage was great. I was in London for a while last summer staying with Fergus Gaffney, whose girlfriend by the way is black, and we went to a few places and you know what it's true they're not as good.

'Are you over for long?'

'We're going back on Tuesday.'

'I see, I see.' I smiled at her. She flashed back the briefest of smiles, enough for me to know that she liked me. Then she started looking around and nodding her head in time to the music. She lit up a cigarette. A pity but no matter, she was a ride.

And what's more her perfume was intoxicating. It required a great effort on my part to keep my eyes away from her cleavage. Too big an effort because after a while I failed. There was no doubt about it but she was a lovely bit of stuff, model material in fact.

'What do you do?'

'Sorry!'

'What do you do for a living?'

'I'm a hairdresser. What do you do?'

'I eh I'm a doctor.'

'A doctor?'

'Well I'm training to be a doctor.'

I thought that would impress her. I was right. She clammed up completely. She finally copped on she was out of her depth.

'Would you like to come outside for a bit of fresh air?' She removed my hand from her back and threw it into my lap.

'No thank you. I'm fine where I am.' Exhaling, playing hard to get. The bitch.

I was just about to ask her to dance when would you

believe it some young fella – he couldn't have been more than twelve years old – bent down and somehow persuaded her to join him out on the floor. Unbe-fuckin-lievable. As she was getting up, stubbing out her fag, smoothing her skirt, the other one came out of hibernation under Balls and touched her on the arm. Brigid or whatever her name was leaned down over the table to confer with her friend, giving me the opportunity to look right down her blouse. For fuck sake, she had no bra. Tits hanging like lampshades, two generous scoops of homemade ice cream, a pair of 99s from Fraser's, the shafts of chocolate flake protruding, tips rounded by the tongue. I would safely say it was the nicest sight I've ever seen in my whole life. I got a bigger horn than Neil Armstrong got when he first saw the moon. Who would have thought? Behind a fairly ordinary purple shirt lay one of the Wonders of the World. They had a good laugh. Then Brigid stood up, closing the door to the secret garden, and went off with your man.

Adrian Gurvitz's deadly song was playing – very romantic. That was usually the signal for to go on the prowl. No partner, unfortunately, as Balls was fully occupied. Just as I was getting up to go, whiskey and red in my hand, I felt a tap on the shoulder.

'Would you like to dance?'

I turned around to see some wee savage from out the country, buttoned up to the last, the blind cunt.

'Fuck sake,' he says when he sees my face, 'I thought you were a fuckin' girl.' Little squeaky voice.

He turned to his friend. 'I thought he was a fuckin' girl. Hahhahahah!'

'I'd say you did all right you big queer.' Says his friend.

'I'm not a queer. I thought he was a fuckin' girl. He's got girl's hair.'

'You should get your fuckin' hair cut hi.' And he laughed, screwing up his ridiculous red face, a small stocky man with a head the shape and colour of a ripe tomato. The sound of his laugh was hideous, his lipless mouth like an axe-wound gone septic. Little curly-haired cunt. I didn't say anything back to them because I didn't want to lose my temper. Anyway they must have known what was good for them because they walked away. I didn't have girl's hair either. I admit it was a bit long but certainly not a girl's. First thing Monday morning I'm going to have it cut. I might dye it as well when I'm at it.

I was beginning to feel a bit hot under the collar. To be honest the shirt was a bit small for me so I unscrewed the pin from my lapels, took off my tie and stuffed it in my pocket. Not exactly a pair of knickers but no matter, there was plenty of time. It was important to get the body temperature exactly right before hitting the floor. Having said that there was no point taking off my tanktop. That was one of the most stylish items of clothing in my wardrobe and you had to put your best foot forward in these situations. The whole point of dressing up was to make a good impression. Even if you got tongue-tied, you were still in with a chance.

I always found asking people to dance one of the hardest things to do. You have to make sure all the conditions were perfect. For example, my bladder was full. It was important to have the fluid balance exactly right too so I decided to go to the jacks.

'Well Patrick!'

'Well Joe!' (My brother Joe. On the prowl too. Good luck to him.)

I was walking towards the toilets when who did I see only Plunkett McKenna coming out. He was looking around him like he was lost, his smile temporarily out of order. I deliberately stood in his path so as he'd bump into me and spill my drink which he did, according to plan.

'Oh Scully boy.'

'What do you think you're doing, you cunt ya? Ha, Look
at my good trousers!'

I lashed out at him with a right fist and flattened him to
the ground. It was quite painful but to be honest I didn't
mind seeing as how I was so excited. What a sound! Bone
on bone, a dull satisfying smack and I loved the way he
crumpled to the floor without a word, just a low moan,
utterly deflated. Looking up at me like a terrified child. As
if to say 'What was that for, boy?'

Big stupid lamb's eyes. I don't know why he looked
so surprised. If I were him I'd be expecting that sort of
treatment all the time. Jesus, I would love to have given
him a good few kicks too, I would love to have stamped
on his head. Jumped up and down on it until his brains
mashed out through his earholes, the cunt, but before I
knew it the bouncers had pounced and fucked me out of
the door.

All in all, in the final analysis, it was worth it. Despite
the fact that I hung around with Shovels I very rarely hit
anybody in public. That's not to say I'm a coward. Far from
it. One time when I was playing for the under sixteens in
the semi-final of the Dr Ball Cup, I elbowed a lad with a
withered arm in the side of the head but, I'm telling you,
he deserved it. Niggly wee cunt, kept standing on my heels,
and mouthing off the whole game, and every time I got
the ball, he'd slap me about the face with the withered
arm like seaweed knowing full well the referee wouldn't
give a free against him. Another time me and Geoghegan
got into a fight in Dublin but generally speaking I didn't
bother with that sort of crack. Shovels by the way didn't
mind if I didn't get involved in his scraps. We didn't have
that sort of understanding, 'I'll back you up if you back
me up.' No. In fact he never mentioned fighting. It never
came up in the conversation. It wasn't even something he
enjoyed doing. It was something he had to do. It was his

duty. If I wasn't mistaken, he was off looking for a fight right now. You're not a preacher without a congregation, as my father used to say.

I got back inside easily enough. In fact one of the bouncers who threw me out was my next-door neighbour and he used to go out with my sister Valerie. In fact he could well be the father of her child. Anyway, he picked me up off the ground and said sorry for thumping me. It was part of the job, he explained, as he helped clean the mud off my jumper. We had a bit of crack and then he let me in a few minutes later through a staff entrance.

It was time to make my move. I spied a little one standing at the edge of the dance floor smoking a fag, tapping her leg, coat and bag at her feet. She was trying very hard not to look pissed off even though she was because her friend, the girl beside her, was engrossed in a conversation with some fella she'd just met. Leaving her in the lurch. The friend was laughing too loudly at everything the fella said despite the fact that she probably couldn't hear what he was saying and what's more he had a moustache and his shirt was tucked into not just his trousers but his underpants as well by mistake. So here we had a situation which was not unusual in this part of the world where the shirt invited the underpants up to have a look out over the top of the trousers. You could tell by the way she was standing right under his nose that she fancied him, staring into his face and all that sort of thing, smiling, and completely ignoring the wee one I had my eye on who was by now giving her vicious looks. Not tapping her leg any more but scraping the floor with her foot as if she was on one of those old scooters like our Valerie had or as if she was an impatient pony. The DJ had stopped playing records and was making one of those long announcements he specialises in. He loves the sound of his own voice but fair play to him, he's got very good taste in music, very.

'That was Queen and "Crazy Little Thing Called Love". Especially for Julie and Shane, from Julie, here's Spandau Ballet with "True".'

I'll tell you one thing for sure, her friend was wasting her time with that fella because I know him. He's from the town and he's a bollox and he does kung fu. In fact he's the only person in the town who does kung fu. He even set up a club a few years ago but as far as I know he's still the only member. These were ideal circumstances, I thought to myself and made my way over to the girl trying to be as careful as I could not to sway from side to side.

My heart was pounding away as usual like the franking machine at work. I could hardly catch my breath but I had to give it a go, she was lovely-looking and, more importantly, available. I sincerely hoped my head wouldn't betray me. It was like a vat, all kinds of drink sloshing around inside it. I could actually hear it splashing against my skull and crashing on the deserted shores of my brain but still. All I had to do was make sense and I was away.

'Look at the underpants on your man,' I slurred, pointing at Frank Hickey's arse.

'What?' she says, looking at me like I was some sort of weirdo. No point trying to explain. She might think I was queer. Try another tack.

'I mean, do you want to dance?' All faculties present and correct sir. Better keep the talking to a minimum. Get her out on to the floor, steady the nerves to a slow song. Talking gets you nowhere, I've always found. You either say the wrong thing or the right thing in the wrong way. Nobody understands anybody else. It would take a philosopher a lifetime to figure out exactly what somebody means when they say a sentence. And I got a B in English for my Inter. Francesca of course doesn't listen to a word I say, she's far more interested in her college friends. No point talking. It only wears you out.

'All right.'

'What?'

'I said all right, I'm dancing.'

I have to say she caught me completely by surprise. It was a lot easier than I expected. She stamped on her cigarette and walked towards the floor.

'Aisling, where are you going?'

'I'm dancing with him. Mind my bag,' she snapped. 'And my coat.' And that's an order.

'I'll see you back here, Aisling. I'll be here.' All apologetic, she knew she was in the wrong.

'You better be,' hissed Aisling. And then to me. 'Come on if you're coming!'

'Young Frank,' I says.

'Young Scully.'

And then I hop-skipped after her double-quick before she got lost in the throng.

I put one hand on either side of her waist and steered her away from anybody I knew. She put her hands loosely around my neck. (It was Adrian Gurvitz again on the turntable. He's very popular around here. The DJ plays it at least once during every slow set and fair play to him. It is a deadly song.) God, she was gorgeous, even if she did look a bit like your man the lead singer out of Soft Cell. Who I believe is a queer. She had short black blow-dried hair and was wearing black lipstick on her beautiful pouting lips. Her tongue was black too. Weird. I suppose you'd call her petite but she had a lovely pair of tits, all the same, lovely little beanbags. You could just about make out the shape of them beneath her sleeveless, knee-length, black chiffon dress. In fact, all I could think of was how much I would love to get my hands on those tits. As she rearranged herself between songs, I managed to catch a glimpse of her bra under her arm.

Jaysus, I don't believe it. There's your man Dracula

wearing the face off Cleopatra, barefoot now completely, inseparable, the two of them drained of strength, after their earlier disagreement, as close as they'll ever be.

'What?'

'Nothing.'

The song finished. I was sure she'd fuck off back to her friend now. That was the custom, one or two dances and fuck off, but no it looked as if she was going to stay the distance, make her wait for a change, rub it in, see how she likes it.

'What's your name?'

'Ehh . . . Patrick. What's yours?'

'Aisling.'

'Aisling. That's a nice name.'

I know it was a stupid thing to say seeing as how it's not a nice name at all but I had to bend down and keep the conversation going for two reasons. First of all, her hot breath on the side of my face every time she opened her mouth was the nicest feeling I have ever felt. She might as well have been licking my spine. And secondly, my cock was getting hard again so I had to try and create a gap between us by arching my back. I didn't want to scare her off just yet and thankfully she didn't seem to notice the manoeuvre.

'You smell nice.'

'Thanks very much. It's Blue Stratos. Francesca gave it to me for my birthday.'

'Who's Francesca?' Flickering her eyelashes.

'Eh my sister . . . eh do you come here often?' (I know, I know, you don't have to tell me but I had to say something.)

'No it's my first time, Cathy was here a few times before.'

'Who's Cathy?'

'My friend.'

'The one talking to Frank.'

'Who's Frank?'

'And that was "Once Twice Three Times a Lady" by The Commodores . . . lady's handbag has been handed in . . . lipstick and a snub-nosed gun . . . special request for Patricia Scully . . . from Plunkett McKenna . . .' That was Balls' idea of a joke. He does it everytime.

'Where are you from?'

'Can you not think of better questions than that?' Fuckin' smartarse.

'No.' I couldn't think of better answers either. The whole thing would have been very embarrassing if I wasn't so drunk. In school there should be a class about chatting up women. Geography, woodwork, smalltalk. I remember when I was sent to the Gaeltacht one summer we had Irish dancing classes. We learned to dance jigs and reels and hornpipes with the chairs. I'd have no trouble getting off with a chair now or settling down with one for that matter. Thanks to my experience.

Aisling was very fresh but for some reason she still stayed. She must have liked limbo. Because that's where we were now.

Anyway, I decided the best course of action was to just shut up completely and concentrate on looking cool. I was very good at that. A fella who works with me in Dunn's tries to be cool all the time, wears sunglasses and walks, waggling his arse. We were going out for lunch one day, crossing the road in heavy traffic, when what happened only wasn't he knocked down. Served him right, the bollox, head up in the air, thinking his shit doesn't smell. I can tell you now it does smell because I smelt it there and then. It's hard to look cool though when you're angling to get a good look at Aisling's arse. The shiny fabric of her dress was clinging to her contours making her case more presentable. 'Your honour, exhibit A, one of the nicest wee arses I've ever seen.' If I were a painter, I'd spend my whole life painting her arse and I wouldn't get anywhere near its perfectly divided perfection. Of course, I didn't tell Aisling what was on my mind. Part of being cool is pretending to have no interest whatsoever in the other person, you show more interest in the new lighting system, the fire exits and your shoes. Which is a very stupid thing to do I suppose considering you're very interested in the other person, very. But that's this place for you. In other countries, I believe, if you fancy somebody, you give them gifts, pay them compliments, you might even tell them you like them. And from what I hear it works even in England. But you wouldn't get far with that strategy here. They'd laugh at you.

'You are very beautiful!'

'Yeah, I'm fuckin' gorgeous, and if you think you're getting into my knickers, you have another think coming.'

No way. That's why if you fancy somebody you'd be more inclined to insult them. 'Jaysus, you've put on an awful lot of weight,' or something like that. That strategy doesn't work either. Nothing works. It doesn't matter if you say what you mean or the opposite of what you mean, nobody has a clue what you're on about. They don't want to know. It's as simple as that.

Every time I glanced down to have a look at her, she caught my eyes, and looked back at me in a sly way as if she was sizing me up. And when I smiled at her, she copied me by smiling back in a forced exaggerated way. I didn't know what she was up to at all. Then all of a sudden she pulled me closer, grabbed a hold of my hands and placed them on the small of her back and pressed the left-hand side of her face into my chest. There was no doubt about it now, she could feel my cock prodding her stomach but she didn't bat an eyelid. Balls used to tuck his cock up under the elastic of his underpants before he went out on the floor. No flies on him. I'm sure she heard my heart too going like the clappers, like somebody jogging on the spot upstairs. All the cells in my body were throbbing like a bunch of headbangers. I was very nervous but at the same time, I have to say, very excited, very.

This went on for a while. At one point she tightened her tummy muscles and pushed harder against me and my chief scout just to let me know she knew he was there. Then she went all sullen again and buried her head in my oxter.

'What's wrong, Aisling?' Not that I really cared.

'Nothing.'

'You've gone very quiet.'

'I'm thinking of committing suicide.'

'What?'

'I'm thinking of committing suicide.'

For fuck sake. That's just typical, bringing up a serious subject when I'm at my most vulnerable. Mind you it didn't affect my erection. If anything it made it harder.

'Why would you do a thing like that?'

'Why not?' She shrugged. Good point.

'Well I don't know, what would your family think?'

'My family *hate* me.' She really spat out the word hate. Who knows, it might be true.

'Well, well what about your friends?'

'I have no friends.'

'What about your one, the one you came with?'

'Cathy? She's a bitch. She just uses me.'

'Well what about me? I'm your friend.'

'You don't know anything about me.'

'Well I'd like to get to know you. Here I'll tell you what. Why don't we get a drink and sit down.'

'All right.' We disengaged and walked over to the side of the floor. (Oh my God! AC/DC and "Whole Lotta Rosie". Just in time.)

'What'll you have?' I asked.

'Vodka and blackcurrant.' Ah, that explained why her tongue was black.

'Right.'

'What are you waiting on?' she says.

'Ehh . . . I have no money left.'

Eyes up to Heaven. 'Jesus, why did you ask me did I want a drink then? It doesn't matter I've some in my purse.'

Off she marches, unsteady in her high-heels, in a huff, brushing past couples mauling each other, me trying to keep up. I actually had money and before the night was out I'd have some more but there was no way I was telling her that. I hardly knew her and wasn't going to let her use me the way girls do. I'm no mug. I did however offer to go up for the drink.

'Don't bother, I'm not an invalid.'

She threw her bag down beside her friend Cathy who was by now grinding up against that clown from the town, stroking his moustache.

'I'll have a pint of Guinness, please, Aisling.' I shouted after her. She disappeared into the crowd at the bar. That's the last I'll see of her, I thought to myself.

'Scully, how's it goin'? What's the crack?'

'Ah young Phelim, no crack, no crack, any luck?'

'No, you must be joking, they're only a crowd of oul' tightholes in tonight. Nuns.' (It wouldn't have anything to do with the fact that you're the ugliest cunt I've ever seen in my life.)

'Who's out with you?'

'Shovels and Balls.'

'Balls is some crack, isn't he.'

'He is yeah.'

'He sure is. What are you up to yourself these days, Scully, we hardly ever see you around.'

'I'm working above in Dublin, private detective.'

'A PI. Good man, Scully.'

'Aye, I'm waiting to hear about the guards. I was supposed to get word this week.'

'Oh right. You could do a lot worse. Any football this weather?'

'No.'

Suddenly, there was a terrible commotion behind us. We looked around to see all the barmen pulling down the shutters the length of the bar and take my word for it, it was a long bar, a hundred foot long. Shattering glasses, almost breaking customers' hands. That meant the licence had expired and the guards were outside. There was a lookout man on top of the Mirage who pressed a buzzer when he saw them coming and it didn't matter if you got your drink or lost your money, but the shutters came clattering down. But don't worry as soon as the guards went away the shutters came up again and normal service resumed.

'Here's your drink.'

It was Aisling, she came back and fair play to her she remembered the drink. Phelim Kennedy fucked off as soon as he saw her. Afraid of his shite of women so he was and this particular specimen was not in his league. We went to sit down. She spent the next half an hour talking about killing herself and how there was no point in living and how everybody hated her and how horrible her family were and how much she hated her job (she worked in a pharmacy by the way) and how men only wanted one thing and how ugly she was.

'Untrue,' I said, 'untrue. I'll have to stop you there. You are not ugly, in fact I'd say you are beautiful.'

I could be a right charmer when I wanted to be. I suppose people think I'm a good listener. I can't think of any other reason why she might be telling me all this bullshit.

'Look you don't know what's around the next corner.' I wasn't quite sure what it meant but it sounded good. My father used to always say it to me anyway. If I was ever writing a book I'd write it in such a way that the readers wouldn't know what was around the next corner.

'I do know. More *misery* that's all.'

'Aisling, Aisling, you're only saying that. Life is . . . is . . . great.' For a split-second, I nearly believed that was true. There was a long pause. I wished I had a fire to look into. You can see everything in a fire.

'Oh well. I probably won't be alive this time next week.' That was going too far. I didn't know what to say but instead of putting my arm around her and consoling her, I found my ears tuning into the conversation two lads were having beside us.

'—a brand new Ford 440!'

'You're not serious!'

'I am fuckin' so serious. I seen it this morning.'

'Jaysus, he must have some money. And is he keeping the Massey 135?'

'Oh he is surely. [*Pause.*] Well as far as I know he is anyway.'

'The lucky bastard, a Ford 44 . . . 0.'

(*Very long pause.*)

'He's got spotlights on her too.'

'Fuck me that's some equipment.'

'I love you!' I said, half asleep.

'You're drunk.'

'I am not drunk. I admit I've had a few drinks but I'm certainly not drunk. There's a big difference. I can prove it.'

'Look, do you want to come outside?' I almost sobered up with the shock. Did she say what I think she said? I'll find out.

'What?'

'You heard me.'

Now this type of thing doesn't normally happen. What normally happens is, you fill an empty lemonade bottle with a mixture of spirits from the drinks cabinet at home, whiskey, vodka and gin, maintaining their levels with water, you go out the back and drink that alone, rocket fuel, then off to the pub, scabbing pints to beat the band, before boarding the bus to the Mirage. There you get tanked up on Pernod and black or Stag until you run out of money, then work your way around the nightclub nicking unattended drinks – pints, shorts, slops and whatever else comes to hand – by which time, it's fair to say, you're drunk, not just drunk, you're one stop short of unconscious. Your head is reeling, colours are magnified, you're swaying like a punchbag. The first volcanic wave of nausea hits the back of the throat, but you fight that back – you know from experience you've a few hours left before the lava will overflow, violently, smothering any memories of the night, good, bad or indifferent, possibly to be excavated at a future date. When you least expect it, the DJ announces the last slow set of the evening.

Fortunately, you've found your tongue. You ask every single girl in the place to dance, some will, most won't – the ones who will will only dance for one or two, then leave to find their 'lift home'. Time is rapidly running out, so you team up with a friend from school, in the same boat, to hunt in pairs, like Toshack and Keegan. You concentrate on the girls who're wearing glasses, the last resort – well nobody else is asking them, they must feel neglected, you reason, hormones raging by way of compensation they'll be chuffed at your unexpected advances. The eyesight may be deficient but the rest of the equipment is in perfect working order, and the chances of a snog are greater, but no, with the glasses they can see right through you, X-ray specs, I presume. Undeterred by rebuff after rebuff, you don't give up hope – far from it. You lurch and leer through 'Wonderful Tonight' by Eric Clapton and the other remaining sonnets, utterly convinced a girl who yearns just like you awaits forlorn in lustful dreams by the door of the ladies' toilets. In vain, of course.

You're still soliciting during the National Anthem in the full glare of the house lights, at odds with the statuesque solemnity of your fellow revellers, and when the DJ plays 'New York New York' by Frank Sinatra – for some strange reason the venue's signature tune – as people leave in noisy droves, and staff hurl empty bottles with violence into trolley bins, you loiter with intent, determined, confident, cocksure, trying to catch the eye of the girl who nearly got away in the queue outside the cloakroom, eyeing departing couples enviously, while you reassure yourself, They come here to meet men, don't they? You and the many men in your predicament whom you don't even notice in your needy pursuit. Beside you, backs to the wall in a line, they surmise the single girls don't want to leave this evening unfulfilled, without an awkward, shy and sticky spat, do they? A story at least to whisper after Sunday mass, a reminder, a hint of their sexuality. All you want is a moment, a gust of hot breath on your cheek, soft hands in yours, clumsy tongues wrestling like baby dolphins. You want to brush against their fabrics, inhale their smells, and share that breathless feeling, when time stops, remember. Hyperventilating now, inarticulate, more inarticulate than the thickest person you know (Eamonn Gilmore from Mulladuff, who's so thick he doesn't even know his own name), you are less eloquent than an ape, blushing uncontrollably, feeling altogether like a big fool, relieved that you're very drunk, in a way, hoping it will end soon so as you can enjoy alone the blissful memory, and what might have been.

You stagger along the five miles into town on your own genuinely expecting to meet her on the road, editing scenarios in your mind – she missed her lift, fifteen in the car, two in the boot, easy to overlook, so she had to hitch.

You say goodnight from twenty paces to warn her of your approach, that you mean no harm, I'll walk you home, she uneasy at first. You give her your new leather jacket, elasticated at the waist, escort her like a gentleman, she relaxes, gushes forth on local topics such as the latest pregnancies. She's an expert, and by the time you reach Maguire's shop on the outskirts of the town, you have your arm around her, and you kiss until dawn at the gates of her house, wave goodbye shyly, linger, walk away, until you're out of view, then run, feet not touching the ground, farting helium, greeting the early morning crows cleaning up outside the chipper.

But of course, I'm not telling you something you don't already know, she's not on the road at all. The only person you meet leaps out of a ditch and shouts 'Yaaaah' like a spectre in a children's book. You jump back and pee in your pants simultaneously, just a drop.

'Did I scare you ha?' he bellows delighted with himself, 'did ya think I was going to kill ya? I betya didn't expect me to jump out on top of you like that didya?' he says, he a huge hulking figure, and yes you are bloody scared as right and don't say too much, your chest feels tight, breathing now restricted, your whole body tense, he's drunker than you, slurring badly.

'Do you do any training at all?'

'I do a bit of football training now and again.'

'No, not that kind of training.'

'What kind of training?'

'You know very well what kind of training I'm on about.'

It's then you notice the tattoo on his arm of Cathleen ni Houlihan and her four green fields.

'What's your name?'

'Patrick Scully,' not wanting to give too much away.

'Can I stay in your place tonight, Patrick, I've no way of getting home?'

You must think fast. 'Ehh, I don't live in the town, I'm afraid. No I live the far side of Cootehill so I do,' I stutter, 'in a house,' I add incomprehensibly. You can't bring a fella like him into your home and not have consequences, and especially with you going on to be a guard, no way.

'You're no good to me then you cuntya . . . c'mere do you want to do any training? Tuesday nights out by—'

'Stop stop I don't want to hear any more, you're not supposed to be telling me things like that.'

'Just tell them Felix McGivney sent you.' And then he stalls.

'Do you want a fight?'

'No.'

'I was in Long Kesh for four fuckin' years, I could batter anyone.'

You finally lose the paramilitary renegade, he mumbles '*Tiocfaidh ár Lá*' and goes for a dump in the ditch and probably falls asleep in his own shit, and you run the rest of the way into town, mightily relieved, fear replaced by supersub, renewed hope with extra time remaining. Did I say hope? I meant certainty, the old stalwart, that she'll be there, whoever she is, hanging around outside the chip van on the main street. It's five o'clock in the morning and they're still doing a roaring trade. You order a burger, a battered sausage, chips in curry sauce and a portion of onion rings. What if she's sitting on the window-sill of the VG, for the sake of argument, with her friend discussing the chances missed earlier on in the evening not to mention future prospects. 'That Scully fella he's a fine catch.' Supposing, just supposing, Jennifer Connolly fancied me all the time and I didn't know it (I used to go to first aid classes with her and one time had to give her the kiss of life), she was there with a salad burger, no onions, red sauce and her friend nudges her.

'Hey Jennifer, speak of the devil.'

'Oh my God!' She buries her face in her hands.

Her best friend, Norma Scotson, or Abnorma as we used to call her on account of her size, says, 'Hey Patrick, come here, this one fancies y—' All hell breaks loose. Jennifer tries to cover Abnorma's mouth.

'Shut up Norma.'

'Were you at the Mirage?'

'I was, were you?'

'I was surely and I didn't see you at all. You must have been hiding.'

'You can see me now.'

'I can indeed and I like what I see. Bye bye Abnorma.'

But like the deadly Santana song, she's not there. You get home, have a piss in your front garden, still holding out for the click-clack of high-heels beyond the garden wall. It might even be your neighbour, suddenly fifteen, she was there tonight, you hardly recognised her at first. Who's the ride? you thought, and did a double-take, and one more take for sure. You said hello, she beamed back, radiating innocence and first-time glee. 'Well Patrick.' She looked so lovely, not the sexless kid playing hopscotch on the street you previously ignored. You felt like hugging her, protectively, if nothing else. You want to whisper in her ear, welcome to the game, but watch out. But she's not there either, she's not fifteen yet.

You go inside, fall asleep at the kitchen table, hair matted in the remains of your curry chips, to be woken by your mother getting up for early mass, disgusted, tut-tutting, but somehow unaware that you've been practically poisoned by alcohol, 'Get upstairs, you're a disgrace, some guard you'd make.' Mutely, you climb the stairs, fall into bed, turn over face down and puke into your sheets, roll them up in a ball, and stuff them into the bottom of the wardrobe, waking your little brother, in long before you, 'Any crack,' he murmurs, 'No crack', 'Did you shift?', 'No, you must be joking, only a bunch of oul' tightholes', 'That's for sure'. You conk out, dream a crazy freefall-dream, until it's time to rise up for half twelve mass. And you think to yourself, Jaysus, I can't wait 'til next weekend. That's what normally happens.

But tonight was entirely different. Here I was outside the Mirage in the rain with a complete stranger who looks like Marc Almond and wants to commit suicide. My own girlfriend Francesca is elsewhere. If only she were here now, almost a year to the day since I started going with her. Since the Freshers' Ball in the College of Media Studies in Capel Street. I remember that night so well as if it were yesterday. Balls introduced me to her, she was doing journalism and he was acting the bollox. I think he wants to be a fuckin' pop star or something. Anyway, fuck the two of them.

The two of us backs against the pebble dash. What happens now I wondered?

'Are you sure you want to go ahead with this?' Barely a whisper.

'Why, are you afraid?

'No, no, it's just, it's just, it's raining. You might catch a cold.'

Before I could make up any more excuses she has me trapped. She stands up on her tippytoes and begins to kiss me with vigour, nearly chewing the lips off my face, tongue plugging my windpipe, almost choking me. I got a bit carried away then myself and started squeezing her tightly, rubbing her back and her arse and even her tits outside her dress. She put her hands under my shirt and dug her fingers into my flesh. I kept one hand on the small of her back and tried to put the other hand down the front of her dress but the neckline was too tight. Her breastplate was bony and as delicate as a robin's. And then we stopped to catch our breath. I thought that was that. I was about to tuck my shirt back into my trousers when what does she do only she lifts my shirt over her head and starts sucking my nipples. That worried me I have to say. For one thing it was extremely tickly, unbearable in fact, and for another I thought for a second she was going to bite them off.

Next thing I know she's undoing my belt. Opening the button, pulling down the zip. For fuck's sake, I'm in trouble now. She rummaged around inside and then grabbed my cock, like the way my uncle would grab a turkey by the neck, and yanked it out of my underpants. I gasped as he felt the rush of air and rain for the first time in all his glory. Aisling looked up at me, straight in the eyes, as she pulled it faster and faster towards her, the knob beating off her dress like a pestle.

I was speechless. Nobody had ever done anything like that before apart from myself. I might as well tell you now seeing as how it won't make any difference, I was a virgin. I had never even taken a bra off before. Don't get me wrong. I'd felt Francesca's tits all right either by slipping my hand up under her bra at the pictures or else under her T-shirt when we were lying in bed the odd time she stayed over at the flat in Rathmines. She'd never let me into her knickers. Not even outside her knickers. Outside her jeans yes if she was feeling randy. So that was about it, a bit of tit and some outside box. Although in fairness to her she did pull me off once or twice, inside my trousers. One night when she was drunk after handing in an assessment and after a deadly night at Wild Bill Crosby and Southern Chicken in The Four Corners she almost ripped him out of his socket. But absolutely nothing like this. Mind you, it was actually getting quite sore, the foreskin wasn't used to being stretched in such a frenetic manner.

Suddenly what does she do only kneel down and take my cock in her mouth as if to weigh it.

'It's not very big, is it?' That was a bit cheeky but I realised it was only a joke. She was just trying to break the ice. 'Here I'll make it bigger.' And she starts sucking away at the lad. It was unbelievable. Like something out of a porn film, which by the way I strongly disapprove of. She must have been sucking it for a good five minutes before she stood up. I thought for a minute she was going to produce an ID card and say 'Police, you're under arrest, pull up your trousers immediately,' but no, oh no, she peels her knickers down below her knees and lifts up her skirt.

'Put it in Patrick.' It was an order I couldn't refuse.

To cut a long story short, I buckled at the knees and stooped down, arse damp against the stony wall, a tremendous strain on my back. I had no idea what to expect but the lad, rigid as a retriever, slid in easily enough, a little pop and he was in. Like putting on a polo-neck that shrunk in the wash, not that I'd be seen dead wearing a polo-neck. Mind you, the foreskin was still a bit tight.

'Push. Push.'

'Well Scully.'

'Ah young Kenneth.'

'Any crack?'

'Ehh, no crack.'

Kenneth McNally, standing right next to us, having a slash against the wall. Me riding a woman for the first time in my life, about to shoot the load inside her.

'What are you up to at the minute?'

'Nothing much, Kenneth, I'm above in Dublin.' The piss slows to a trickle. After what seemed like ages, he shook it and put it back into the stable.

'Is Joe out?' (Joe my brother.)

'He is yeah, he's inside.'

'Has he got the car?'

'He has yeah . . . I don't think so . . . I'll tell him you were looking for him.'

'Right you be!'

'Right, good luck, Kenneth.'

Off he went. And off I went inside her. I released the greyhounds. It was like shooting somebody with wee wet balls of paper from a peashooter, only bigger of course. The cock more or less fell out of her, shall we say 'area', straight after the performance. He took a bow and went back in behind the curtain. I pulled up my trousers and Aisling pulled on her panties. They must have been soaking wet.

'What are you looking at?'

'Nothing, eh was that all right?'

'I'd say that was your first time, was it Patrick?' The same sly smile as before.

'No. No it was not. No definitely not.'

All I wanted to do at that point in time was tell somebody, anybody. I now knew why it was called losing your virginity. It wasn't like losing a fiver, or a family heirloom, or a limb or your father. It was worse than that. It was like committing the seven deadly sins all at once, pride, lust, anger, the whole lot. I was damned, my soul pickpocketed by a wee tramp. Who the fuck could I tell? I couldn't tell Francesca. I could hardly tell my mother, Mammy I rode a woman, she'd never speak to me again. I certainly couldn't tell Balls. No, Balls got on very well with Francesca, too well in my opinion. They were great friends, in the same class and all at college. So there was no way. As for Shovels, he wouldn't really be interested in that type of thing unless of course I battered her as well. And I certainly couldn't talk to Aisling herself about it. In fact I never wanted to see her little face again, a trace of acne surfacing now beneath her smudged make-up.

She went on back into the Mirage. I wondered if her friend was still there trying to get off with that big show-off, Frank what's-his-face? I'd say Aisling couldn't wait to see her face. 'Where were you?' and shock her with the news.

'You did not?' That'll teach Cathy to leave her hanging around like an eejit.

'I'll follow you in in a minute.'

I felt like a convalescent, some yellowing stick-insect who'd just come out of hospital after a long lay-off with some unacceptable illness. All at sea. Unfamiliar with the outside world. The new gadgets. Dirty as sin. The first thing I did was I puked my guts up, then walked around in the cold, crying, like when you drink a whole bottle of gin and hide in a wardrobe and just cry because you don't know anything and you're unknowable and nobody wants to know you anyway. I realised, I shouldn't have done it. I shouldn't have done the dirty on Francesca. I should never have hit her. Poor Francesca.

You've been waiting for years for your fantasy to come along and then all your fantasies come along at once, handjob, blowjob, ride, all in the space of five minutes with a mad bitch from Armagh.

And I never got to feel her tits, that's all I wanted to do, was to gently polish her lovely little tits with my palms. And maybe lick the sweat from her collarbone.

Fuck Francesca. It's all her fault. Anyway, I went back inside. Who's the first person I meet at the door only Mick 'Miguel' Donnelly, so called because he looked Hispanic, with his jet-black hair and a little black moustache.

'Scully how's it goin'? I've been looking for you all night.'

'Good man Miguel. I was looking for you too. But sure you can't move in there. It's black.'

We shook hands, a bit of spunk still on my hands, but he wouldn't notice, he's so fuckin' slimey.

'What's that you've got on your face? You've big black marks all over your face.' Winking at his compadre whom I didn't recognise.

'Were you eating turf?'

'No!'

'Or maybe you're thinking of joining the army?' Winking again.

'No, the guards.' Me wiping Aisling's lipstick off my face.

'What's the crack?'

'No crack at all, here, that's all I could get.'

I handed him two engagement rings I took from the shop.

'You can keep the tie, Scully, there's no market for second-hand ties.' His friend laughed. I put the tie back in my pocket. My balls were still pulsating. Every weekend I went home I took a few rings from the shop, or a watch or gold earrings and sold them to Miguel. He gave me twenty-five pounds for each ring, fifty pounds for the pair, not bad for a night's work, I think you'll agree. I'm in charge of the security cameras, that's my job, you know, to monitor everything that's going on in the shop so I'm able to take what I want, no problem. I wouldn't, only Mr Dunn is a miserable bastard, like I said before, a fuckin' slave driver. He only pays me fifty quid a week. Miguel probably makes a fortune, at least a hundred pounds a ring, I'd say. They're worth three times that. But what the fuck.

'Good luck, Miguel. See you next month.' Although somehow I doubt it.

5

I was hovering near the entrance for a while, like a blue-arsed fly, trying to decide whether to collect my jacket and clear off once and for all or stay. There was great excitement within due to the announcement of a certain song. Everybody had their hands up in the air, like a bunch of charismatics praising the Lord or basketball players, 'Here give me the ball you cuntya. I'm unmarked.'

'Hands up, baby hands up . . . give me your heart.' A really deadly song. Ottowan, I think it was, the kind of song that got absolutely everybody out on to the floor seeing as how you needed no rhythm whatsoever to join in. But I wasn't in the mood. Me and Francesca danced together to that song many times. Suddenly, Jinky Doyle comes up to me and tells me that Shovels was getting a right hammering in the car park, very happy with himself to be first with the news. Now normally I would have said to myself, 'That's grand, none of my business,' but this wasn't a normal night. Without thinking, I ran out of the door and steamed in to help Shovels. The 'fracas', as it would have been called in the local papers, seemed to halt momentarily while the participants clocked the new arrival. Shovels looked more surprised than they were and slightly offguard received a right hook to the jaw as the fight resumed furiously. Jesus, there were fists and boots flying everywhere, a few rocks and even a crutch. There must have been at least four of them, big wide fellas, hard as trees. Three of them were on top of Shovels who was still on his feet, all roaring abuse, except for one of them who was busy biting his ear. I meanwhile had pulled the fourth one off, put my head down and started flailing away with my fists. A crowd had gathered by now, to mock or be shocked or to shout encouragement. One or two of them would try and wade in, 'break it up, break it up,' but in reality were looking for an excuse to throw a thump themselves. They didn't get very far, however, repelled as they were by the electric fence the combatants had erected around themselves. I looked up to see Shovels facing the wall and lashing out with his feet like a donkey, landing a beautiful kick on the leg of the lad who was using the crutches, hopefully rebreaking the bastard's leg. All I know is my fella, a fuckin' Californian Redwood, was knocking lumps out of me but I didn't care. Why would I care?

After watching the mêlée for their own amusement for a while the bouncers finally leapt in. There were plenty of shall we say verbal slingshots being bandied about and blood flowing but the fight was over. 'Nothing to see here, back inside.' Shovels, his ear hanging off and his shirt torn, was on fire. There was blood streaming from his nose and the nearest thing to a smile on his face I've ever seen. He was animated, snorting like a horse, almost, I would say, satisfied.

Later on after we got cleaned up, Don Caulfield, the bank manager's son, said he was having a party above the bank because his parents were away.

'Do you want a lift?'

'I do,' I said, 'and Shovels?'

'Shovels, no problem, Scully.'

'RBI 157?'

'That's right,' says Don. 'How did you know?'

'Oh I just knew.'

I still knew my registration numbers. No flies on me. Don was a bit of a dryshite but a good wee footballer. Both myself and Shovels played with him in the under sixteens. In fact, he was one of the ones who went on to play for the county minors. As far as I knew, he was repeating his Leaving at boarding school for the third time. His mother was very friendly with my mother, they used to do the graves together.

So there was Don driving, his sister, I don't know her name, in the front, quiet as a mouse, myself and Shovels in the back, and a fella Shovels worked with on the sites who was stocious and wanted a lift home, Lavey or something like that. Shovels asked Don if it was okay.

'No problem, Barry.'

That was Don, always ready to please and not sure whether to call Shovels Shovels or not.

I'd never met the fellah before and to be honest I was glad. He was unsavoury. About thirty years old, very long black hair, different era altogether, and just out of jail. Sinewy. No thanks. The fact that he kept pinching me and calling me a wee girl didn't help. That was the second time that evening I'd been mistaken for a girl and I wasn't happy about it. He thought it was great fun. But there was very little I could do to stop him on account of his reputation for fighting, breaking windows, robbery, country and western music, smuggling, cattle rustling and arson. If anything he was more violent and hostile to the human race than Shovels.

There wasn't much crack in the car and us on the way to a party. Shovels was far away as usual, at peace, as if he were listening to classical music in his head, although I doubt if he was. The two in the front were mortified, not a squeak out of them. They just wanted to deposit this lunatic as soon as possible outside his bungalow and put it down as a bad experience. But worse, much worse was to come.

He opened the door on a bad bend and leaned out of the car until his elbow was touching the road, sparks literally flying. Laughing and screaming like a maniac.

Watching him do that reminded me of something else I was told about him. Lavey – no, Lavell, that was his name – was the arse skiing champion of the area. Arse skiing was a craze that became popular on country lanes in the locality during the long summer evenings of 1980. I suppose you could call it an endurance sport, inspired by a television show that was presented by a wee bald smartarse from Australia. The way it worked was you'd get two cars, side by side, say a Datsun Cherry and a red Escort, or two tractors of even horsepower. You'd tie a rope to the tow-bar of each vehicle and you'd have two contestants sitting on the ground about twenty feet behind the cars, holding on to the ropes, sharing a last-minute joke. They'd usually be brothers. Suddenly the cars'd rev up and take off down the road at speed. And the first person to let go of the rope was the loser. There were no winners in my opinion. None of our crowd ever got involved but I was, however, at a meeting once in Dun Bainne. Needless to say it was an illegal activity and a lot of money changed hands. Not just illegal but stupid if you ask me although some of the brighter participants would wear good thick jeans which only cost a fiver from the stalls in the town on a Thursday. I'd say there were about fifty people there in attendance, mostly from the same few families and four races altogether. Everybody was taking it very seriously indeed, running after the cars and urging on their favourites, 'Hold on!' At first you'd swear there was smoke coming from their arses but I suppose it was just dust. They'd last for maybe fifty yards at the most before letting go of the rope and rolling to the cool grassy verge in agony. Eyes streaming, teeth clenched, screaming in pain, holding themselves off the ground in the crab-position while waiting for their supporters to arrive and pour water over their shredded flesh. I have to say it was a horrific sight. Denim flaps exposing flaming gravel-studded arses. It bothered me more than it bothered them. Some of them, I was told, were back in the hot seat within a week. Ha? It's not as if they had any other great use for their arses unless they take down their trousers now and again to let itchy animals relieve themselves on those coarse surfaces. Who knows? Looking at Lavell now, leaning out the door of the car, he had a hard flat rump, a shelf of toughened skin, the mark of a champion arse-skier, so I'd well believe he was involved.

We pulled in to let Lavell off. Another car pulled in behind us, headlights on full.

'Youse go on home,' says Lavell.

I could hear four doors slamming behind us.

'Get the fuck out of here,' says Lavell, jumping out of the car, and banging the door after him.

I could hear a boot opening and closing behind us. Voices menacing darkly, silhouettes emerging in the beam of the headlamps.

'Now you're for it Lavell.' Or words to that effect.

Shovels and me got out and stood behind Lavell.

'Go home Shovels. Take the girl with you.' (Meaning me I think the cunt.) There were four lads facing us armed with a hammer, a jack and other club-like implements – I couldn't tell you exactly what they were.

'This has nothing to do with you, it's Lavell we want.'

'Do youse not hear him, it's me they want. Go on home'

We didn't budge.

'Don, get the guards,' said his sister, the first words she spoke all night.

He didn't need to be told twice. And skidded off towards Carrickhall. Fuck Balls O'Reilly, I thought to myself, especially fuck Balls, the treacherous cunt. Where's he now when there's trouble? There's only me and Shovels. Fuck the party, fuck Francesca, fuck Mammy, fuck Joe, fuck the guards, fuck the under sixteens, fuck the county selectors! Me and Shovels, that's all. We'll sort them out, on behalf of this man, Lavell. Whatever he did he didn't deserve this.

'Don't say you weren't warned!'

'C'mon you bastards!' says Lavell. A tight ball of fury.

It was over in seconds. Lavell put his head down and charged in. He managed to absorb a few blows and kick in the right headlamp of the car. Good thinking, but unfortunately he was grabbed by two of them and carried away before he could summon total darkness to our aid. I was flattened anyway in the same instant with a belt from a wrench and fell to the deck.

There was a lovely smell of fresh mud in my nose, as I lay down, snuggling up. Thud. Thud. Thud. Loading sacks on to a pallet, hundredweight sacks of flour, one on top of the other. No pain at all. He kicked me in the head, in the stomach, on the arms, on the legs, on the arse, to a nice steady beat. He could have gone on all night for all I cared. Oooh! One on the mouth, for good measure. But I felt no pain. I was beyond pain. And I didn't even try to resist and I didn't give a shit because as long as this pummelling continued I didn't have to think about Balls and Francesca. Or what I did to Francesca by mistake when I found out.

PART 2

Francesca's Diary

Friday, 29 October 1982

Wow, what a week! I can't believe it's Friday already as I put quivering pen to paper. I'm still slowly recovering from Wednesday night's Freshers' Ball although my headache, like the husband of a slighted aunt, has no intention of abating until retribution is made. My nausea, like the aunt herself, weeps silently in the other room. As long as I don't try to stand up, or move a muscle or even blink ever again, I'll be okay.

And yesterday, I was so hungover that I couldn't do a tap. I could hardly get out of bed. I tried valiantly to make it to college in the afternoon for the Psychology lecture and more importantly the post-mortem but felt queasy and stopped halfway. If on the side of the dual-carriageway there was a trough of tea every hundred yards I might have triumphed. But there wasn't. Woozy, I almost fainted. A trio of boys on horseback, malnourished centaurs all, trotted by. One shouted, 'Do you want a ride love?' The others sniggered. 'You wagon!' Charming young men. One of them, trying to keep up, was riding the tiniest pony I've ever seen. It couldn't have been bigger than a rat. I'm sure the Ragged Kid thought he was John Wayne all the same and from the top of the nearby tower blocks nobody was any the wiser.

I crawled back to the digs, stayed in bed for the rest of

the day and drank tea, each cup a monsoon on my parched, rusted implement-strewn paddy-field.

Mary-Rose Hanratty, a girl from Portlaoise, and I were in stitches trying to piece together the details of the evening in the canteen this morning. We were like two senile ladies in a nursing home trying to remember anything with only a torn photograph for reference.

Mary-Rose had been on her ear. Her landlady heard her being sick into the toilet at seven in the morning and became very concerned. Mary-Rose told her that it must have been food poisoning from a hot dog. The poor landlady, not suspecting a thing, wanted to call her parents immediately and sue the retailer.

I broke my pledge never to drink without forethought or hesitation or indeed regret and got absolutely pissed too. I must have had about ten Bacardis and Coke. I understand everything now. And don't know why people don't wear tanks of the stuff on their backs. I'm sure I disgraced myself but wasn't that the idea? Will anybody remember? And if so will they bat an eyelid?

And I met a man as Mary-Rose and half the college reminded me this morning. Some wag had even pinned a sign above the door to the lecture room which read 'Francesca loves Patrick'. Kindergarten stuff. It was too highly embarrassing for me to reach it and remained there like an admonishment for all to see for the whole day. But I'm jumping the gun.

At first I wasn't going to go to the ball. I didn't know anybody and certainly wasn't going to turn up on my own. Feeling quite sorry for myself, my hopes for the year already dimming, I bumped into Mary-Rose at the coffee-machine that afternoon. We got talking with scalded tongues and quickly realised that we were in exactly the same position.

Alone in the by now eerily quiet and it must be said

filthy recreation area, we made a split-second decision to go and almost leaped out of our chairs. We bought tickets (the last two apparently) and arranged to meet in the Shoebox, the pub across the road, at half four. I wore my new grandfather shirt and jeans, and thought I was the bees-knees until M-R walked in. She looked stunning, tall, full-breasted, rosy-cheeked, with long auburn hair – oozing womanhood. She wore a red dress which she had made herself and a headband that was actually the cord of her father's dressing gown.

The Shoebox was crowded, the more vocal and outgoing members of our class were already ensconced down the back flooring pints and making an outrageous racket. They'd only met ten days ago but you'd think they'd fought together through love and war and sporting success, and survived a ferry disaster. Singing, shouting, some only managing guttural sounds to express their satisfaction, boys punching each other playfully, spilling drinks, one or two couples snogging.

We perched at the edge of the colony, scoffing at their antics, hoping, praying somehow to be absorbed into it during the night. Our plan worked to perfection, for within a short time we met one of the most beautiful men ever, Xavier O'Reilly (from Monaghan). I recognised him instantly because he had been elected class rep earlier in the week and was Chairman of the 'Lefties', one of the societies I've joined. Oh and he was also the guy I had fallen helplessly in love with on the first day. ('Hello, my name is Xavier O'Reilly, I am an ambassador from the planet Uggh, I have come to observe your ways.') Thin and unshaven with the most gorgeous floppy fringe and a pair of mittens, I was smitten on the spot. He was so friendly and charismatic, with a smile that would refresh you like a summer shower. A glance from his big brown eyes cut through me like copper wire through cheese and left me weak and squishy by the locker doors. He was so funny and lively, always playing the fool, yet was unable to conceal a deadly intelligence. The holes in his Dennis the Menace jumper revealed the Albert Camus T-shirt beneath.

My heart skipped several beats, a whole bar in fact, as he jumped over the back of our seat to join us. Almost toppling the table in the process, he nestled in between myself and Mary-Rose, sweat pouring from his face. Then adopting the tone of a reporter, he pretended to interview us, as if we were visiting celebrities, using his balled fist as a microphone. He bamboozled us with rapid-fire questions and quips and confounded us with his verbal trickery. A bombardier, a conjuror, a spider spinning yarns; we were willingly entrapped in his cunning lingual web. He asked us blunt personal questions about our family backgrounds, underwear and favourite sexual positions. But he did it with such an innocent face, you couldn't but respond and be amused. I think he took a particular shine to Mary-Rose, I mean, she is beautiful. Well, although he was too slick and diplomatic to give her his undivided attention, he did address her more often and more intently than me.

But soon we were engrossed in conversation with everyone present. It's amazing how wrong your first impressions of people can be. Lads I had condemned as right dickheads turned out to be amenable and down to earth, and vice versa. After a few drinks, we were able to relax a bit and actually say stuff out loud unlike anything we'd ever said before. I experienced an incredible pulsing sensation in my spinal column. It was as if somebody had opened a bottle of champagne in my back and the bubbly was cascading into my brain. I was reminded (sort of) of the time I won the junior cross-country at the community games when I was ten.

Earlier in the week, while walking down Pearse Street, I noticed a bunch of scruffy children hanging on to the back door of a moving container lorry. It looked very dangerous. One of the little urchins hadn't managed to make the leap and was running after them in the middle of heavy traffic, crying, afraid that he'd lost his friends for the day. He had no choice but to keep running for fear of being run over. The truck, approaching lights, slowed down and one of the lads, his brother I suppose, held out an arm, and managed to lever the snivelling brat on to the tiny and precarious platform at the back of the forty-foot trailer. Although I thought for a minute that they were all going to be killed, it was in a way a beautiful sight. I felt indebted to Xavier and the others for giving me a leg up and bringing me along for the ride.

Half an hour before closing time, a friend of Xavier's from Monaghan, Patrick Scully, walked into the pub wearing a shirt and tie and a pair of brogues that had seen better days. He stuck out like a sore thumb but seemed like a pretty nice guy. X, buzzing around as ever, flower to hive, introduced him to me and left to forge more bonds. I was more or less landed with him for the rest of the evening, having been separated from M-R earlier on. But he was grand. A stocky, fair-haired man with a boyish clean-cut face. He was handsome-ish in a high cheekbones, piercing blue eyes, *Village of the Damned* kind of way, and exceptionally neat. So neat that I wanted to toss his hair and stick a safety pin in his nose. It was obvious that he knew nobody apart from X and that he was even more reserved than me, if that's possible (a kindred spirit perhaps?). Endearingly flame-faced and flustered, he drank steadily while I did most of the talking, or should I say aimless wittering, which was unusual to say the least but like I said I was roaring drunk.

After the pub, we all hopped on a bus and singing jauntily went to the Ball. When I say 'Ball', I don't mean the type of formal occasion frequented by flouncing débutantes and mannerly monocle-wearing men moving stiffly to the sound of an orchestra, although it was priced like one. No, instead of an orchestra, a punky band called the Golden Horde provided the 'entertainment', followed by a disco. The venue was the National Ballroom, a building that was more suited to storing hay.

Once inside, before I had time to get my bearings, Patrick asked me out to dance. He was a terrible dancer as I'm sure he'd be the first to admit. I have never seen anybody, not even the most backward bogman from the hills above Killeeny, dancing like P with his hands in his pockets. For some reason, I hugged him after that first dance. His innocent, sensitive face visibly brightened. We stayed on the floor, Patrick trying not to catch my eye, looking around for clues, tentatively taking his hands out and shaking them ever so slightly, gaining in confidence. It was hilarious to watch. I got hiccups, I was laughing so much.

The others had dispersed throughout the hall like syca-more leaves. Mary-Rose was necking a Languages student, saw me and made a 'what the hell' face. But I met hundreds of people during the night. Vaguely familiar faces, i.e., the ones I'd sat beside at lectures fumbling for words, I now embraced like old friends. I exchanged greetings and phone numbers with students from other faculties, people I'd passed in the corridors or to whom I'd lent a pen in the library. I threw my arms around complete strangers. Patrick stood by, cheerful and attentive. At one stage Xavier grabbed Patrick and together they pogoed to some heavy metal like a pair of kango hammers, P for the first time letting himself go. They pulled me in between them to form a scrum and we reeled around the room banging into people, not giving a damn. The hall was like one big pinball machine, us a ball of energy. We eventually broke free, bruised, dripping, delirious.

The music was so loud I couldn't hear what anyone was saying but I nodded in agreement anyway. Our ecstatic faces said it all. I could hardly see either, partly because I was so drunk and partly because my glasses had steamed up. But each time my eyes refocused, P was waiting for me with another drink and a vulnerable smile.

He had just done an interview for teacher training earlier that day. (That's why he was in the shirt and tie.) His description of him singing '*Óró sé do bheatha bhaile*' for the interviewers had me in stitches. According to P they were practically shielding their ears from the pain and tried to get rid of him as soon as he finished the rendition. Patrick claimed that it wasn't his croaky voice that they objected to but his strong Monaghan accent. For a moment, I thought he was serious. The only reason he went for the interview in the first place was to get his mother off his case. He told me that he knew he wasn't going to get Pat's, and wouldn't accept a place if he did because he was expecting word on the guards in the near future. In the meantime, he said he was managing a restaurant but didn't elaborate. A man of few words.

At the end of the night, I said my goodbyes to all and sundry. There was no sign of Mary-Rose at all. Others including X had left noisily in taxis, shouting an address that I couldn't catch, leaving just P and I. Patrick shrugged his sizeable shoulders and offered to walk me back to Phibsboro even though it was completely out of his way. A proper gentleman, I thought. The spooky streets of the inner city for once held no fear. He talked, volubly, on the way about Castlecock and his childhood there regaling me with stories about a fella called 'Balls' and a host of crazy characters.

At the door of the digs, more sober now and suddenly aware of the early-morning chill, I thanked him for his kindness and said goodnight. He lurched forward to peck me on the cheek and paused, hoping I suppose that it would develop into something else. I mean, I liked him but not *in that way*. I stood on tiptoes, nevertheless, and kissed him back, on the lips. Oh well, I thought, I mightn't get a chance like this for a long time again. There was an uneasy moment. Oh dear, I thought, he doesn't want me *in that way*. A milk float hovered past. The milkman shouted 'Give her one for me!' shattering the silence and the frosted glass that had closed between us. We collided and kissed for a minute or was it five? Eyes closed, time distorted by alcohol, I could have been anywhere with anybody. Embarrassed by my corny fantasies, I prised myself from Patrick. He, elated I think, shook hands and asked me to meet him for a drink in town next Wednesday. I said, yes. He was actually a good kisser. He had walked me home. He hadn't let me put my hand in my pocket all night. He was respectful. Potentially interesting. And above all a friend of Xavier.

Wednesday, 3 November 1982
I was to meet Patrick outside the AA shop on Suffolk Street at six thirty p.m., his idea, not mine, based on the notion that if one of us was late, he or I could study the car accessories and manuals in the display window. The fact that neither of us had a car was immaterial, it seems. Exhausted after a gruelling day at college, ideas, impressions, snippets of conversations still whirring around in my head, like kids at a carnival, I had a bath and got the bus into town. Dublin was gridlocked. The buses moved a few feet, braked, screeched to a halt. The crowds of pedestrians on the footpaths seemed to lurch in sync. Dublin was a stop-start sort of place. You couldn't go anywhere at any time without meeting either somebody you knew or somebody else who wanted money, directions, or just a chat. You couldn't walk out of a shop without banging into a man carrying pallets. Taxi-drivers cruised, picking their noses, looking around for diversion and/or passengers, only accelerating

to prevent other cars joining the stream of traffic. Work, manual, clerical, was done in bursts. Even the rain stopped and started according to the most whimsical of plans. The city wheezed and coughed and groaned, a tubercular city with a defiant life-loving heart. I still got a thrill each time I stepped off the bus in the city centre.

Patrick was wearing a shirt and tie (again) not to mention a light grey leather jacket elasticated at the waist which didn't amount to a lovely ensemble at all. There wasn't a hair out of place either. Damn that blow-dryer. I touched his arm and told him he looked very smart.

I hoped that I was going to be pleasantly surprised, no, that I was going to be trembling in anticipation. That he was going to be waiting for me, if not with Xavier then with a bunch of carnations and a big grin. That he would sweep me off my feet and carry me through the amused, approving throng to a horse-drawn carriage and beyond. He did hint on the phone that he had a surprise for me. I imagined this encounter many times during the week. I suppose I'd created a whole personality for Patrick considering I didn't know him at all and to be honest couldn't remember that much about the Ball. I had even forgotten what he looked like. But I'd convinced myself that he was special.

He forced a smile and said, 'What kept you?' I assumed that was a joke, I mean, I was only a minute late. I gave him the benefit of the doubt and put it down to nerves and insecurity. Or was that me projecting? He looked me up and down and if I'm not mistaken behind me too. I felt like saying 'Nobody followed me and I'm not wearing a bug, see no wires.' He looked disappointed whether it was because of my 'tardiness' or because I fell some way short of his recollection, I don't know. But my self-esteem deflated in that instant. What was I supposed to do, tap my heels three times, close my eyes, grow taller and suddenly sprout breasts?

I pointed at his tie and asked him if he'd been to another interview. He looked confused for a second, then told me that he'd been in court for the afternoon, that he'd been called as a witness to a stabbing but didn't go into details. I asked him how was work. Again he hesitated and changed the subject to nothing. I thought all guys were supposed to have a story, true, false or embellished, a topical anecdote, on the tip of their tongues, that illustrated their humour and heroism.

We walked across the road and went into a pub called O'Neills. It was full of Trinity students, rich kids who dressed like Oscar Wilde and discussed abortion loudly. Our conversation, about the best place in Dublin to get a big sandwich, was a bit stilted at first. It was like as if we had just met in a dentist's waiting room and weren't sure who was first in the queue. P wore a haunted, hunted look which invited a certain amount of sympathy, at least as much as you'd have for a budgie trapped behind a radiator, and prompted further investigation. I was determined to make him open up, salvage the 'date' in some way, but it was like drawing blood from a stone.

A pair of unsophisticates, we eventually settled down and he told me a bit about his family, not that I really wanted to know. He has a mother and a brother and a sister and a psychotic friend called Shovels. Big deal. But did he have a witty and urbane alter ego? He did not. At least none that I could detect. His father died when Patrick was thirteen. Now we're getting somewhere I thought, but no sooner had I squeezed that information from him than his eyes reversed into his head and the garage door came down.

I had a mild panic attack while Patrick was up at the bar ordering more drinks (only Coke for me, I'm afraid, no more alcohol until the mid-term break or until later on this evening, I thought, if the situation doesn't improve). In the few minutes that he was gone, I got measles, mumps and rubella, shingles and shakes and eating disorders but they all cleared up fairly sharpish. I suddenly realised that I wanted to be anywhere else but there. In a tent with a snake or my mother.

At one stage, Patrick went to the toilet. When he came back, he was quite upset. He said 'There was a pair of fuckin' queers in one of the cubicles.' That was the first time I'd heard him use such strong language or indeed show any emotion. It really seemed to bother him. But what does that mean? Is that a clue? Is everything everybody says a piece of the puzzle? I don't know.

Patrick had loosened up sufficiently after two pints of Smithwicks to teasingly mention the 'surprise'. I couldn't wait. What on earth could it be? A compliment? We left the pub and strolled down to the Savoy cinema, rigidly observing a mile-wide distance between us. Patrick had two free tickets for *Tootsie* which he'd got from a newspaper. It could have been worse, I suppose. He had queued up from four in the morning to be one of the lucky first hundred people to claim a pair. When the office opened at nine, he was still the only person in the queue.

The film was fine. I enjoyed it up to a point, he didn't at all. I could sense that he was bored and tense, fidgeting and shifting in his seat. About five minutes before the end of the movie, Patrick slipped his left arm around me, leaned over to kiss me and in the same clumsy lunge put his right hand under my jumper, knocking the ball-bearings left at the bottom of my popcorn box right out of my lap. I squealed and pushed him away.

'Patrick, what are you doing?'

'Nothing.'

Apart from anything else, I wanted to see the end of the film. The whole row behind us laughed. P silently fumed. I couldn't believe he had just done that. He couldn't believe that I had rejected his advances. How could he get his calculations so awry? Celsius/Fahrenheit. Did it really happen?

After the cinema, we had to go to the Palace Bar where we met a friend of Patrick's called Dermot Geoghegan. Now I really didn't get a good feeling from him at all. He made my flesh crawl. He was very tall, wore a beard to hide his evil face and carried a crash helmet. I think Patrick said that he was a courier. The thing that unnerved me most about him was the way he stared straight into my eyes and smirked whenever I spoke. It was very intimidating. Even Patrick seemed ill-at-ease. He laughed nervously every time Geoghegan cracked a joke and glanced over at me almost apologetically. The two of them became animated once the conversation turned to the mad antics of the mysterious 'Balls'. Apparently, he put a frozen chicken into the oven while it was still in its plastic wrapping. And on another occasion, he climbed out of the emergency window at the back of a double-decker bus to avoid an inspector. It transpired that 'Balls' was none other than Xavier O'Reilly and that they all lived in the same flat.

Thankfully Dermot Geoghegan left before closing time. On his way out, he kissed me on the lips and patted my head, much to Patrick's annoyance as well as my own.

Once again, Patrick walked me home, despite my protestations, stopping only for a bag of chips and a spice burger. He hardly said a word on the journey, embarrassed, troubled perhaps by my earlier rebuff. I felt strangely callous.

It's hard to believe he's a friend of Xavier's, I mean, he's not the most exciting person I've ever met in my life but I can't fault his generosity. Once again, he insisted on paying for the Cokes and the chips. I was mortified but he wouldn't take 'no' for an answer.

I got the distinct impression that he doesn't particularly like me, that he certainly doesn't fancy me, that any girl would do. I mean his face didn't exactly light up on the odd occasion our eyes met. I didn't expect him to ask me out again but on the off-chance that he did, I resolved to say 'no'. I would tell him that I really liked him which wasn't untrue but had too much to do at college which was true and didn't want to go steady with anyone at this time which is a lie. When it came to the crunch on the doorstep of the digs, I lost my nerve and said 'Yes, I'll see you next week.'

2

My mother used to call me her special little man.

'How is my special little man today?' she'd say. 'Are you ready for school?'

'No Mammy, I'm not going to school today,' I'd reply, seriously, 'I'm staying here to help you.'

'You're going to school Patrick if I have to drag you up the hill by the ears.'

'I have a sore throat. I can't go,' I'd tell her from under the dining-room table, and me absent-mindedly pushing a dumper-truck to and fro on the carpet, the toy vehicle full of Lego bricks but minus a wheel. And all the time there'd be strands of wool winding tightly around the back axle, reminding me of the time I wound a spool of thread around my wrist until my hand went blue and only for Nurse McNulty, my mother's friend, finding me and snipping my new nylon bracelet, I would have lost the hand. That's what she told me anyway. I always hated the nurse even though she probably saved my life on that occasion. Mammy would tell me to scram whenever she called around which was nearly every day even if I had something important to show her. And the nurse who by the way never wore a nurse's uniform would snap at me too, 'Do what your mother told you, you little pup or I'll put you across my knee.' And they'd both laugh.

'You'll have a sore head if you don't hurry up,' she'd reply, *still humouring me. 'C'mon now, out of there and off you go to school, my little parcel!'*

I'd cough feebly and she'd suddenly lose her patience and fly into a rage. She'd chase me out the door with the wooden spoon, me trying desperately to protect my bare legs from her thrusts. I could never figure it all out. Here was me, about six years old and easily her best friend. And there she was doing her damnedest to get rid of me morning after morning without fail. What made it worse was knowing that the baby, Joe, had her all to himself for the whole day. (Valerie told me years later that when I was about five and Joe was about three and a half, I got up in the middle of the night, took him outside into the garden and locked him in the kennel. I don't remember the incident at all. Anyway, sorry about that Joe.)

For ages, I felt very lonely and, I would go as far as to say, abandoned at the school gates. I'm sure it was all fine once I actually entered the yard and got caught up in a noisy throng running around the school, playing tig, or releasio screaming like an apache and throwing mud. But for some strange reason, I prefer not to recall the good times. Don't get me wrong, I'd love to recall them but I simply can't at this point in time. Happy memories you see are not relevant to my story. If, for the sake of argument, I had been the first person from Castlecock to break the speed of sound, or travel back in time, or make contact with aliens, or discover a cure for cancer, or win the Young Scientist's Exhibition, then maybe a nice pleasant story about a popular boy genius would be appropriate. 'I had any amount of friends, won a medal for Irish dancing, jumped into a lake and saved a lad from drowning, and never missed a penalty in my life.' If I hadn't thrown my life down the drain in a moment of madness, that type of anecdote would have been just the ticket, the candle to illuminate the past.

I didn't like the National School from day one. Man, o man, as my father used to say under his breath, especially when stooping, I didn't like it one bit. If I'm not greatly mistaken, your first big shock on this earth is being born. Squirted into a strange and incomprehensible place. There's no preparation for that sort of trauma, no assault course in the womb or anything like that, no expert advice whatsoever to the best of my knowledge. But four years down the road, just as you're getting used to your surroundings, you're picked up and loaded into the catapult again. The second big shock therefore is being packaged in a pair of short pants and once again propelled into a hostile environment.

I'm afraid I still haven't forgiven my mother for betraying me, forsaking me on that first fateful day on the top step at the entrance to the school, delivering me into the care of the Brothers. I'd say that I must have looked as bewildered as the puppy we bought once from a man who called at the door with a pram full of whimpering pups. Dara, as my father called it for some reason that always made him and him alone smile, crouched on the kitchen lino and pined for three days with a face as desolate and inconsolable as Ireland during the Famine. I must have looked a similar sight, with my well-fed and well-scrubbed little face, streaked with tears.

I could have been the cake, a freshly-baked sponge gateau divided into two hemispheres, one on top of the other, separated by lashings of cream and jam bursting out the sides, my mother made for the jumble sale above in the Parish Hall to raise money to repair the roof of the church. There was nothing wrong with the roof of the church as far as I could see but in case it was ever struck by a meteorite it was good to know there was an emergency fund.

'Hey I'm just out of the oven, you can't give me away. I'm still warm, for God's sake. Have a heart, Mrs Scully! Please, put me in a tin, I promise I won't go stale on you.'

'My special little man, oh, my special little darling man, wake up Patrick! For God's sake, Doctor, will he be all right, Doctor? Are you doing the best you can?'

I realised to my dismay when I heard my mother bleating by the hospital bed that I wasn't dead at all, only unconscious. I was alerted to her presence not so much by the sound of her voice but by the smells – of fresh fruit and recently-laundered paisley-patterned pyjamas – that wafted into my nostrils after landing together in the same plastic bag on the bedside locker. For a moment, those beautiful fragrances cancelled out the odours of disinfectant and medicine that up to now distinguished the ward.

Sometimes I can't believe my mother, the way she carries on. If somebody belonging to me was in an accident and ended up in hospital, I wouldn't have the time or the presence of mind to think of bringing a pair of pyjamas. But in her agitation at my distress, Mammy still remembered to bow to convention and decorum, thinking to herself, 'No son of mine will be seen dead in a hospital gown' and 'I must buy apples and oranges and grapes or I won't be allowed in to see him.' She knows right well I don't eat fruit, except for blackberries. I could never understand that. You're feeling very sorry for yourself in your hospital bed and instead of cheering you up with a bar of chocolate or a magazine or a game of pocket Mastermind, visitors feel the need to bring you fruit. I'm telling you, if we were meant to eat oranges they'd grow in Ireland, for fuck's sake. Fruit. I bet you any money she was wearing her good scarf too and that she sprayed a bit of perfume on her wrists as she hurried from the house.

The young doctor who by the way sounded to me like a bit of a smartarse was obviously ignoring her as he prepared yet another injection.

'Joe, what are we going to do Joe? He might never walk again. I'll have to carry him around on my back, like a sack of spuds.'

'He'll be all right Mammy.' Joe, wanting to touch her, put his arms around her and give her comfort but unable to do so, imagine that, a boy as sensitive and affectionate as him unable to put his arms around his own mother, as paralysed as me in the bed.

'He just got a bad hiding, that's all. Don't worry, he'll be right as rain in no time.'

I could picture Joe, trusty old Joe, as clear as day, standing awkwardly there at the foot of the bed trying his best to placate her, his lips pursed in that serious expression he always adopted when he didn't know what else to do with his face. I'd say he was concerned about me all right but at the same time a bit embarrassed by her behaviour.

'Has he brain damage, doctor? Is he going to be a veg-etable? Will I end up feeding him through a tube? I only want to know the truth.'

'No Mrs Scully, not at all. I know his face is not a pretty sight at the moment but I assure you he's going to be fine.' (See what I mean, a smartarse!) 'I see no reason why Peter ehh Patrick shouldn't make a full recovery.'

What would the likes of him know about anything? And him, barely out of medical school. All doctors are the same, they're only in the game because they got the required points. Take Grainne for example, Francesca's best friend, or Granny as I call her sometimes on account of her cardigans, she's just a swot. I wouldn't like to be treated by her when she finally qualifies. And they're all raving alcoholics too, doctors, so they are, with their tweed jackets and a free basket of eggs every Friday from a grateful patient, wrapped up individually in newspaper. They're only interested in the money and the perks. You go into them after cutting your leg with a chainsaw or breaking your ankle and they can fix that all right. They can mend bones and staunch the flow of blood. Sure a carpenter or a plumber could do that if he put his mind to it. But if you go into them with anything seriously wrong with you, they take a wild guess and hope for the best. They send you to somebody else up in Dublin to be on the safe side. A lot of them have very sick minds too. Granny told us stories about her fellow students that would turn your stomach. According to her, they're always messing with the corpses and taking certain body parts into the pub for the crack. That's a fuckin' disgrace if you ask me.

I wasn't surprised at all to read in the paper that 'physicians' as they like to call themselves, the big-headed bastards, compared to people in other occupations suffer from the highest levels of stress and heart-related disorders. In other words, they're their own best customers. Like publicans. So I don't trust them. They're only a crowd of hypocrites. I have no time for them at all. Dr Christian Barnard himself couldn't fix me. The fuckin' chancer.

'The fact of the matter is, Mrs Scully, your husband, I mean, son *is* severely concussed and has several bruised ribs and as you can see he's also missing a few teeth but, miraculously, he hasn't broken any bones.'

'None at all?'

'None Mrs Scully, he's a very, very, lucky, lucky man,' spelled out the doctor with a big grin I'd say as he jabbed the needle into my rear end. And that was supposed to be a painkiller.

By the way, 'Lucky', my arse! 'Lucky' in my opinion would be if I woke up and asked the fella in the next bed 'what day is it?' and he answered 'last Wednesday'. That would be my definition of 'lucky'. If the last three or four days were all a bad dream. 'Lucky' would be I suppose if I woke up and I turned out to be a dog, as happy as Larry, with no responsibilities whatsoever and no important decisions to make, ever. Always ready for action, you know, if somebody got up at an unearthly hour for a glass of milk or a ham sandwich I'd be up in a flash to lick their hands and receive whatever crumbs came my way even if I'd curled up to go to sleep just before they opened the fridge door. Jaysus, I'd love to be a wee terrier or a sheepdog, giving people nothing but pleasure all day long. Getting too much love and overeating are as far as I can see the only two drawbacks a dog has to watch out for. Our dog, Dara, once upon a time got violently ill after finding the remains of my parents wedding cake in a wardrobe. It must have been there for the best part of fifteen years. But apart from that one error of judgement, he lived life to his heart's content. If you were a dog, the only time you'd ever annoy a human being is the day you died. 'Lucky' would also be if I were some bastard like Balls O'Reilly who always landed on his feet. Failing that, 'lucky' would be I suppose if I were dead.

You know, I don't think my mother would have been that disappointed if I had been brain-damaged in the mêlée after the Mirage. Do you know what I mean? It would have suited her down to the ground if that particular outcome had been God's will. I could nearly sense her working it all out in her mind during her vigil. She'd be able to keep a close eye on me from now on, protect me from all the 'loose women' that according to her were crawling all over Dublin – if only she knew the truth – and feed me and talk non-stop without me answering her back. I could see it all. She'd have me lying on a camp-bed in the sitting room, plugged into the wall and covered in a garish blanket, another cross for her to bear, her very own tale of woe to share with her friends, listening to Gay Byrne on the radio, dying to ring him up and confide in the whole nation.

You see, Mammy is obsessed with injuries and diseases and deformities of every description. She is an absolute authority on operations, amputations, biopsies and triple by-passes. Tumours and malignant growths, carbuncles, bumps, mumps and inappropriate lumps are all badges of honour in her estimation, to be worn by sufferers with pride. She judges friends and strangers alike according to the pallor of their skin and the latest surgical indignity they have been obliged to endure. And of course a special place in her heart is reserved for victims of the Big C. Oh yes, a reverent hush descends upon the house whenever *cancer* is mentioned and let me tell you it is mentioned often. Bowel cancer, breast cancer, lung cancer, throat cancer, cancer of the hair, any kind of cancer at all will do her as long as it is terminal. And in her book, those afflicted by that incurable curse are considered royal. But her bread and butter are ulcers, your common-or-garden ulcers, and gall bladders and hernias and kidney stones. While she's on the subject of any of those relatively minor ailments, you'd want to see the eyes enlarge in her face, like those of a jeweller through a what-the-fuck-do-you-call-it eyepiece, inspecting a precious gem. Man, o man!

She is a glutton for gore. She just can't get enough of car crashes, and accidents in the workplace (especially involving the loss of or damage to an eye), street fights, domestic violence, severe burns, bombings and shootings, knee-cappings, stabbings, gougings, drownings, suicide attempts and ritual sacrifice. One of her favourite stories was the one about the young fella who was pumped full of air with a tyre pump as a practical joke by two lads working in a garage, and later died. As a direct result of that incident, she was always warning us, 'Never walk past a garage'. The more horrific and painful and gangrenous the wounds, the more she wants to hear about them, the more detail she demands. Most of her information she got from Nurse McNulty, the midwife and community health nurse and general busy-body I mentioned earlier who when she wasn't scalding the bedsores of old farmers was to be found standing in our kitchen with a cup of tea in her hand, swapping tragedies with my mother. Jaysus, I could never stand it.

'Poor Mrs Flynn. She's killed with the thrombosis.'

'No?'

'Yes, she can hardly walk.'

'Ah the poor devil.'

'Mind you, it's not as if she did much walking anyway.

She was always on her knees.' (Mrs Flynn worked for the priests.) 'Scrubbing and polishing. The whole church above is shinier than Aladdin's lamp. You'd have to wear tennis shoes going to mass to stay on your feet . . . Big purple veins like ropes. I was in with her this morning. Her own house is like a pig-sty.'

'Ah, the poor thing,' my mother would say, glancing down at the back of her own legs, imagining what it would be like to have swollen limbs bulging through her support tights, and having to walk like a wardrobe.

'And I heard old Mr Hanratty isn't well.'

'Which Hanratty is that?' the nurse would ask, furiously racking her brains, recalling every Hanratty who ever set foot in the state from the beginning of time to the surface of her brain and speed-reading their medical records of which she had intimate and encyclopedic knowledge, make no mistake about that.

'Hanratty, the cobbler,' my mother would announce in triumph, having for once trumped the nurse with an ace. I don't think that she derived any great enjoyment from the misfortunes of others but she did like to be first with the news. I can't blame her for that.

'Is he not well?'

'No he had a heart attack.'

'When?'

'Yesterday morning. Half past ten.'

'Go away.'

'Isn't that right Joe?'

Joe'd be passing through the kitchen with a glass of water on his way back to the bedroom to finish off his homework. He'd answer in a monotone, to disguise his excitement.

'Yeah, young Noel McEntee was in the shop at the time collecting a pair of his mother's shoes when the man just grabbed his chest and keeled over. He took half the shop with him too so he did as he hit the floor and was buried under a mountain of footwear. Wee Noel was afraid to arrive home without the high-heels and had to search the rubble high up and lowdown to find them. He found them at the heel of the hunt anyway and gave them a good rub with his sleeve and as far as I know left the shop without paying. There's talk he didn't pay anyway but spent the money on himself because he was seen getting sick on jellytots. Anyway it was only about four hours later when he told his mother that Hanratty was in fact dead.'

'Well it served him right,' said the nurse.

'Oh Brigid, God forgive you!' My mother, trying to smother an involuntary laugh.

'I never met a man as rude as that man in all my life. He'll be no loss, that's for sure. Sure his own family haven't spoken to him for donkey's years.'

'I believe he liked a drink?'

'Humph,' she'd snort, and take off like a drag-racer, rattling out insults left, right and centre. 'I never saw a man to drink as much as that man did. He was in and out of Malachy's more often than the staff.' (Malachy's was a mental home.)

'The smell off him . . .' Added my mother, helpfully, but to no avail. There was no stopping the nurse once she'd started.

'I left a pair of sandals in there three months ago and I haven't seen them since.'

'Typical.'

'Paddy Boylan told me one time that he left his right shoe to be soled and heeled and when he got it back wasn't there a set of teethmarks on it? I swear to God, would you credit that? Good riddance to bad rubbish, that's what I say . . . blah blah blah . . . that man has caused me more trouble. Sure there last Christmas, I was just sitting down to eat my Christmas dinner, I'd just literally taken the turkey out of the oven, when didn't his wife ring me, distraught is not the word, to say that he'd forced his way into the house and kicked them all out on to the street, wife, children, teddy bears, the whole lot.'

'No!'

'Yes. And then he poured a can of petrol all over his head and threatened to set himself on fire if she didn't take him back. Myself and the doctor and the guards managed to talk him out of it. We were wasting our breath if you ask me.'

They would never have talked about people like that when my father was alive. He wouldn't hear a bad word about anybody, not even about the worst bowsie in the town (who by the way was probably Miguel Donnelly). In fact, Nurse McNulty knew better than to call at all in his day unless he was out at work. And to be fair, my mother didn't show that much interest in pain and misery back then either. It was not until her own mental health began to deteriorate after the oul' fella's death that she became so engrossed with the nurse and they realised that they both shared such a macabre passion.

'And come here to me, how is Nuala Carney?'

'Her skin is the colour of that wall.' The wallpaper in the kitchen was a sort of muddy green. 'She's riddled with the secondaries. It's spreading like ragweed.'

'Ah no, the poor dote. It's very sad and I always said that she's a lovely person. A real lady.'

'I don't know about that.'

'No. She is, Brigid. She's a lady. A real . . . *lady*.' My mother would sit back and congratulate herself both on her what's known as magnanimity and on her exquisite choice of compliment. It was only on rare occasions that she'd ever stumble on a description that pleased her so much.

'God I remember her only six months ago at the parent-teacher meeting. She looked lovely, really lovely. She was *radiant*, and so . . . so *friendly* and, and *elegant*. A . . . a lady.'

'Well you should see her now, there's not a pick on her. She looks like a ghost. They opened her up last week above in Dublin and took out half her intestines.'

'Is that a fact?'

'That's a fact and you know she was too weak to go under the anaesthetic.'

'Ah stop!'

'Oh yes, they had no choice but to cut her open and her wide awake. You'd have been able to hear her screaming down here in the house if only she'd the breath to scream. Aw, that one has only days to live. Mark my words, Laura.'

'And her husband is such a lovely man. A gentleman.'

'What does he do?'

'Isn't he a manager out at the packaging factory or something. Joe . . .' Joe'd have come back into the kitchen pretending to look for a roll of Sellotape for to stick stamps in his stamp album, his homework put to one side for the time being as his natural curiosity got the better of him.

'Quality control manager out in Pretex and a born-again Christian. The son Eamonn is in my class. He's taking it very bad.'

'I didn't know they were born-again Christians.'

'Aye, they're in the Charismatics.'

'Do they speak in tongues?' Mother.

'Eamonn doesn't anyway. At least, I never heard him anyway if he does. Although as far I know he's got a tambourine.' Joe.

'Is there a God at all, I wonder?' my mother would implore, usually just before joining her hands together and offering up a brief and silent prayer. And then she'd stand up. 'Isn't it just awful what some people have to put up with? Will you have more tea?'

'Just a drop. That's grand.'

And on and on and on it would go. Like some sort of an

endless medieval version of the card game, Twenty-five. God, it sickened me. If I happened to be in the house at the time, and let's face it I usually was, I'd stay in the front room, switch on Radio Luxembourg on my pocket transistor and glue it to my ear. Even if you had the best three-in-one music centre money could buy, you couldn't get a clear signal from Radio Luxembourg. No way. If every television and fridge and washing machine and hair-dryer and lawnmower as well as the rest of the electrical goods in the country were switched off, there was a very slim chance of hearing what was going on. But it was the only popular music station available so I had no choice but to try and tune in. The squealing and hissing and crackling I had to put up with sounded like someone deep-fat frying a herd of live pigs. But at the end of the day a migraine was a small price to pay for escape from the duelling harbingers of doom in the kitchen and access to the airwaves and high seas of pirate radio and rock'n'roll. Wouldn't you know it though? One of the best DJs ended up with Multiple Sclerosis. My mother would have been an avid fan if she'd been aware of that.

You see, I've discovered that the thing about a small town like Castlecock is that you don't exist unless people are talking about you, good, bad or indifferent. In Dublin, you don't exist, full stop. Not as a person anyway. As a victim of crime maybe, or as a customer or as a statistic or as 'the weirdo who lives next door'. But here at home, where I belong, they're genuinely interested in your welfare, if only to pass on the information to somebody else. If there was a drought in the town – and I'm not suggesting for a moment that there's going to be – the parched inhabitants wouldn't ask for water, no. No, no. 'Any scandal!' they'd whisper before dying in your arms, desiccated, like a coat of figs. I'll tell you, the people in this town are like the pillars of an Ancient Roman viaduct, do you know what I mean? Conveying gossip above their shoulders, instead of water, in exalted fashion. I'm tired of hearing how great the fuckin' Romans were. They never made it to Ireland, did they, with their armies and their sewerage systems? They did not. A few chip shops and that was it. Where are they now, tell me, if they were so fuckin' clever? And as for the Greeks and the so-called cradle of civilisation, what have they got to show for themselves? Jackie fuckin' Onassis, that's what, and she's not even Greek. The Irish always had the right idea. Apart from the failure of the potato crop in the last century and a few other hiccups, we as a nation have gradually improved in all departments from the beginning of time. I'd say that within another thousand years approximately, Ireland will be a Superpower. Don't say that I didn't warn you!

Anyway, as I was saying, nobody gives a damn about the Falklands War, or the hole in the ozone layer or the antics of the Ayatollah Khomeini. Nobody gives a shit about the disappearance of Shergar, or rising petrol prices or glue-sniffing in the inner city. No. Current affairs, as far as the people around here are concerned, have more to do with who said what, where and when, to whom and what were they wearing at the time? That's all that matters. Who was at mass on Sunday? Who was fiddling the dole? Which shaggy-haired rogue was caught in bed with another man's wife? Who was putting red diesel in his car? Who do the gippos think they are, camping in our town? These were the pressing questions on everyone's lips. But by God, they'll have no shortage of things to talk about from now on. I've made sure of that. They won't know what hit them.

And on and on and on my mother and Nurse McNulty would go.

'Did you know the young lad who fell off the tractor?'

'I knew the family well. I've been getting eggs off them for years.' (The country people give eggs to the nurses as well as the doctors.)

'To think that the poor cratur was only ten years old.'

'Eight, he was only eight.'

'Eight years old . . . what an appalling tragedy. How did it happen?'

'Uhh! It was the same old story, they were taking in the hay, with a tractor and trailer, and of course, as usual, there was a crowd of young ones up on top of the hay, I don't know how many times I've warned people about that, when doesn't young McNally, Brian I think you call him or was it Liam, stood up and started showing off in front of the other ones doing an impression of Joe Dolan, lost his balance and fell off. Into the middle of the road he fell and was run over by a milk lorry coming the other way.'

'Sacred heart!'

'He died instantly. It was his next-door neighbour driving the truck. McConnon, he was devastated.'

(*Pause.*)

'And am I right in thinking that the father lost an eye only a few years ago.'

'That's right. He fell on a nail. Out mending a fence when he slipped. Fell on to a big rusty nail sticking up out of an old post. He was lucky, he could have lost his head.'

'And didn't the cousin commit suicide last summer. Shot himself, I believe.'

'What? Where did you hear that? He didn't shoot himself. He hung himself in the hay shed.'

'We were told he was shot. Isn't that right Joe?'

Joe'd be just sitting there by now having abandoned all pretence at being otherwise engaged, addicted now to misery like everyone else in this Godforsaken town.

'That's what I was told anyway.'

And finally before she'd leave, the nurse would ask my mother. 'How is your Patrick?'

'No change, I'm afraid,' she'd sigh, spoon-feeding me

with rice pudding most of which would dribble down my chin.

'Sure it's probably all for the best. Keeps him out of harm's way.'

All around the house
Looking for Mickey the mouse,
If you catch him by the tail
Hang him up on a rusty nail
And give him to the cook
To make a bowl of soup.
Hurrah boys, hurrah boys, how do you like the soup?

I couldn't believe my banjaxed ears. Mammy was singing me a song she used to sing every day without fail when I'd rush in the door after school for my toast and honey, hot milk and tickles. I don't remember the next verse because to tell you the truth I never stayed around long enough to hear it. I had too much to do in those days, too much energy to burn. There was another tree to conquer, another Rodney Marsh trick to master, not to mention whole jungles of dockweeds and nettles to raze to the ground. I suppose she was singing in an effort to revive me from what she hoped was at least a coma. She must have seen the programme on television a few weeks ago about the lad who went into a vegetative state after heading a football. I saw it myself. A few hours after the ball hit him on the head he complained of a pain and promptly collapsed. It showed diagrams and all of how the brain – like a lump of jelly – was flung against the skull on impact. In his case, however, there was a happy ending it seems. Months after the accident, the family left a tape recorder beside your man's bed playing his favourite music over and over again, Queen I think it was, and before long he woke up. Well my mother's music, for want of a better word, was having exactly the opposite effect on me.

I knew I could probably regain consciousness in the blink of an eye if I felt like it but instead I closed my eyes tighter than ever. And concentrated on stemming the flow of blood to my brain, not that I was very good at mind over matter or that type of thing. I'm sure poor Joe was mortified too at this stage. I could just picture him there his face on fire, hoping the ground would swallow him up while the other patients in the ward sniggered and exchanged glances at our expense.

In my first year at the high school I used to go home in the middle of every day for my dinner. As soon as the bell went, me and Mickey Mohan, my next-door neighbour, made a mad dash for the door, got on our bikes and raced home. I had an oul' Triumph 20 that used to belong to Valerie but I stuck stickers of Leeds United players all over it so it didn't look too girly and made sure to use very bad language whenever I was riding it. I had a couple of deadly patches sewn on to my coat as well, one said 'Up Leeds' and the other, 'School is a Drag', although by the time I reached secondary school I didn't think it was. In fact I quite liked school when I was twelve years old. After Stephen Lyons, I'd say I was probably the best in the class. I was usually first to finish a spelling test and was very good at pronunciation too. I was so good at pronunciation that sometimes in the middle of my turn reading from the English book, I would deliberately mispronounce a word. For example, instead of saying 'old man', I would say 'oul' man' just so as the rest of the boys wouldn't think I was trying to be a fancy bigshot. But the teacher, who knew right well that I was play-acting, would fire the chalk duster at my head and order me to say it properly. A cloud of dust particles would rise above my hair like a mini-explosion in a cartoon. A wee bomb.

I used to read a lot of books as well when I was younger, mainly encyclopedias and my father's detective novels. But I never told anyone that I read. I knew what was good for me. If the lads *ever found out, I would have been tried at the children's court and convicted of cissy stuff. Some people seem to think that I'm stupid but I assure you that I'm not. I did exceptionally well in all my exams up to and including the Inter Cert. There was no two ways about it, I was a naturally bright pupil despite my best efforts to deliberately make mistakes in my homework and fail to answer questions in class.*

It's funny, in primary school, it's all right to boast about being the best in the class.

'I'm the best in the class!'

'No I am!'

But one year later for some unknown reason those claims become a liability.

'I'm the worst in the class!'

'No I am!'

And after a few years of this kind of crack I was actually the worst. I would say that I'd wilfully turned idle, lost my interest in reading, and spent all my time messing with Balls O'Reilly and staring out of the window and by the time the Leaving Cert came around it was too late to rectify the situation. If I had only buried my head in the books, I could be studying medicine now. I'd make a better doctor than Grainne or that wisecrackin' bollox on duty in the hospital. If I was in any doubt about a diagnosis, all I'd have to do is pick up the phone and ring my mother.

Anyway, where was I? Oh yes, once me and Mickey Mohan hit the Main Street, we'd jump off the bikes, he'd let his fall on the footpath, I had a stand, and we'd head straight into Fraser's, the newsagent's. I had to collect the Irish Press *for my father and the local papers as well if it was a Thursday. If there was one thing my father loved it was the papers.*

Once a month I was allowed to get Shoot!, *the English soccer magazine. It was a weekly magazine but I was only allowed it once a month seeing as it was all about soccer. My father played Gaelic Football for Donegal in the fifties so I suppose I was lucky to get it at all. Although I loved Gaelic, I preferred soccer and always dreamed that I'd play at Wembley some day. Sometimes if oul' Norman's back was turned, me and Mickey would steal a few packets of football stickers before we left the shop.*

And then we'd hop on our bikes again and continue to race the rest of the way home. I normally won the contest even though he had a proper racer. That's because I was very fit and my opponent had asthma. I took after my father I suppose. He was still playing for the senior team in the town when he was forty-five years old.

During that daily routine was the only time I ever hung around with Mickey, except after dinner, of course, when we'd race back up to the school again. I would safely say that we never actually spoke to each other on the way. We had an arrangement that suited us both very well. No complications or misunderstandings. He was a very quiet fella altogether, Mickey Mohan, and to be honest I have no idea where he is now. He could be dead for all I know or in America. His family moved away and that was the last anybody heard of them. Balls who was my best friend even then took sandwiches to school because his parents were too busy to make dinner what with the shop and everything.

By God it was all action in our house at dinnertime. As soon as my mother put the dinner down on the table, me and Joe would have a race to see who'd finish it off first. I used to let him win because he'd only start crying otherwise. Big baby. Then I'd go and read the paper from cover to cover before my father came in. I loved the papers too.

'Well Paddy, a mhic, anything in the paper?'

That meant I had to give it to him. But usually I'd have it read in plenty of time. I was a very quick reader. Daddy would put his hat on Joe's head, sit down at the table and read headlines out loud to my mother as she was getting his dinner ready. 'Council Meeting Ends In Blows! Boys oh boys, they've no sense at all.'

I loved the local papers most of all, especially the court reports.

There was great excitement in the house if my father's name was mentioned.

'Mr Kevin Deehan of Aghasedge was accused of painting "God Bless the IRA" on the wall of the fire station . . . Garda Patrick Scully [hurray!] saw a man whom he recognised as the defendant running from the scene . . . later found Mr Deehan hiding in a skip with white paint on his trousers . . . when asked what was he doing in the skip, Mr Deehan replied, "I was asleep" . . . The defendant claimed that he had been helping his brother to paint his house. They finished early and went drinking . . . Defendant said he couldn't remember how much drink he had taken but that he had a "skinful" . . . he had separated from his brother . . . suddenly became very tired and went to sleep in the skip . . . according to Garda Scully [hurray!], the defendant became abusive and called him "only an oul' bollox, an MI5 bollox" . . . Justice McGinlay told Mr Deehan to "cop on to himself" . . . fined £5 for defacing public property and ordered to pay £5 to the court poorbox . . .'

I would read them out loud to my father who chuckled softly to himself between mouthfuls of buttered cabbage as he remembered some other details of the incident that went unreported. I used to cut out the best stories and put them in a scrapbook which as a matter of fact I still have. There was very little doubt in my mind in those days about what I wanted to be when I grew up. I wanted to be a guard too of course. As far as I was concerned, the Hardy Brothers and Nancy Drew didn't know what they were talking about. Agatha Christie didn't have a clue about crime either. Serious crime for me had very little to do with killing people on a train, or stealing valuable paintings from an art gallery. For a start there were no trains or museums in the area. No, breaking the law in my book meant not displaying a tax disc, burning a neighbour's hay shed, being drunk and disorderly, IRA membership, nicking copper wire, from a building supplier's yard, to hold up your trousers. That's what it was all about. My father was very proud of me whenever any

*of his colleagues were around which now that I think of it wasn't
very often.*

*'What are you going to be when you grow up?' they'd ask in
their Southern accents.*

'A sergeant.'

*'Ho-ho, ya boy ya, do you hear that Pat, if you don't hurry up,
he'll be calling the shots around here.'*

'Hahaha.'

*And then he'd say to me 'Go out there and let them see you solo
the ball.' And I'd run around the garden for the next hour, with
unlimited energy, imagining that I was playing for Monaghan in
every round of the Ulster Championship, against Cavan, Donegal
and Armagh, and in the All-Ireland semi-final against Cork and
in the final too above in Croke Park. I broke all scoring records
and saw my name in huge block capitals on the back page of the*
Northern Standard. *'Scully brings Sam home,' 'Sam' being the
Sam Maguire cup, the most important trophy in the land.*

*My father was always getting clapped on the back for his
sporting achievements. There was above average respect for people
like him. One time when I was about nine years old we all had to
go to Donegal to see him getting a Hall of Fame award from the
county board. It really was a great day.*

*The best part about it was that I didn't have to go to school.
Instead, Mammy made me put on my good suit, dark blue velvet
jacket and trousers, light blue shirt, dark blue tie. Joe had one
exactly the same. In fact she had them both specially made for
Joe's communion the year before. The two of us looked like a pair
of wee guards. The only difference being that Joe had a dicky bow
on instead of a tie and you don't see guards wearing dicky bows.
(Maybe they should wear them, and that way, people mightn't
look at them as the enemy, scallywags mightn't view them as such
a threat. You know? They might be more inclined to co-operate
with them and have a laugh. Who knows? I can't see it being
introduced in the near future though.)*

Our dog, Dara, a black sort of a cocker spaniel wanted to come with us but wasn't allowed in the car. Daddy was very particular about the car. Anyway the dog followed us for about five miles, up the town, begging to be let in, a shoe in its mouth, where are you going without me?, out the road, nearly lost him, no wait here he comes flying around the corner, wait for me yez bastards I've got the shoe, stuck behind a tractor for ages, surely they'll let me in now that I've come this far, out of breath, heart about to pack in, in tears. Joe was in tears too when he finally gave up the chase. We thought he'd get lost out the country or get in trouble for savaging sheep or something.

It took about five hours to get to our destination partly because of the constant driving rain and partly because my father wouldn't go as much as one mph over the speed limit. Also, seeing as how we took the shortest possible route through Northern Ireland we were stopped at army checkpoints twice, once on the way in and once more on the way out. Jaysus, me and Joe got very excited when we saw the lookout tower and the huge concrete walls and the British soldiers with their blackened faces and their weapons and their walkie-talkies. We especially enjoyed going over the ramps.

'Hurray!'

'Sssssshhhh!' my mother hissed nervously. 'They can hear everything we say.'

The first time we were stopped, after queuing for about half an hour, the car was searched and the young squaddie gave my father cheek. I'd never seen anybody give him guff before. We looked at each other in the back with disbelief.

'Can I see your driving licence Paddy?'

How on earth did they know his name?

'Where are you going?'

'Donegal.'

'Where are you coming from?'

'Castlecock.'

'Where do you live?'

'Castlecock.'

'Why are you going to Donegal?'

'I'm attending a Gaelic Games function.' He was too modest to tell the whole truth and too straight to lie. A lie would have made things easier because that answer didn't please the soldier one bit.

'Are you in the fucking IRA or something?'

'I am not.'

'Who have we got here?' looking in through the back window. *'Are these your little baby terrorists?'*

'Yes!' said my mother, leaning across.

'I didn't ask you.'

'They are not terrorists,' my father said softly.

'I have a good mind to take you in for questioning Paddy. What will your little bombers do then?' My father tightened his grip on the steering wheel and looked straight ahead. *'Go on!'*

We drove on. *'Bastards!'* he muttered, *'bloody bastards.'*

We travelled in relative silence without further ado through a drab, unchanging landscape and grey towns.

'Now, is this a Protestant town or a Catholic town, I wonder?' Mammy asked herself every so often and tried to reach a conclusion by reciting the names she saw above the shopfronts and pubs.

'McConkey, Nicholson's, Fortune and Sons, Spar, Wallace, Leavy, O'Neill, Armstrong, Spence, Fashion.'

As a rule, she classified people by religion as well as by illness. Mind you, in her book, being a Protestant was a type of ailment. She whispered the words, *'Protestant'* and *'cancer'* in the same tone. There was a Protestant school in our town, and sometimes on the way home from our school, if we had nothing better to do, we'd throw stones at the proddy goats.

When Daddy went up to collect his award for outstanding service to the county, there was a huge cheer. Mammy was crying. Daddy was supposed to make a speech which he had been writing all week but only said *'Thank you'* in the end. Then we all had our photo taken for the Donegal News. I noticed that my arm was missing from the photo when it was printed the following week. It looked as if I had only the one arm and I was very upset for a good while *after that. I was wearing a Leeds United ring at the time on my finger, one that I'd sent away for in* Shoot!, *and was holding it up to the camera, so that might be a reason. I'll never know. A drunk man wearing a wig came up to me and said 'Your father was the best man ever to play for the county.'*

We stayed the night with our granny, me and Joe in the same bed. Next day when we got home there was no sign of Dara. He'd been knocked down and was killed stone dead.

I knew my father and his friends would stop watching me walloping the ball against the hedge after a few minutes and start talking about the IRA but I didn't care. I was happy enough. They were always harping on about the IRA. I didn't even know who or what they were but I knew one thing for sure, they were very, very bad. They were a scourge. Mythical creatures, who dressed from head to toe in black clothes and killed children.

One morning, there was a bulky envelope lying in the hall with five bullets in it. I brought the package up to my father before I went out to school.

'Look what we got, Daddy!'

He grabbed them off me and hit me on the side of the head. There was no note or nothing, just the five bullets.

My mother went into hysterics, 'We'll have to move Paddy, we can't stay here.' He didn't say a word. He closed his mouth and sealed up his face, breathing heavily.

'Bastards,' he said, 'bloody bastards!' He was on the tablets after that. They both were, for the nerves.

Of course, they weren't real killing bullets at all but a set of shotgun cartridges. I realised much later with mixed feelings that we hadn't been singled out by the men of violence. No. Anybody could buy shotgun cartridges. A child could buy them across the counter at the post office. The family was simply the target of some local madman with a grudge. Some drunk who spent the night in the cell. Some farmer my father ticked off for parking his tractor in the middle of the main street. Someone who'd nothing better to do.

*   *   *

'Poor wee Paddy! Would you look at the state of his hair all matted with blood? Wouldn't you think they'd cut it. Nurse, nurse!' I suddenly experienced a touch of the old *déjà vu*. Three years ago, I was lying in practically the same bed with practically the same mammy fussing over me and the same goody two shoes brother Joe tagging along reluctantly.

It was the day of the under sixteens final against Ardfeart. For weeks beforehand, I'm telling you here and now, that game was treated as one of the biggest events ever in the history of the town. It was more important than the famine, Catholic Emancipation, the War of Independence, or any uprising, sporting, political or domestic. The only thing that came close was a barmen's race a year earlier on the main street. Jaysus, that was some crack, ten lads running from outside the courthouse to the launderette, each one holding up a tray laden with drinks, a right disaster. But nothing compared to the forthcoming match of the century. The whole town was talking about it. I couldn't walk up the street but there'd be people shouting at me, 'Up the Castle,' and 'C'mon, you boy ya!'

My mother was proud as punch. She wouldn't stop boasting about me. I heard her telling the man who delivers the Catholic newspapers that I'd play for Ireland one day. There was no point telling her that Ireland didn't have a Gaelic football team.

'I thought he was going to be a priesht!' replied the man in his Kerry accent.

'Well he'll be the first priest to play for Ireland, won't you Paddy?' And then she'd toss my hair. I'd try and dodge her outstretched hand.

'He doesn't like me tossing his hair.'

'He's the big fella now.'

'It's a pity his daddy won't be here to see his big day.' A big tear, magnified by her glasses, would form in her eye. Like a larva. 'And he got six honours in the Inter.'

'He's a credit to you.'

'He's my special little man, aren't you Paddy?' Wiping the tear away with the cuff of her blouse. To hear her heaping praise on me and Joe, you'd think we were a pair of prize pigs in a pen at the Spring Show above in the RDS. And her shovelling compliments in on top of us, regaling her audience with examples, real and imagined, of our merit.

'My Paddy did this, my Joe did that.'

(Mind you, in recent years, she's slightly changed her tune. 'My Joe did this, my Joe did that.')

'Will ye win?' The man.

'We will surely, we'll slaughter them.'

'Good man, the girls will be falling all over you. Does he have a girlfriend, Mrs Scully?'

I always hated that, the way they used to talk about you and look at you as if you were still four years old. I was fifteen, for God's sake.

'I thought priests couldn't have girlfriends.' I said out of the corner of my mouth, thinking that might shut him up. I thought wrong.

'Shpeaking of which did you hear about Mrs Flynn?' The man.

'No.' Mammy.

'She had a shtroke.'

'Sacred heart, and wait 'til I tell you Mrs Malone had a brain tumour . . .'

Even the teachers were nicer than usual. For example, if the homework wasn't up to scratch or if I, say, stuck a compass in somebody's hole, I'd get off scot-free. I could have stolen a car or killed a man and got away with it. They'd say, 'ahh he's a lot on his mind. He's a special case.' In fact, me and Balls, who by the way was only a sub, got drunk the Wednesday before the game in his house when his parents were away. We stole a bike from outside the garda station in broad daylight, me sitting on the saddle and him pedalling in an upright position. There was no crossbar. We *spun around the town for a couple of hours causing havoc. Balls robbed a Rubik's Cube from a stall on the main street. He couldn't make head nor tail of it so he simply peeled off the coloured stickers and rearranged them until he had the puzzle solved. We terrorised the town. We even called in to the parochial house to see Father Farrell. Holding hands, we told him that we were homosexuals. It was Balls's idea. I couldn't keep a straight face and the priest lost the rag and hunted us out of there. When we were finished with the bike, which I think belonged to one of the Carolan girls from the Hill, we threw it over the wall into the river. Nobody for once passed any remarks. I'll tell you one thing I couldn't wait for the big day.*

Ardfeart had beaten us twice already that season in the league although the last game was very close. They won 3–11 to 2–9 and I scored a goal and four points. But this was the one that mattered. The Dr Ball Cup. We were all highly motivated, nobody more so than Shovels. At training during the week, Brother Padraig who was a very fierce man decided to thump each one of us in the stomach. By that I mean, he stood in front of you bawling into your face, 'We're going to kill them,' and hitting you repeatedly until you joined him in the chorus. Shovels of course didn't take too kindly to that and thumped him back right in the middle of the chest. Brother Padraig, he had no nickname, landed on his feet two yards away. Now, although Shovels was very big he was no match for the Brother. Wiry and demented we were absolutely certain that he was going to kick seven kinds of shite out of Shovels. We all went quiet. Brother Padraig squared up to Shovels, stuck a finger in his chest, turned to us, and 'If only the rest of yez could be like Barry Malone, that's the type of attitude I want to see.' He carried on hitting us but nobody else had the nerve to hit him back. Balls needless to say wasn't there. He was far too cute to go training. No, he was taking some young one to the cinema instead.

Sunday came. It was a lovely bright day. I met Balls after mass and even he who has very little interest in football was excited. He pulled me and another few of the lads into a huddle and started taking off Brother Padraig. 'You're to pass the ball wide to Scully.' Some members of the congregation who must have thought we were all mad cheered when they heard this. I went a bit red but I didn't mind.

(By the way, his imitation was accurate, I played right-half forward and although I don't like to boast I was very fast, so the Brother did encourage the boys to play it out to me. Mind you having said that, dwelling on the ball was considered to be a capital offence. Going on a solo run, or dribbling the ball with your feet, or selling a dummy or anything fancy like that or drop-kicking it or holding on to it for more than a second was severely frowned upon by the Brother. Anything above and beyond booting the ball down the field as far as possible after preferably decapitating a member of the oppositon was known as 'showing off', a crime punishable by immediate substitution and possibly a three-match ban. 'Think about it,' the Brother would scream at a newcomer who'd be trying to demonstrate a bit of flair to impress the selectors, 'just think about it you morons,' pointing at his head. 'Imagination loses games.' He was probably right too, for the longer you held on to the ball the more chance you had of being upended by a hairy heat-seeking missile on legs. 'Skill gets you nowhere. Passion is all you need,' the Brother would rage almost stopping your heart with his fist. And the whole town would agree with him. They'd turn out in droves for even the most insignificant under twelves' game, firing water-cannons of invective at the referee and the opposition but most of all at their own little men in red and green. You couldn't do anything right. If you scored a point from an impossible angle, they'd say, you should have gone for a goal. If you scored a great goal, they'd say, 'A fluke, it was definitely a fluke.' 'He should have passed. O'Neill was in a better position.' 'Oh You're right there.' 'He's a flukey wee cunt.' The pharmacist, a fussy old woman, would turn up on the sideline still in her starched white shopcoat, 'Kick the ball, kick the fucking ball'. It didn't seem to matter that I had

*caught the ball beautifully, if I may say so, a two-handed catch
above my head and had acres of space in front of me. No, as far
as they were concerned the ball was a bomb primed to explode,
the possession of which could bring bad luck on the town like a
skull on the mantelpiece.)*

*We didn't linger too long outside the church. There was no point.
We hadn't been out the night before so there was nothing much to
talk about.*

*At one p.m. we met outside the Lock Inn and all piled into the
back of Sylvester Duffy's Hiace van. I never saw anything like the
state of Shovels. He was still in his working clothes from the day
before. (Like I said before, Shovels was the only one of us who had
a proper job.) You could tell by looking at him that he hadn't made
it home at all from the night before. He told me that he went for a
few drinks after work, ended up out at the Mirage, got tired on the
way home and went to sleep in a car parked outside somebody's
house. As far as I could see he was still pallatic. But I knew from
experience that it wouldn't affect his performance on the pitch.
There was about sixteen of us squashed into the back of the van
like battery hens but Sylvester didn't seem to give a whit. He did
a circuit of the town, beeping the horn, as if anybody needed a
reminder of what was about to pass. We stopped briefly outside
the house of a no-show. It's hard to believe that some people like,
for example, 'Muck' Duffy would skive off on the day of a big final.
No pride or else big match nerves, one or the other, but either way
he cried off. Off we went then to Monaghan town for the final of
the Dr Ball Cup. Singing songs. 'We've got Patrick Scully on our
team, we've got Patrick Scully on our team, we've got Patrick
Scully on our team, we've got the best team in the land.' Liam
McCabe led the chorus. Fair play to Liam. 'IRA all the way, fuck
the Queen and the UDA, with a knick knack Paddy whack give
the dog a bone, send those British bastards home.' Deadly crack
altogether.*

*Three-quarters of an hour later, the van stopped outside the
ground. I was last off, seeing as how I was almost smothered*

under the whole full-forward line. I threw my boots out of the back door and stepped out, right foot first. But didn't my toes get caught between two slats of a drain? I was off-balance, my leg went back and I broke my ankle. I heard a snap and knew immediately the joint was broken. I was roaring with the pain but the lads thought I was just messing. Brother Padraig who arrived just after us in a car pushed everybody else aside, 'I'd say it's broken all right, he's no use to us, Sylvester, take him to the hospital.'

Jaysus, I was bawling crying and it wasn't because of the pain. I couldn't play in the final and the County Selectors were going to be there. I had trained hard all year and indeed done extra training at home but to no avail. Balls played instead of me, can you believe that, his very first game of the season. By all accounts he wasn't very good, but the team won. We won the cup but I didn't even get a medal. Four of the lads went on to play for the county. I know I would have distinguished myself too if I'd had the chance. Shovels of course got sent off for spitting, not at one of the opposition but at the opposing captain's mother who was abusing him from the touchline. Opinion was divided in the town for months afterwards on his behaviour. My mother and Joe arrived at the hospital as I was getting the plaster on. Joe was furious because he was missing the match. He didn't have that much interest in sport but the whole town was there and he didn't want to miss out on the crack.

4

Francesca's Diary

Thursday, 11 November 1982

The party was an utter disaster. When Patrick first mentioned it to me, I got the impression that there was just going to be a few of us sitting around a candle listening to records and drinking wine. I imagined that Patrick, Xavier, that 'yeti' who lives with them, Gráinne maybe and one or two others from the class would be in attendance. We'd play cards, Geoghegan or one of the lads would suggest strip-poker for the millionth time in his life, clinging to the delusion that sometime somebody will say 'Yeah okay, that sounds like fun.' Which is a bit rich from a guy who hasn't changed his clothes in about four years, who wouldn't denude himself in front of his wife, if somebody was ever dumb enough to marry him, who was born in a pair of FCA boots that would take him the best part of an hour to remove. Xavier would cheat outrageously at Switch, Gráinne would suggest Charades to hoots of ridicule and shortly afterwards go home in a huff, leaving me to grapple halfheartedly with P on the floor, while Xavier bedded whoever was available, lucky bitch, and Geoghegan fell asleep on the armchair, stoned, but still managing a nasty sneer.

But no. News of a party travels fast. All week, the only questions on everyone's lips were where and when? There was a buzz of anticipation in college on the fateful morning like something you'd find on the eve of a coup d'état. I guess we were all expressing some sort of a spontaneous desire to keep the good-time momentum of the first few months going for as long as possible.

Patrick, unaware of the mounting hysteria, had asked me to come to the flat in the afternoon to help him clean up in time for the party. That was a bit optimistic. If he'd called in the Irish army this day last week, he'd have been cutting it fine. The place as ever was like a badger's set, dark and filthy with an appalling smell. David Attenborough could have done a whole series from the kitchen. The cohabitants were supposed to lend their assistance but needless to say disappeared off to the pub at the earliest opportunity. Such cheek. And it was Xavier's idea to have a party in the first place. I have no idea how able-bodied adults can live in such disgusting conditions. We managed to eradicate most of the vermin in the flat and stack whatever flimsy furniture there was into a corner. Kindling, that's all it was good for. Patrick I must say surprised me with his appetite for hard work. When I asked him for washing-up liquid, he said 'Elbow grease is your only man,' and proceeded to polish like a man possessed. He almost frightened me, he was in such a frenzy, a dervish, a Tasmanian dust-devil, brushing, scraping, scrubbing, not stopping to treat his wounds, cuts and scratches and bruises and burns, hoovering until the bag burst and then hoovering some more until the antique appliance itself exploded.

From about nine onwards, the hordes arrived. Patrick, a little Dutch boy's finger, could do nothing to stem the tide at the door. He was furious with Xavier for inviting so many. Half of Dublin was there, or so it seemed, hardly any of whom he knew. At least, I recognised most of the people who came from college, complete with six-packs and plastic bags full of cans, traffic cones, hub-caps, rusting registration plates, uprooted plants, trees, an elaborate mat from the foyer of the Shelbourne Hotel and, believe it or not, a bust of Isaac Newton. Gráinne was there too and Maeve Quinn from UCD whom I hadn't seen since the summer along with two of her friends.

Some of Geoghegan's courier colleagues decamped to the kitchen and like a flock of leather-clad vultures consumed everything that was in the fridge i.e., a jar of pickled gherkins, ice cubes and some mouldy sausages.

They were belching lecherous louts, the dregs, carcasses full of mud, performing obscenities for each other's amusement, stealing drink, groping girls and generally giving everybody a hard time.

People rivered in continously as the pubs emptied, joined by tributaries of curious passers-by. One lad tried to gate-crash by doing an impression of a Thalidomide victim. He had managed to conceal his arms inside his jumper, making it appear as if his hands began at his shoulders. We weren't sure whether to laugh or be outraged. A friend of Xavier's, Mick King, who has a handicapped brother was in no doubt. Infuriated, he broke the lad's nose with a crash helmet which was the first object to come to hand.

Meanwhile, the couriers were smashing glasses in the kitchen which by now had become a suburb of Beirut. Checkpoints manned by various extorting factions. Breaking stuff, it seems to me, is a natural highlight of any social event, any wedding, christening, or congregation of more than four, once drink is taken. People spontaneously feel the need to sing, and later to, well, smash things – glasses, bottles, headlamps, windows, skulls.

Another crowd were smoking joints in the lads' bedroom, tearing Patrick's birth certificate into strips to make roaches, and whatever else they found among his paraphernalia in the shoebox he kept under the bed. They passed around joints and tiny pipes, broken bottles and even a hollowed parsnip.

Patrick, incensed but powerless, never the best on red wine, wandered inconsolably from room to room. Music was blaring from the tape deck but the place was so crowded there was no space to dance. The mob throbbed and glowed, like a giant brain on a life-support system.

The guards were called at about half past one, either by somebody in the flats above or by somebody who wanted to get out. Three of them arrived at the door but could move no further. Their very presence however prompted a few of the revellers to leave, thank God, satisfied at last that they'd been to a decent party that had got the ultimate blessing of a visit by the boys in blue. Patrick, who was frowning so much that he had a set of shelves on his forehead, agreed with the guards that the party had gotten out of hand and promised to do his best to clear the flat. He also mentioned that his father had been a member of the force. By this time, Maeve and Gráinne had left. I would love to have gone with them but felt compelled to stay and give poor Patrick some moral support. I felt so sorry for him. Xavier was asleep in a drunken heap in a corner surrounded by alcohol spillages and cigarette butts. Somebody had poured sugar all over his head and into his trousers. Finally at about four in the morning the tide turned and people began to drift away, summoned by the sandman, including the threesome who had been in the bathroom for half the night. (Thanks to them the garden had become an open sewer.) Other courting couples rose and separated, dazed and self-conscious and disappeared without farewells into the night. A few stragglers remained in stupors. We decided to let sleeping dogs lie. Geoghegan and the couriers had barricaded themselves into the kitchen. God only knows what they were doing now. And God help anybody who breached their defences.

And then came the part I dreaded most. Patrick somewhat sheepishly asked me to stay over. I really wasn't in the mood but didn't want to let him down any further. And I didn't have enough money for a taxi.

We both crawled into his recently vacated, still warm and sweaty bed, fully dressed. As usual, there weren't any sheets. The only bedclothes were a blanket and an unzipped sleeping bag that looked as if it had been shredded by a maniac. He put his arms around me and tried to coax me towards him. I tensed without wishing to offend him but my somewhat spiritless gesture was futile due to his persistence and a mattress that annoyingly sagged in the middle. I could feel his heart beating like a caged thrush, no, an albatross, through his shirt, damp with perspiration and testosterone. I could smell the beer and worry from his breath as he attempted to find my mouth in the dark. I got the impression that he almost didn't want me to notice his advances, that in a bizarre way he wished I wasn't even there, or that I was asleep, that he really didn't want to have to do this with a real person but knew he must.

He forced his tongue into my mouth and swished it around like a paint-roller, his teeth, aggressive soldiers brutally quashing a demonstration. I was floundering for air as Patrick got more and more amorous, writhing like a shark on top of me, the end of his tie getting caught in my nose, stifling me even further. He put his hand under my T-shirt and pawed at my breasts. Then after burrowing under my bra, he pinched my nipple between thumb and forefinger and tugged it, in his mind, I'm sure, gently. It was quite painful but I bit my tongue, knowing he'd remove his hand when the bra-strap cut off his circulation at the wrist. With the wind in his sails, he became more daring. He released the offending mauler who immediately teamed up with his erstwhile mate and together they thoroughly searched my stomach and sides as if they were looking for a secret stash. One went around the back on a decoy run while the other hovered suspiciously at the top of my jeans.

Patrick tried to slide his hand into my knickers, and just reached the pubic hair when I seized his arm and pulled him away. My actions couldn't have been more blunt. He tried again, convincing himself no doubt that I was simply adjusting my position. I resisted. He tried again and again and again and again, obstinately certain that I'd relent, succumb to his charms. Finally, I broke free but before his heart dropped below the trap-door, I stuffed my hand down his trousers and gripped his fat friend. I quickly built up a head of steam. It was an unpleasant job but somebody had to do it. Thankfully, despite the obstacles and the confined space, it didn't take long. (It was a bit like doing a three-point turn in a shed.) I think I shrieked when the hot liquid squirted all over my hand. Romance, ehh? Patrick moaned and buried his face in the bed. It was the first sound he'd made since we'd stepped into this nefarious dimension.

Neither of us was particularly drunk. So we didn't talk. Within a few minutes, a humbled Patrick turned towards the wall, like a Tridentine priest turning his back on the congregation to mumble the Latin rites. I turned the other way. I have a sneaking suspicion that he lay awake until I stole out at first light. I know I stared into oblivion for the remainder of the night, grilling myself. What was I doing here? Where did I go wrong? I had no feelings for him, no matter how hard I tried. I'd probably like him a lot if I met him outside this, do I call it, a relationship? But now somehow, he's inside my head, a lodger. It's madness.

I had never ever felt so lonely in my entire life. I'd certainly never felt this alone on my own. As an only child, I am quite comfortable with my own company. Although not proud of the fact, I am probably at my happiest in isolation from others, in a low population density, one person to every square mile, the Tundra. I like to eat alone, go to the cinema alone, run alone. I don't blame Patrick. He's on a parallel track, a slow goods train. The signal box is derelict. I was beginning to wonder would I ever feel relaxed with any man?

Before long I found myself rolling inexorably towards his compact frame, the mattress having one last giggle at our expense.

Tuesday, 16 November 1982

What a day. We spent the whole afternoon in the canteen. Time stretched and yawned like a holidaymaker in a hammock. There must have been about fifteen of us just sitting around drinking coffee and talking and laughing and pointing. Xavier of course held centre stage with Mick King, who's a nice guy but sports a pony-tail. Oh dear. The pair of them didn't let up for a second, slagging off each other, the rest of us, anybody who had the misfortune to pass, the public at large, making faces, punching shoulders, following people, eating sugar and salt and all sorts of odious concoctions. It was hilarious, I suppose.

It all started when myself and Mary-Rose were leaving the canteen after lunch, queasy after a plate of greasy chips. Xavier stopped us at the door and forbade us to leave. He had called an emergency meeting of the Left-handed Bass Players Society and our attendance was apparently essential. Mick King was debating that night and we all had to help him write his speech on the motion, 'This house thinks debating is clever,' or something like that. And afterwards the 'Lefties' were holding a drinks reception. Xavier had booked a room and a DJ and secured two free kegs from the Guinness rep with whom he had become very friendly. He doesn't miss a trick.

Ignoring our feeble protest, he ushered us to a table where

the rest of the gang was already seated. At about two o'clock the canteen emptied as the more diligent students and staff went back to work. Soon we had the hangar to ourselves, the laughter thundering off the walls. I was dying to go to the toilet for ages but stayed put afraid I'd miss some of the crack or be victimised in my absence. Xavier had already done a devastatingly accurate impression of Patrick which was disloyal but very funny. I went scarlet. Not saying a word myself but not uncomfortable, assured in my supporting role, wired on caffeine. Nobody but nobody escaped their savage tongues. Needless to say, little work was done on Mick's script.

More details emerged about the damage done at the lads' party last week. It appears that somebody actually stole the public payphone from the hall, lock, stock and barrel, in the early hours of the morning. It must have been the couriers, fulfilling the common urge to leave a party with a trophy. But what a souvenir! They'd also tried to break into a couple of other flats in the house, virtually kicking in the heavy wooden doors and terrorising the occupants. And somebody ripped a drainpipe off the outside wall probably with the intention of making a gigantic hash pipe. There was hell to pay. The landlord threatened to evict Patrick and Xavier if they didn't cough up the cost of the repairs, a bill that was going to amount to at least two hundred pounds. We organised a whipround to raise funds towards a contribution. I was elected treasurer.

From the canteen we went straight to the Shoebox, recklessly abandoning any lingering notions we might have had about doing something constructive that day. Hours later, we swept back gaily on a magic carpet to college for the debate, waving sympathetically at those pedestrians outside our spell. The amphitheatre was crowded with a giddy audience, all stamping their feet and banging the tables as one, their voices unifying in an expectant din like the chorus of a Welsh choir. I could feel the hairs standing up on the back of my neck, thrilled to be part of the instrument that created this joyous uninhibited sound. I was nervous too for Mick. It was one thing speaking in public but for a man to do it while wearing a dress and make-up beggared belief. He was so brave. I can't imagine how he must have felt, exposed to the ridicule of so many, looking just like a girl having let his hair down. He didn't win but was easily the popular favourite especially after baring his behind in summing up his argument.

We squeezed through the corridors from there to the reception like a good-natured bunch of marathon runners, parading Mick King as if he were the Olympic flame.

I got pissed at the gathering and spent ages talking to Xavier who wasn't his usual ebullient self at all. I suspect that's because Mick was getting most of the attention. We discussed Patrick but I didn't want to say too much because I didn't know for sure how close they actually were. He told me that Patrick was a bit odd, surprise surprise, but was fundamentally a decent chap, and that he'd become very disillusioned lately and urged me to give him a chance. (I took that to mean that he himself didn't fancy me. Boo-hoo.) He confirmed my inkling that Patrick was lying when he told me that he managed a restaurant. He's unemployed of course having failed to get a college place. According to X, he's always making up stuff like that.

During this chat, I suddenly remembered that I was supposed to ring Patrick earlier on but didn't budge because I didn't want my time with X to end. I was, God forgive me, feeling weak in his presence, my nostrils filled with the scent of his patchouli oil, and the rest of my senses sharpened by alcohol.

Eventually the bubble burst and X was pulled away. Feeling shallow and a little sentimental, I sneaked out to the payphone at the end of the corridor and rang Patrick. He answered on the first ring before I had time to prepare my opening gambit. He was hurt and furious and claimed that we were supposed to have met. (I didn't say I'd meet him, I said I'd ring.) My excuse however backfired badly. Slurring my words, I told him that I'd stayed late in the library to finish an assessment. As I was telling him this, X and the gang crowded around me and started moaning loudly and shouting obscenities as if there was an orgy going. Patrick hung up.

Wednesday, 17 November 1982

I rang Patrick first thing in the morning, having decided never to contact him again. I'm so brave, so in control of my life, I thought, as Mrs Dungan made my breakfast and forced me to wash it down with a LemSip (her idea of a daily tonic). If only willing someone out of existence were easy, or stonewalling worked in practice. If only. A successful person I suppose can do that, treat other people's feelings like stains on his Louis Copeland suit, and dryclean the irritating problem away. With dread I dialled his number, apologised for my behaviour and arranged to meet him for lunch at a café in town.

I expected him to be still in a big sulk but on the contrary he was smiling when I met him, like an underdog. He had quite a disarming smile which softened his features and made him even more defenceless than usual. With his poor-me demeanour and brittle confidence, he was the type of person that you really really didn't want to let down or offend in any way.

I handed over the proceeds of our collection, a total sum of eight pounds, which would just about cover the cost of their landlord's ulcer medication.

Patrick, touched by the gesture, was worried in case he ended up having to find the rest. Xavier, although he was on a grant and his parents were loaded, had a finger in more pies than Mr Kipling, and was the type of person who found briefcases full of money but wouldn't lift a finger, in Patrick's opinion. He wouldn't give a shit if they were all turfed out on their ears. In fact, being homeless for a while would appeal to his sense of adventure and abandon. Of course, they couldn't even approach Geoghegan on account of his notorious temper. It actually annoyed me to think that Patrick was going to be the scapegoat. On the dole, he finally confessed, spending his pittance on hazlitt and frozen peas, his spare time on fibs, not even claiming rent allowance because of his stupid pride.

Sitting there in the café, looking out on a sheep looking in, who must have strayed from a farmers' demonstration on nearby Kildare Street, watching chunks of beetroot fall from the ends of Patrick's enormously stuffed roll, and later strolling, hand in hand, through Stephen's Green, I persuaded myself that I could live with this. Yes, I would be content to meet Patrick maybe once a week for a film and a drink as long as there wasn't anything else involved. I mean, it's healthy to have friends outside your own immediate circle, although if Patrick had his way, I wouldn't see anybody else but him. ('Those Lefties are a bad influence.') You can't always choose your friends, no more than you can choose your family. You don't even have to like your friends that much, do you? You're lucky to have somebody, anybody. And you don't have to be idiotically happy all the time, I mean, if you were, there'd be nothing to look forward to, would there?

5

I'll give you an account of a typical day in my life. Take
April 3rd 1983 when Gaffney was home from England and
staying on our couch for a few weeks.

I met Francesca outside the AA shop on Suffolk Street as
per usual. She was in a great mood because she'd just got
her J-1 visa for America. And I was supposed to be delighted
that she was going to work in America for the summer with
Grainne and a couple of girls from her class.

'It'll only be for three months, Patrick, and anyway the
break'll do us the world of good.' I don't see how it will do
me any good whatsoever. We went for a burger in the New
York Burger Joint, a very nice restaurant around the corner,
done up like a police station. The waiters and waitresses
were dressed up as cops and all. It was my first time here.
In fact to tell you the truth, it was the first time I was ever in
a proper restaurant ever. (Mind you, my father took us all
to a hotel one time in Donegal when we were on holidays.
Myself and Joe had chilled orange juice to start followed by
a basket of sausages and chips between us. About a hundred
grizzled sausages. We were delighted. I'd never seen food in
a basket before. My father had a steak and my mother went
on hunger strike. She didn't approve of dining outside the
home, eating something that she personally hadn't boiled
the fuck out of. She didn't trust people in the catering trade

one bit. And you know I can't say I blame her. I've heard since what goes on in the kitchens, spitting, pissing, picking stuff up off the floor. I wouldn't be surprised, if the chef had wiped his arse with that steak before he sent it out to my father.)

Anyway, it was Francesca's idea and she was paying. I suppose she was feeling guilty and wanted to soften the blow. And rightly so. I told her, in between the first course and the second course, that maybe I'd go to America too, just to test her reaction. Instead of saying 'Oh that'd be great' she came straight out and said she'd prefer it if I didn't. Can you believe that?

'I want to go with my friends.'

'You just want to get away from me, don't you?'

'No that's not fair, Patrick, it's just I've never been any-where before.'

'Well neither have I. Why can't we go together?'

'Jesus, Patrick, we're not married.'

That's Gráinne putting words in her mouth. She never approved of me from the start. And now that Francesca was living with her in a flat, around the corner from where she used to live in digs, she was coming more and more under her influence. And come here hi, what's so terrible about a boyfriend wanting to go to America with his girlfriend?

'Look I can't really explain, Patrick, I just *want* to go with my friends. We've it all planned and everything. Do you not understand?'

'No.'

'And anyway Patrick, you wouldn't get a visa.'

'Right, that's it, you can just fuck off.'

It was true, there was no way I'd get a visa, not even a holiday visa. I had no money in the bank, and no permanent job or college place to come back to. And who'd give me a reference? Balls?

To whom it concerns in America,
Scully is a man of his word. If he says he'll come back,
he'll come back.
Signed, Balls

I had no criminal record either but was known to the authorities for protesting outside the British Embassy at the time of the hunger strikes. Shovels roped me in, assuring me that it would be great crack abusing the Brits. And it was too until the guards started chasing us down the road. They took photographs and everything. Now, I'm no Republican but I was very upset about those fellas dying above in Long Kesh. Fuck Thatcher anyway. It is all her fault. And she only sleeps four hours a night. No wonder she doesn't have a clue. If I only slept for four hours a night I wouldn't know what was going on either. I'd be walking around like a zombie. Luckily for me though I didn't sign the petition. I never sign petitions. They always fall into the wrong hands. If you want to get into the USA you can't be a Communist, a criminal or sign a petition ever, even one saying 'I think America is great.' No, in their estimation, you're a potential troublemaker if you put your name to a piece of paper, period.

Typical of Francesca to bring that up, that business about the visa, the bitch. Talk about rubbing salt on the wound.

'The Manhattan with chips?'

'Here,' whispered Francesca, fighting back the tears.

'The Double Skyscraper with baked potato. Side order of chips, corn on the cob, coleslaw, mushrooms and green salad.'

'You can shove it up your hole!' I blurted. The waitress didn't bat an eyelid but turned on her heels and sauntered back to the kitchen, a pair of plastic handcuffs bouncing off her arse. I think she was European. She was very sexy anyway.

'Patrick!'

'Fuck off, you,' I bawled at the top of my voice. 'Right, just fuck the fuck off!'

The whole restaurant went quiet. Except for a woman at the next table who turned to her friend and piped up. 'I wouldn't let a man speak to me like that!'

I wasn't sure if she was giving out about me for shouting or Francesca for not answering back. Either way she had no right to butt in. She didn't have both sides of the story. 'It's none of your fuckin' business, you old windbag.'

I could feel my face going puce with the anger. I grabbed my good jacket off the back of the chair, knocking the chair over in the process, and stormed out. I was starving, my mouth was watering at the sight of that burger but once I started there was no stopping me. It was bad enough her going to America in the first place without consulting me until the damage was done, but it was much worse her more or less telling me it was all over between us, adding insult to injury. But I was wise to her game. I could read between the lines. She'll probably end up having it off with a lifeguard. And I'll tell you one thing for nothing, no woman is going to make a fool out of me.

It is at times like this you need hills, miles and miles of marshy undulations, tighter isobars or whatever the fuck you call them, contours on the map. There's no point walking off in a huff if you're going to be impeded every inch of the way by a mother bending down to wipe her child's nose, or by a party of old, out-of-season tourists dressed in luminous-green trousers bewildered because the streets curve, or two bastards in suits, solicitors probably, walking out of a pub without looking where they are going, laughing much too loudly, and bang into you, knowing full well if there are any injuries and it goes to court they'll win (it's who you know), or a bunch of fuckin' students pushing a bed for charity, or a wizened old bagman pushing a pram or a bike without tyres, Dublin's full of them, cursing the day they were born. Jaysus I hate Dublin. Back home whenever I was in a bad mood and, I have to say, that was often, I'd put on my wellies and head straight for the horizon. When I heard that my father died, I walked off the edge of the map, and believe me, that was possible, the world is flat where I come from. I kept going until I collapsed from exhaustion. And wasn't found until the next day, by a farmer, asleep in the long wet grass among spiders on stilts and a wagon train of fat slugs. And I felt an awful lot better. My father became real for the first time that night in a dream, more real that he ever was when he was alive and has remained that way to this day in my mind. And that's sad. That's the saddest thing I know.

I was waiting at the bus stop on Kildare Street for the bus to Rathmines with about ten other hopefuls including one old woman who looked at me as if I were some sort of cannibal and tightened her grip on her plastic shopping bag that was full of lightbulbs, me praying for the bus to hurry up, when who comes around the corner in floods of tears – only Francesca, as I knew she would. I would have been far happier if she had actually seen me getting on the bus but no.

'I'm sorry Patrick.'

I ignored her at first, staring straight ahead, like an early Celt on top of the Hill of Tara.

'Patrick, what do you want me to say? I'm sorry, okay.'

'Sorry for what?'

'Sorry for mentioning the visa. If it makes you happy, I won't go.'

'No, no, no, don't let me stand in your way. You do what you want and I'll do what I want . . . so I will.'

The bus came and went. We stayed put, sitting on the steps leading up to a statue. Dr Joseph O'Brien, Physicist (1848–95). Look at him standing there, proudly, unaware of us at his feet. Birds shitting on his head, surrounded by a moat of drunks' piss, the traffic pollution covering his bronze frockcoat in black grime, choking him yet his gaze remains unflinching. Fair play to him, Joseph O'Brien, Joe, like our Joe. I could see it all. Dr Joseph Scully, Tremendous Inventor and Sound Man (1966–). Our Joe is going places all right or so I'm told ten times a day.

She touched my hand. 'Cheer up, it's not the end of the world.'

'You'll meet some Yank and go off with him. I know it. They're mad about Irish women.'

'Don't be stupid.'

And she kissed me on the cheek. We huddled together to keep warm for the next hour or so, kissing occasionally, not giving a damn about the many people who stopped for a gawk. We had arranged to meet Balls and his new girlfriend Sheila Mannion, a lovely bit of stuff, and Fergus Gaffney later on to go to a new comedy club but that rendezvous was far from my mind at that precise moment. I felt so close to Francesca just then that I was seriously thinking of asking her to marry me. No messing. She was the one for me. I would have been happy to spend the rest of my life locked in that particular embrace, the hunger pains in the pit of my stomach indistinguishable from the pangs of longing I felt for her. And I'm not exactly what you'd call a romantic. I wouldn't, for example, be a great one for the flowers and the chocolates and the candlelit dinners. No. Romance for me isn't lying in bed after some heavy petting, lighting a cigarette, then, trying to adjust the coathanger on the back of the television so as to get a better reception and dozing off in each other's arms to the closing credits of *Dallas*; or doing the tango at sunset on a beach on a tropical island, beside the ruins of a World War Two plane, with our own personal midget in tow to make cocktails; oh no. Romance for me is painting creosote on to a wooden fence at the back of the house at home, alone, reflecting on the last encounter and looking forward to the next; or being at mass together, in our Sunday best, giggling uncontrollably, on our knees, my eyes on the back of her left leg, following the meandering line on her tights until it disappears up under her good grey skirt, and me with an evergreen shoot in my trousers. That was my idea of romance. I haven't fulfilled that particular ambition yet but I'm working on it. Another bus rumbled past like an overstuffed hedgehog. Thanks very much. It's a pity the moment had to pass. It's a pity she was going to America.

Anyway off we went to the so-called comedy club. Gaffney, Balls and his girlfriend were waiting for us in the pub. The show itself was on in a tiny room upstairs. It had already started by the time we got there. At the door, there was a smartarse collecting the money. He obviously thought that he was one of the comedians. 'Fares please,' he says, as if he were a bus conductor. Balls and his one went on ahead after paying the student rate. Francesca showed her card and went on in at the same reduced price of admission. Of course I didn't have my card with me (Balls had got some friend of his in the Student Union to forge one for me but I forgot to bring it) and ended up paying the full whack and what's more, much to my annoyance, I had to fork out for Gaffney too. He only had sterling on him. I'm not saying he was a cheapskate but he had the whole morning to change his money. Gaffney I might as well tell you was one of those fellas who thought the sun shone out of his arse. Especially since he went to London. He's behaved as if he's doing us all a big favour by staying with us. Fergus, I'm afraid, had become very big-headed, English accent and all.

Anyway Gaffney said 'Cheers mate' (do you see what I mean?) and went on ahead to join the others while I waited for my change. In the meantime the comedian on stage turns to me and says 'What's all the commotion? Are you coming or going?' And stuff like that.

'I'm coming,' I say, my whole head going red like a boil on a builder's back.

'Where were you until now? Have you got a note?' And so on. He picked on me for a full five minutes, despite me staring straight into his face, as if to say 'If you don't shut up, I'm going to fuckin' kill you,' the whole crowd looking in my direction and having a great laugh at my expense including, it has to be said, Francesca. That's loyalty for you.

'You're only a bollox,' I said and laughed, hoping the rest of the crowd would join in. But they didn't. Silence. What a crowd of fuckin' dryshites!

'See ladies and gentlemen this is what happens when cousins marry!'

Well they just loved that, they fell around the place laughing at that, even though your man was wearing a beret and a stripey jumper and wasn't remotely funny. I can take a joke as well as the next man but I didn't go there to be humiliated. I wouldn't mind but the thing is I didn't even want to go in the first place. It was Francesca's idea. Mary-Rose or one of them knowalls she hangs around with told her all about it.

To make matters worse we had to stand for the whole show in extremely cramped conditions, like pigs on a lorry. Everybody – and I mean everybody – was smoking, even Francesca who doesn't smoke. The big-shot Gaffney had duty-free and was handing them out to beat the band. I gave her a dirty look which she ignored. The bastard with the beret who was the MC made snide references to me all night but did I get any support at all from Francesca? I did not. She turned a blind eye to me as if I weren't there, as if she was ashamed to be associated with me. Even during the interval, she was deep in conversation with Fergus Gaffney.

God only knows what they were talking about but if I know him he was up to no good. He always had a reputation as a, what you might call, a ladies' man. Our Valerie and her friends thought he was a ride and they were about three years older than us. They were always quizzing me, Does he have a girlfriend? Will he be at the disco? Will you warn us the next time he's staying at your house? which was a stupid request because he never stayed, nobody ever did, not even cousins. My mother worried in case they brought lice or germs or pornography or explosives into the home. Admittedly Fergus is tall with dark hair, dark bushy eyebrows, dark eyes and fairly dark skin in comparison to everybody else in Castlecock although personally I think he looks like a fuckin' Mongol.

It was a terrible waste of money. The comedians were all useless except for one lad from Monaghan, a pale skinny fella who was very droll. Although I could probably do better myself. Balls went up to him at the end to congratulate him. I was half-thinking of going up myself to tell him he was on the right track as opposed to that cunt with the beret, at which point they both looked around at me and sniggered. *Et tu*, Balls. Another traitor.

I can't say that I enjoyed the walk back to the flat in Rathmines. It was very tense and nobody said a word. I had heartburn to boot after drinking on an empty stomach and it was raining. When I say raining, I mean drizzling continuously. You don't think you're getting wet in those conditions but the rain is so thin it gets under your clothes, under your skin too, in a way a downpour wouldn't. At least if the heavens officially opened you'd have an umbrella or some sort of a hood.

After a while, we stopped outside a chipper. By law, whether you are hungry or not, you have to stop for chips on the way home. As it happens I was absolutely ravenous after the fiasco earlier on.

Suddenly Balls turns to me in front of the others for no reason. 'You've no sense of humour, do you know that?'

I could tell straight away that for once he wasn't messing. I didn't agree with him but I was so flummoxed that I couldn't think of anything to say in reply. And needless to say, nobody came to my defence.

'You used to be great crack Scully.'

I don't know what possessed him to come out with that. I was hardly going to debate the issue in the street, 'No Xavier I beg to differ. I'm still great crack. In fact, I'm funnier than you.' And provide recent examples of my sense of humour to be judged by Balls and his panel of experts. The difference between me and him is that I don't want the world to know that I'm great crack. And he, to this day, telling stories of mine and jokes too as if they were his own, no acknowledgement whatsoever. Something must have been eating him. Well whatever it was he shouldn't have taken it out on me. To be honest I was almost in tears and that's very unlike me. Why would anybody say a thing like that? Even if I thought that about somebody else I wouldn't say it to his face in public. That was out of line. Francesca went in to get the chips.

'Plenty of vinegar on mine,' I shouted after her. I love vinegar. She was buying for me and Fergus Gaffney. Balls and his one weren't hungry. Or so he said, hands all over her, saving his appetite to savage her back at the love-nest. I'll tell you one thing for nothing, he wasn't getting any of my chips. In fact, I was thinking of never even speaking to him again.

Sheila, that was her name, said she was getting cold, in heat more like it, so herself and Balls moved off towards the flat for a ride leaving me and Gaffney looking at the ground in silence. Turned-up jeans, too, and loafers, he thinks he's fuckin' Elvis. Thankfully, it wasn't long before Francesca emerged with the chips and we were on our way. The two of them walked together ahead of me and talked like old friends even though they'd only met for the first time in the pub. I caught up and stepped in between them. But I hate it when there's three people in a row. You never get to stay in the middle for long. Suddenly, you bend down to blow on a chip, and you find yourself on the left or right of the group, excluded from the conversation.

I had only eaten about four chips when the brown paper bag, drenched in vinegar, tore and the chips fell out on the footpath. I could have killed Francesca.

'You did that on purpose didn't you?'

'What are you on about Patrick?'

'You drowned them in vinegar, knowing full well the brown paper would tear. Didn't you?'

'You asked for loads of vinegar, Scully,' said Gaffney.

'This is none of your business, Fergus, I didn't ask for the brown paper to tear, did I? Did I? No I fuckin' didn't.'

'I'm sorry Patrick,' she mouthed, 'I didn't mean it. Here, have some of mine.' I slapped the bag of chips out of her hand. They scattered all over the road.

'How do you like it? Now you know what it feels like.'

With that Francesca burst into tears.

'There was no need for that, Scully,' says Gaffney, looking at me with contempt, 'it was a simple mistake. You know, you're a stupid prick sometimes!'

'Why don't you fuck off back to England, it's got nothing to do with you. She's my girlfriend.'

Gaffney, disgusted, looked away. 'Are you okay Francesca?'

'Yeah, I'm fine, you go on ahead, I'll see you later.'

And off he went frowning, trying to catch up with the other pair to tell them, 'Scully is a right cunt.' No sooner was he gone, than Francesca totally out of character reared up at me.

'Don't you ever ever do anything like that to me again!'

I gripped her by the elbows to try and calm her down.

But she wriggled away. There were still plenty of people milling about on the street, stopping in their tracks to spectate, probably thinking that I was the guilty party. This type of entertainment was always a bonus at the end of a night on the town. Some of them'd be wondering should they intervene? Should they report the incident to the guards in case it exacerbated out of control into a full-scale riot? Then they'd carry on, after doing nothing, their curiosity and their conscience satisfied. Of course most of the bystanders, starved of visceral action, would be half hoping that we were tinkers and that slash hooks would be introduced at some stage.

'Sssshhh! Stop making a show of us.'

Half an hour later we had only moved about a hundred yards and hadn't got much further in the argument either. Francesca could be very stubborn sometimes.

'I know I asked for loads of vinegar, that's not the point, the point is, I didn't ask you to drown the fuckin' chips.'

'Will you please stop harping on about the chips? I said I'm sorry. How many more times do you want me to say it?'

'Are you stupid? Is that it? You're the one at college and you don't know that wet brown paper tears easily. Look at me when I'm talking to you.'

'Shut up! Just shut up. I don't care about the flipping chips. That's twice you've lost your temper with me today and I did nothing wrong. Do you understand? Nothing. I just can't stand it any more.'

She was screaming now like a banshee. That's all I needed. My own girlfriend disgracing me on the street again. If there is one thing I hate it's that.

'Shut up Francesca!'

'You and your flipping chips. Next time you can go in and get them yourself.'

'I will. I obviously can't rely on you to do anything right.

If you weren't too busy flirting with Fergus Gaffney all night—'

'How dare you? I was not flirting with Fergus Gaffney. I was talking to him. There's a difference. He happens to be a very nice fella.'

'Huh, you don't know what he's like, he's only interested in one thing. And don't think I didn't notice the way you were looking at him, and smoking his fags, "I'll see you later, Fergus." You fancy him, don't you?'

'I'm sick and tired of this. I'm going home.'

'Go on, admit it!'

She turned and bawled at me. 'All right then if it makes you happy I do. Now are you satisfied?'

There was a pause. A streetlight flickered out above me. The fuse must have blown. The traffic stopped. The rain stopped. I slapped her across the face. I only slapped her once, but saw it in slow-motion three more times. She stood stock-still. Her face drained of blood. Her tears dried up. I reached out to grab her arm. She froze. My hand was repelled by what I can only describe as a forcefield. She looked into my eyes, as if she was Drogheda and I was Oliver Cromwell. And off she went back the way we came. Running like a bird, a duck with a damaged wing.

I suppose she thought I'd run after her and say sorry. 'Sorry Francesca, I was trying to hail a taxi.' And beg her to come back to the flat. Why should I? What would be the point of that? End up staring at the ceiling with nothing to say to each other, listening to Balls and Sheila Mannion hard at it in the bed next to us, me wishing I was in the bed with them. In her mind, she'd be saying 'There's no way he's going to let me walk home on my own.' Normally I wouldn't. It was at least two miles to Phibsboro, it was the middle of the night and according to the *Evening Herald*, there was a psychopath on the loose. If he didn't get her, she'd still have to chance her arm with all the winos and

knackers and other citizens of the dark. But this time, she'd
gone too far. We'll just see, I thought, how well she gets on
without me.

Of course, in one way, I wanted to chase after her,
apologise on my knees and hug her to my chest. I wanted
to feel her glasses pressing into my cheek. I wanted above
all to stroke her hair. She kept her hair very clean. I knew
I shouldn't have let her walk off like that. It was far too
dangerous. But in another way I was willing for something
bad to happen, that she'd at least get a fright. And you
know then maybe she might appreciate me a bit more. On
the way home, I ripped the wing-mirrors off about twenty
cars. I juggled one, from a Renault Four I think, five times
on my foot. That's a record.

Anyway that was a typical day.

6

Francesca's Diary

Thursday, 4 April 1983

I've finally found the excuse and the moral courage to leave Patrick. He slapped me. He actually slapped me in a fit of pique. And for that I'll never forgive him. He left me to walk home alone in the most violent city in Western Europe. And for that I'll never forgive him. He has single-handedly, in Disaster Des fashion, managed to undermine what were otherwise the happiest most carefree days of my life. And for that above all I'll never forgive him. The bastard.

The girls were right all along. I was right all along. I overlooked his moods and his tantrums, his snide comments, his selfish, obsessive, increasingly erratic behaviour. Like an absentee landlord, I let the resentments of the peasant fester. I've pitied him. I've tickled his tummy. I've even tried to love him, for God's sake, hoping for a fairy tale, waiting naïvely for the day he'd shed his amphibious skin.

All for what, a slap in the face? It wasn't even sore or in hindsight a shock. He'd been extra jumpy for days, since he'd heard that I'd gone to a Macra na Feirme dance in Wicklow with Pól O'Neadún. You can't get away with anything in this country. I hadn't even told Gráinne I was going or Mary-Rose. I thought at first Patrick had trailed me or hired private detectives but it seems that a cousin of that odious slob Dermot Geoghegan was there and relayed the scandal. Patrick was waiting at the college gates on the following Monday in such a temper that he threw a bottle of Lucozade against a wall. And it's not like him to waste anything. He called me every name under the sun, harlot, Jezebel, whore, tramp, mostly terms of abuse he couldn't possibly have known. Either he consulted a Thesaurus or a Bible before he left the flat or perhaps he drew from the folk well of the incensed cuckold that sprang in every man's head. Not that I betrayed him. Pol, his gaunt face, shaved to the jawbone, tried to kiss me in the car on the way home. I nearly got sick. I went because he asked me to, 'I know you probably have a boyfriend but . . .' and I felt I owed him that much. I didn't even want to be there, not because I was afraid of Patrick's reaction. Far from it. I didn't want to revisit the set on which so many episodes of my badly-written soap had been staged. I wasn't curious or nostalgic. I didn't want to make smalltalk with the suspicious survivors of poverty who'd stayed behind in Killeeny and its environs. It was awful. Pol tried his best. He'd scrubbed himself with a wire brush and washed his father's car. He presented me with an orchid and a box of Maltesers, played Bach and Liza Minelli on the creaky tape deck. But he was just too gangly and too nice. And the band were atrocious, an outfit called Bonanza, grinding out the dreariest country and western standards, the musical equivalent of munching dry cream-crackers. But there was no telling Patrick that, no sharing what wry amusement could be derived from the fiasco.

And a few days later, for merely talking to a friend of his I get a slap on the face. Once again, Patrick Scully had suffered an imaginary slight. And everybody else was to blame. He was never wrong. If you presented him with documentary evidence, irrefutable proof, a list of witnesses willing to testify that he was wrong, he wouldn't concede an inch. In his mind, they'd be tackling him, not the truth.

Last month, for example, he wanted to visit the zoo in Phoenix Park. He had never been there before. His father, he maintains, was supposed to take him and his brother Joe once but unfortunately died the week before the big day. And, not surprisingly, Patrick's mother didn't let him go on the school tour the year the zoo was on the itinerary. She was convinced he'd be savaged by polar bears. (She's a very odd woman, Mrs Scully.) I'd been to the zoo once as a child. I remember I was wearing ear-muffs. I was given an ice cream that I didn't want. My parents were fighting. I got lost in a crowd and didn't mind, thinking logically that I'd probably never see my parents again but would be found by a nicer family and remain with them for ever. That didn't come to pass.

Instead of marvelling at unusual animals, we got the wrong bus and ended up in a housing estate in Finglas. Patrick insisted that we get the number 11. 'The number 11 definitely goes to the Park . . . there must be a diversion . . . the driver is lost . . . well they must have changed the route.'

Never wrong, he stormed off, the skin on the back of his bullish neck bunching up like undulations on the moon. Nervously I set off for Phibsboro.

There were still people dilly-dallying on the street, stalling for time, drifting home towards the suburbs, tasting the smog-flavoured night air or just looking for mischief. By the time I got to Portobello Bridge, this aimless sort of activity had ceased and the city had tucked itself into bed. I took giant steps, head down, determined that Patrick's cowardly actions weren't going to bother me any more, angry but relieved that I was free at last to breathe. Aware that a man was approaching, I coiled and cast my eyes upwards. Too late. He filled the footpath. 'Excuse me!' I whispered, too scared to speak, as I almost walked into him. He caught me in his arms, and quickly let go, search-me blameless. I got a very good look at his face in that instant, automatically memorising every pore. Although I'd never seen him before I could describe him better than a friend or TV celebrity. He had black hair, bready skin, and a moustache that didn't quite cover the outbreak of spots around his nostrils. About twenty-five years old with thick lips, he wore a green army-style jumper and blue jeans. I tried to round him, expecting him to step aside. He blocked my path. I screamed. Reeking of whiskey, he said, 'I just want to ask you a question, love. Do you know anywhere I can get a cup of tea?' I said, 'No sorry!' and pushed past him. He grabbed my arm, 'Look love, I only want a cup of tea.' 'Get off me!' I wriggled from his grasp and immediately crossed the road.

I knew exactly what he meant. Could he have a cup of tea with me, preferably in my house? A girl on her own at this time of night must be a goer or a simpleton. Either way, easy prey. How did he expect me to answer? 'No mister, there's nowhere open but why don't you come home with me and I'll put the kettle on.' How optimistic, desperate or downright dangerous was he? He crossed the road too. Alarm bells rang, air-raid sirens sounded. At first I thought he was just a drunken chancer but something about the shifty way he moved, the speed of his decision to follow me, suggested otherwise. Jets of adrenalin were suddenly released into my bloodstream.

In panic-stricken flight, I turned to the right, down to the canal, instead of going straight on down Camden Street, which would have been brightly lit and populated even at this time of night, albeit, thinly. I suppose I turned to see if he'd turn too, to test him, to confirm my suspicions before I was forced to bolt. It was such a stupid thing to do. The canal was dark and slimy like a rigid eel, lined by trees. It had an unsavoury reputation at the best of times, and was very very quiet.

I walked faster but could still hear the squeak of his runners behind me and his thick denim-clad thighs rubbing together as he tried to catch up. I could practically feel his stinking breath on my neck. But I was too afraid to look around, to betray my fear, a large part of me still hoping that he was a figment of my imagination, that he wouldn't be there if I didn't look.

I've often thought people were following me. Maybe people follow people all the time, discreetly for their own innocent amusement. I don't know. I can see the appeal of such a hobby. Once you think somebody is following you, it's hard to put it out of your mind even in broad daylight. But nothing prepares you for the absolute certainty that you're being stalked. For the dread that begins in the pit of your stomach and spreads, like the Third Reich on a map of Europe, to your bowels, and your legs, and your torso, and in all directions to your extremities.

Maybe he genuinely wanted a cup of tea. Who am I to assume, to judge and condemn? For all I know, he could have been a Typhoo addict. There was a man in Killeeny, Pól O'Neadún's father, who drank forty-five cups of tea a day, who got up five times every night, for a fix. And while he sipped his tea he read, and reread all the classics, the philosophers, learned works on art, religion, and history, the papers, magazines, the *Guinness Book of Records*, instruction manuals for electrical goods, clothing labels, and cereal packets. There was nothing he didn't know. He was known by the imaginative people of Killeeny and beyond simply as the 'Professor'.

With my newly-activated and ultra-sensitive radar, I spotted a pedestrian on the other side of the street, going in the same direction as me, us. I jogged over to join him, asking if it was all right to walk beside him for a little while. At last I could permit my head to turn in time to see my pursuer hail a taxi and disappear.

Hyperventilating, I thanked the man, a creepy sort of guy in his early thirties who wore a paper-thin windcheater, navy-blue with stripes down the arms. He had greasy blond hair and carried a plastic bag in his hand, the name of the shop worn away by his sweaty hands. He smiled at me lecherously and muttered something no doubt X-rated under his breath. Maybe he had a mushy palate from chewing too much liquorice as a kid and his mangled words were innocent. But I became edgier with every pace as his gibbering became more suggestive, then lewd, then obscene. He asked me did I have a boyfriend, and what sort of things we did, and did I take it up the arse? Suddenly he stopped and my heart stopped. Oh no, out of the frying pan into the fire, I thought and spun in mid-air like a flying pixie.

Laughing, he watched me flee, sprinting along the canal bank until I reached a familiar landmark, Leeson Street Bridge. I turned left towards the Green, still running, past the infamous strip of basement nightclubs, busy with office parties and night-owls. Basted in sweat, yet cold, tense but exhilarated, I ran on. Past a man whistling as he sold baked potatoes from a wagon, a customer buying two, one for himself and one for the stuttering tramp who warmed his hands on the generator, a man vomiting in a doorway, a bouncer pounding a punter's head off steps. Kerb-crawling taxis. The rain had abated, leaving colourful spots of reflected neon to light my passage. I left behind the Georgian buildings, dowdy dames, ashamed of their underground dens, the drinking, dancing and degeneracy, their gangrenous feet.

Every voice, every car splashing through a puddle, every cat and car-door slamming, every noise startled me. Every shadow was a gunman. I found a rhythm and made it from Stephen's Green through O'Connell Street to Parnell Square without incident in less than fifteen minutes. That coincidentally was the route of a student march I attended a while ago, a pro-choice rally. We seized the streets and afterwards went on the piss. It was great fun except Xavier cold-shouldered me again. He hasn't given me the time of day since New Year's Eve. And of course, my mother spotted me waving a banner in a clip on the nine o'clock news. So she won't be bothering me for a while.

From Parnell Square I increased the pace towards Phibsboro. I was on the home-stretch and I still felt strong. Faster and faster I ran, the fear draining from my pores. My lungs put my heart and brain and other organs to shame. Tingling, expectant, I emerged from the claustrophobic chrysalis in which I'd been contained and soared like a butterfly. I was suddenly the sexiest woman alive. The damp air caressed my face and neck, my lathered clothes massaged the rest of my body. Empowered and free, I felt I could do anything. I could hold my own in any company, charm the trousers off any man. I mentally wrote all the essays I had to hand in this term. I wrote a thesis too and a novel. Why not?

On and on, I ran, up Dorset Street, my path now illuminated by hundreds of tiny bulbs and flashes, a constellation of glow worms, my progress cheered by hundreds and hundreds of well-wishers. Running now in a flat-footed style to keep my feet in the slithery conditions, arms pumping, elbows back. Now, tiring, leaden, digging deep, I hear the voices of the crowd urge me on, 'Go on Fran, go on!' Each exhalation a spirit, another demon exorcised. Barefoot, practically naked, in a singlet and shorts, Charlie Haughey waiting on the finishing line, I raised my arms and breasted the tape. I was home.

I broke into tears.

7

Things went from bad to worse towards the end of May. For a start, I always hated the summer. I was a prime candidate, year in year out, for hayfever and summer colds. There were two things I was allergic to and they were a) pollen and b) the sun. To make matters worse, I developed a big boil under my nose which caused me great pain and adversely affected my breathing. It also made me extremely self-conscious in public, extremely. I tried everything to draw out the pus but I'm afraid all my efforts were in vain. I squeezed it, lanced it with a hot needle, applied poultices of all descriptions and degrees of silliness – facecloths, cotton wool, brown bread, white bread and even slugs but to no fucking avail whatsoever.

Francesca was avoiding me like the plague and I'd say it had a lot to do with the hideous deformity that was blocking my nasal cavities. She didn't want to be seen with a fella like me. I didn't need to attach electrodes to the sides of her head to figure that out. No. No matter how much you love someone, you can't stand the sight of a big boil on their face. Oh she had excuses all right. Francesca was a great woman for excuses. She was 'in a tizzy' about her exams and had to study around the clock. She had to go home at the weekends to visit her ailing mother. That was fair enough. I could accept that, only she managed to make time for Gráinne and prepare for the trip to America. One day, I was going to get a sandwich on my lunchbreak when I saw her looking at sleeping bags in the window of the Great Outdoors. All she had to do was ask for the lend of mine. But no, she had to get her own. And a money-belt and a new pair of jeans and a haircut. I followed them around for about an hour until she went into the hairdressers, probably for a bob. Personally, I thought her hair was fine the way it was. And I would go as far as to say that it was disloyal of her to change her hairstyle on the eve of her departure. It was certainly not me she was trying to impress. I could never understand why women doll themselves up before they go out when their boyfriends aren't with them. That's not right, in my opinion. At one point, Gráinne almost caught me spying on them. They had stopped to join a huge crowd who were watching lads break-dancing beside a ghettoblaster on the street. There were about five or six young fellas in matching tracksuits, doing robotics and rolling around on their arses, a bunch of fuckin' knackers if you ask me. I dodged into the entrance of Switzer's department store as Gráinne turned around. Not that I felt bad about following them. A man has a right to know what his girlfriend is up to. Thanks to Francesca I was late for work and had to face Mr Dunn's music which by the way was not a very pleasant sound.

Straight after her exams, she was gone. She couldn't wait to get away. We had a blazing row the night before she went and in the middle of it all, she broke off our relationship permanently for the fourth or fifth time that year. In the heat of the moment, she told me that she never liked me from day one, that she wished she had never set eyes on me and swore that she'd never see me again. And then she ordered me out of the flat before I could put forward the case for the defence. I know she was probably very emotional but that's no excuse.

I was annoyed with her so I left, cursing the ground she walked on.

And off she went to the States and there was nothing I could do about that. Fuck Christopher Columbus anyway for discovering the shithole. Unlike the *Nina, Pinta* and *Santa Maria,* I was rightly sunk now. Absence makes the heart grow fonder, they say, so who knows, I thought, no sooner would she get on the plane than she'd be regretting the tiff and writing a kiss-and-make-up love-letter. I vowed that we'd start off on the right foot when she returned in the autumn.

Balls was acting the bollocks too. He was far too busy these days to talk to the likes of me even though on paper we lived in the same flat. I was only a security guard in a shop. What good was I to him? He was hanging around with a fella called Mick King and a crowd of gobshites above in the college, and stayed over on the northside most nights smoking dope and taking advantage of loose women. I never liked that prick, Mick King. About a month ago he was down in Castlecock with Balls and a few of his foot-soldiers. Shovels took an instant dislike to him on account of his pony-tail and headbutted him on the nose. I can't say I was sorry. Anyway I only ever had Balls to myself these days on the bus home when his 'wacky' friends weren't in tow but he too's packed his bags and fucked off for the summer. A crowd of them went to London to work in offices or on building sites depending on the number of hobnails in their boots.

I couldn't prevent them from going, Francesca and Balls. I didn't have the authority to seal off the airports and seaports. Believe it or not, I was very sorry to see them go, make no mistake about that. To be honest I felt a bit left behind. I saw a child a few days ago up in Stephen's Green with a couple of balloons in his hand. He let them out of his grasp for just a second to suck on an ice-lolly and they floated above the trees, big smiles on their orange and green and blue faces as they soared away. And he started crying and I thought to myself I know exactly how you feel, *a mhic.*

Joe secured a summer job too delivering frozen food so he was on the road a lot of the time and when he was at home he was invariably wrapped up in the arms of his besotted girlfriend, Jennifer.

Everybody I knew was moving on while I stood still. I was running just as fast as they were but unfortunately I was running in a swamp. Every night I dreamt that I had the ball in my hands and was heading full steam towards the goals, but the more I exerted myself, the further away the goalposts receded. And even if the net was right in front of me, there was nothing I could do because my legs had turned to jelly. Holding on to your friends or just maintaining a grip on things generally was like keeping mice at a crossroads. Mind you, I could never understand that expression, why the fuck would anybody want to keep mice at a crossroads? That's the last place I'd keep them. A cul-de-sac would be more suitable or better still a box.

Meanwhile, I was stuck in the shop, literally stuck. My shirt was glued to my back with sweat and I could hardly move in the stifling heat. Thanks to a new triple-pack of tight-fitting underpants I developed a minor rash on my groins. To top it all, I was sneezing bloody pus. I couldn't have been more uncomfortable if I wiped my arse with sandpaper.

The sun was dazzling and very hot. Objects lost colour and definition. For a while, I thought, I was going blind. Having said that, there was no way that I was going to wear sunglasses. I wouldn't be seen dead wearing shades and end up looking like a ponce. So I settled for a permanent squint.

The summer as per usual sapped me of energy and me on my feet from nine to five. I was withdrawing into myself more and more by the hour, unable to concentrate on the questions the American tourists would ask me.

'Excuse me sir, where's the Book of Kells? Where's Trinity College? Are we anywhere near Sligo? Are you Irish? What's a bodhran? Do you have appliances in Ireland? Thanks for your help, if you're ever in Massachussetts, look me up, here's my card.' They'd buy Waterford Glass and big ugly chunks of pseudo-Celtic jewellery and have it posted to them later on in order to avoid paying the VAT. One of my jobs was to make up their parcels and send them off. That meant spending hours in the post room out the back packing at my own pace. It also meant making the occasional foray into the stock room.

It was so easy, it hardly seemed like stealing at first. I didn't have to put on a stocking mask and shoot somebody in the leg with a sawn-off shotgun. No, that wasn't my style. Most of the smaller items were contained in unlocked drawers and trays and supposedly watched over by Dunn's daughter, Niamh, but she was on the phone all the time to her friends and didn't know what was going on right under her nose. So I whipped wedding rings, engagement rings, earrings, necklaces and charm bracelets, one or two wee pieces a week. I wouldn't even say that I was doing it for the money although my wages were a disgrace. In fact when I first entered the world of petty crime, I didn't have a clue what to do with my plunder. I was hardly going to wear it. Like I said earlier, I didn't want to look like some sort of ponce like that fella Mick King, with all his earrings. And then I met Miguel Donnelly below in the Lock Inn one night and remembered that he'd been in jail for theft. I had a list of every criminal in the town at home. I kept my own records, culled from the local paper and from hearsay, in a shoebox under the bed. We got talking over a few pints and he agreed to look after the merchandise on my behalf in return for a percentage of the profits. I wouldn't even say I stole to get one over on Mr Dunn even though he was a bastard and it was the least he deserved. No, the truth is I don't know why I stole but if you were to ask a psychologist it probably had something to do with boredom and deficiencies in other departments of my life. 'Patrick Scully just wants to live out some sort of gangster fantasy.' You tell me. All I know for sure is that I liked the weight of a gold bangle in my hand and the feel of a fine chain running through my fingers like sand. The biggest thrill wasn't actually pocketing the valuables. Like I said, it was easy. Too easy. As long as Dunn wasn't on the premises, you couldn't be caught even if you wanted to be. I probably wouldn't have done it otherwise. No, the thrill for me was moseying around the shop with the illegitimate hardware on my person, or walking down the street after work with a slight bulge in my trouser pockets containing my secret ill-gotten gains. I might as well have been transporting classified microfiche in the heel of my shoe, on the run from a man in a bowler hat with a poison-tipped umbrella. I was on a mission beyond the ken of the last-minute shoppers and struggling mortals I met on my way.

I couldn't stand the staff. The sales assistants treated me like a second-class citizen and as far as Mr Dunn himself was concerned I was his personal gopher. He was always sending me out on messages, 'The kettle's banjaxed, leave it in to be fixed; there's a power cut, we'll need paraffin for this lamp; Scully would you ever get me an ice cream; I want a set of golf balls.' I brought him back the wrong golf balls once upon a time and he flipped the lid, dressed me down in front of everybody including customers so he did and sent me back to the sports shop. If there is one thing I always hated it was returning goods to a shop. That was by the way one of my mother's favourite pastimes and one of her principal faults. She was never satisfied with anything, the pliability of vegetables, the sell-by dates of sausages, the settling of contents during transport, the dents in a tin of beans, and the price of, well you name it. By the time she was finished inspecting the goods they were damaged irreparably but I still had to put up with the embarrassment of leaving them back. And when Dunn was out on the golf course, some of the girls would take advantage of me too. One girl in particular, Siobhan who had a huge pair of tits that she tried to hide under a floppy jumper, would send me out for buns. I got on all right with one of the other security guards, a fella called Kevin Egan, but he had a moustache and almost certainly a screw loose. He was a corporal in the FCA (the reserve army) and you couldn't have a single chat with him without the subject of guns and ammunition and military drills coming into the equation. A man obsessed, I'll tell you, I wouldn't like to be one of his recruits. I'd say he had posters of Adolf Hitler on his bedroom wall. He used to march around the shop and even salute at Mr Dunn. 'Yes sir, Mr Dunn, no problem.' And he loved trouble, man o man, you could always rely on him to back you up in an altercation with an obstreperous shop-lifter. And you could have a bit of crack over a sandwich at lunchtime.

Every day that summer was the same. Once or twice I woke up to find a postcard from Francesca in Chicago to break the monotony, but otherwise it was the same old routine. I'd walk into town first thing in the morning, try to look busy for a few hours, while the boss irritated by the lack of business so early in the day, would begin criticising my appearance. He'd look me up and down and ask me why didn't I polish my shoes and brush my hair, and iron my shirt even though my deportment was in my opinion excellent. He'd physically feel my chin for stubble too which was tantamount to sexual harassment if you ask me. One day he attacked me for not wearing matching socks, I'm not joking, and forced me to buy a pair of heavy, knitted hiker's ones with shamrocks down the side. Like everything else in the shop they were at an exorbitant price and geared towards tourists from the frozen North of Canada. They came all the way up to my knee. My feet swelled and suffocated in the thick wool. I don't know why Dunn didn't just cut my legs off and roast them on a spit.

The afternoons dragged on forever. I'd wilt and stare into space like an automaton, my mind blank, totally devoid of thoughts.

One Tuesday, late in the day when the whole city seemed to have slowed down to a near standstill, thanks to the oppressive weather, I was startled out of my reverie by a familiar face from Castlecock. It was Budley Moran, the Budley. God knows what he was doing in the shop, probably buying a retirement present for his grandad, a crystal clock or something like that of no use whatsoever to a person set in his ways. I pretended I didn't see him and thought if I stood there like a mannequin he wouldn't notice me either or if he did he wouldn't be sure it was me. I often find that when you meet somebody unexpectedly, outside of their normal situation, you can't be certain of their identity. If, for example, the Budley saw me hitching to Dundalk, or coming out of Fraser's with a cone, he'd say to himself, 'That's definitely Scully.' But if he saw me judging a fuckin' beauty contest in Disneyland or smiling on television outside The Four Courts, he'd say, 'Jaysus there's a fella looks awful like Scully but it couldn't be him, sure what would he be doing there.' It's the same thing, if you're used to seeing somebody naked you wouldn't recognise them in their clothes and vice versa, I'd say. Anyway after looking at me from every conceivable angle he satisfied himself that it was indeed me and came over. I immediately reddened. The last person I wanted to see was somebody from Castlecock.

'It is you, Scully, I'd know the head of you anywhere. What are you doing here? I thought you were in charge of the casino on the Holyhead ferry.'

'I got seasick,' I said quick as a flash. I didn't even remember telling the Budley that particular yarn.

'Aye I'd say you did all right. What are you doing now . . . security?' There was nothing he'd love more than to be able to go home and tell everybody about Scully's dead-end job. Budley was one of the town's equivalent of a KGB man. There were people like him stationed everywhere, their job to report back to headquarters on the behaviour of anybody who dared to leave the town.

'I've my own company,' I said, 'my clients consult me on various security matters. What are you up to yourself, Budley?'

'Me? I'm selling these prints of well-known Dublin land-marks,' he answered, holding up a portfolio.

'Well you'll have no joy here,' I informed him. 'The Dunns only deal in quality goods.' I got him there but it was a close shave.

Before I knew it, I was hanging around with Geoghegan. I didn't really have much choice. Going home to an empty flat and slouching in front of the television isn't exactly my idea of fun. I mean, we could only get RTE, and not without interference. I rest my case. Anyway I'd meet him after work three or four nights a week in the Palace Bar. We'd start off with a few pints of Smithwicks, and quickly move on to the shorts, skulling double vodkas to beat the band. We made an unlikely pair, him in his biker gear and me in my shirt and tie; him with his twisted mind and me with my melancholy. Within a couple of hours, however, we had plenty in common. We'd be both footless for example swapping tall tales and giving guff to drinkers at nearby tables and unless some of his old cronies joined us we'd be the best of buddies by closing time. Sometimes if the mood took us we'd end up in Buffalo Bill's at a hoedown, as it was known, more interested in drink than women, who seemed to be beyond reach within a gauze of smoke. To be honest I ached for female company but Geoghegan's fierce beardy countenance frightened them off.

Jaysus, it was so hot in there you'd nearly sweat yourself sober. So we had to drink at twice the rate, trebles of Smirnoff with ice to slake the thirst, followed by lethal cocktails invented by Gaygo to blot out the present. I suppose we got involved in the odd scrap here and there and possibly broke the occasional shop window. I have a hazy recollection not to mention scars on my hand that would indicate confrontations of some sort.

There were times when we'd find ourselves at a party in a sordid flat in the middle of the week, not knowing whose party it was or how we got there. The person who was throwing the party would have long ago forgotten why they were having one. We'd be the last to leave, Geoghegan's friends wrecking the place on the way out after shitting on the floor and covering up the mess with the couch. Man o man, they were some savages. They'd piss anywhere, on the street, through letter-boxes, into people's cups and almost choke laughing. I couldn't even piss in front of my brother, Joe.

One night Geoghegan led me to a park in Fairview. Again the details are a bit of blur but I vaguely remember an altercation on the grass. It wasn't until two days later when Geoghegan proudly presented me with a cutting from the *Evening Press* that I began to realise just how serious it was. Apparently 'the assailant or assailants' kicked the shit out of a queer and left him on a life-support machine. Personally, I find it hard to believe that I was involved and am convinced that it was just Geoghegan's idea of a sick joke. Bragging about an incident like that. If we were the culprits and I

doubt it, I must have blanked it out of my mind completely
and that's not an easy thing to do no matter how drunk
you are. Mind you, I do have disturbing dreams in which
Geoghegan rugby tackles a man to the ground in a park
at night and I know for a fact that he used to play rugby.
But still there's no way. Not that I give a shit. Don't get me
wrong. I'm not saying the man was asking for it but he was
a fuckin' queer.

I still went home now and again, on Friday nights, but to
be honest I couldn't tell you if things were any better there.
Half-cut, I was in no condition to pass judgement and the
weekends flew by like telegraph poles from the carriage of
a train. I'd substitute Shovels for Geoghegan and we'd get
drunk in the Mirage. I suppose we had a bit of crack at night
but during the day I just lay in bed, doing nothing. All day,
Saturday and Sunday. My poor mother was overwrought.

'Is Francesca having an abortion? Is she, Patrick? You can
tell me I'm your mother?'

'No!'

'Is she pregnant? I won't disown you, love, just tell me
the truth!'

'She's not pregnant.'

'Are you on glue?'

'No!'

No matter how miserable I felt, I wouldn't touch glue.
That was for losers. Joe told me that Mammy hid the jar
of Evo-Stik under her bed just in case.

I'd get up at about twenty to five on Saturday for the
football results on the teleprinter, have a bite to eat and go
out. On Sunday, Mammy would call me at twelve o'clock,
knowing full well that I had no intention of getting up
for mass.

'Time for mass, Patrick.'

Most of the people I knew in Castlecock had jobs for the
summer, or permanent jobs, were preparing for college or

pushing prams. They had passed Go. Personally, I felt that people were putting on their indicators and overtaking me. I was driving a vintage car in the Belgian Grand Prix. The ship was sailing off without me.

8

In the middle of August, I decided to go to London. I was getting sick of Geoghegan and his violent tendencies. He was always on at me to go out queer-bashing again and when I'd refuse he'd start taunting me and calling me a cowardly cream puff. He was a fuckin' psycho, that fella, so he was. Sometimes if he was bored, he'd get me in a headlock and wouldn't let me go for ages. And one time he gave me a Chinese burn for absolutely no reason.

I was sick too of slaving away in the shop, day in day out. Anyway, the plan was quite straightforward. I saved up as much money as I possibly could. That meant cutting back on the drink for a few weeks and eating a bit less as well as working overtime and stealing a bit more. On the appointed day, I packed my rucksack and got the nightboat from Dun Laoghaire to Holyhead. I didn't tell anybody that I was going. Not a soul. I had asked Mr Dunn for a week's holiday, all right, but I didn't tell him where I was going. And I didn't tell him that I had no intention of coming back. I didn't even warn any of the lads that I was coming. I thought I'd surprise them, for the crack.

There's a lot to be said for disappearing without trace. For the best part of twenty-four hours, on boat and coach, I was missing, lost to the world, although I doubt if anybody was looking for me. I revelled in my anonymity and let my hair down by a) taking off my tie and b) not shaving at all during the journey. For all anybody knew I could have been a fugitive or an amnesiac, trying to piece my fractured life back together again. Jaysus, letting the old hair down felt good, I must say. I should do it more often, I thought.

The ferry was packed with holidaymakers and hooligans and youth groups in matching T-shirts. They were all running around causing a big hullaballoo, playing Space Invaders and shopping in a duty-free frenzy. I had a plate of chips in the restaurant where, in a cordoned off section, a gang of brooding and heavily-tattooed lorry drivers were trying to play cards. They were very unhappy with the noise of the aimless merrymakers and with their own mounting losses.

And then there were the casual migrant labourers, strung out along the bar, hardened by disappointment. These were serious men, their faces, varnished by too much whiskey, bent down to meet the rollies, cupped in their hands. Unlike myself they were *permanently* lost, in some dark and derelict place. Whereas I was about to climb out of the mine shaft and find myself in a green and pleasant field with a pair of brand-new binoculars.

Anyway, I sat up at the bar and ordered a drink. The barman refused to serve me, arguing that I had to be over twenty-one. And the cunt didn't look a day over sixteen himself. I was about to turn away, after all I had a bottle of cut-price Jameson in my rucksack, when one of those men I was talking about, an oul' lad called Jamesy, shouted for the drink on my behalf. He was wearing a green anorak, dusted with dandruff, and had a mop of greasy grey hair brushed back in the style of a lawyer's wig. We shook hands and I pulled in beside him.

We nattered away for a couple of hours, man to man. Here I was on a ship for the first time, making my own way in the world, answerable to nobody. There was no stopping me now. Jamesy had just been back to Leitrim for his sister's funeral, a woman he hadn't seen for more than thirty years. They were all gone now, he said, and good riddance. And then he laughed loudly, clinked my glass with his, and swallowed a double. They'd done him out of his rightful inheritance, the bastards, and treated him like a leper. And what good did it do them, dead in the grave with only the worms and a nagging conscience for company. He admitted to me that he had a drink problem but that was no excuse in my opinion for their abonimal-abom-abominable neglect of my friend (belch) Jamesy. We got very drunk and he offered me some great advice. Keep your head down and your eyes open and never trust a soul. We became lifelong friends and swore that we'd keep in touch although we didn't exchange addresses or telephone numbers. I said goodnight and went out on deck to suck in huge gulps of sea-air and gratefully accept the sea's gift of spray on my face. It was well after midnight. I could have jumped overboard there and then and nobody would be any the wiser. You wouldn't hear the splash above the disco music and the drone of the engines. Even if you were standing right beside me, you wouldn't hear as much as a plop. Can you believe that? A life, a personality could disappear with only an indistinguishable gloop. Gloop and gone. Never to be found again. Shivering with the cold and buffeted by a maelstrom of emotions, I climbed into a lifeboat which was hanging over the side of the ship on a pair of metal arms, like a cradle. I skulled the whiskey and chucked the empty bottle into the Irish Sea. I felt safe and warm in there under the tarpaulin and fell asleep and dreamt I'd been awakened at the turn of the century approaching a South Sea island by the screeching of an extinct bird. Oul' Jamesy was in the dream too, an old sea-dog and my right-hand man and faithful ally ever since the time I saved him from the savages. I remained there, the smell of kerosene fuelling my fantasy until the ferry docked at Holyhead.

Man o man, that ten-hour bus journey to London was an ordeal. If London was hell, and I'd heard tell that it was, then this ride was pure purgatory. An interminable penance especially designed to test the mettle of poor fucked-up Paddies going to work or worse. Jamesy was on the bus, too, down the back, snoring. I tried to sleep but couldn't on account of the cold that had been injected into my bones on the platform at Holyhead. Why are railway stations the coldest places on the planet? Can you tell me that? It could be the hottest day of the year, the temperature in fact could be the highest in living memory, it could be too hot for wasps, you could be wearing a duffle coat and a balaclava and Damart mail-order thermal underwear but you'd still be frozen solid if you had the misfortune to be stuck waiting for a train at somewhere like Limerick Junction. I'd safely say that you'd catch a cold at Bombay Railway Station. The fact that the door of the coach was jammed open didn't help but somehow or other I eventually managed to sleep. There was one break of fifteen minutes but I stayed on board because I had just contorted my body into a position which took up at the most a square inch of space, the only position on the bus where the draught couldn't get at me. The driver told us in no uncertain terms that it was our own lookout if we were left behind. He didn't care and, after the respite as if to underline his point, he hopped into his seat, revved her up to the last and jerked off at speed. I looked around to see if Jamesy had made it back on time. Well as it happens he hadn't or else he was under the seat but either way I wasn't going to get involved. I didn't want to cause a fuss. I didn't want to rock the boat. And anyway I had more pressing matters to consider. No sooner had the bus pulled off than I realised that I was bursting for a piss. I couldn't ask the surly bastard to stop again because I knew he wouldn't and

I didn't want to draw attention to my plight. And of course there was no toilet on the coach. I held it in for as long as I could but with the sun high in the sky about eighty miles from London I had no choice but to let it go. The underpants absorbed the first few gushes but by the time I managed to stem the flow, the urine had soaked my good trousers and trickled down my leg. It was a warm and prickly sensation, embarrassing and uncomfortable but a great relief all the same. Nobody thank God noticed my predicament and my clothes had nearly dried out by the time we disembarked at Victoria Coach Station.

Exhausted I made my way by tube towards Gaffney's flat in North London, near Archway. His was the only address I had. The journey underground was a disaster. First of all, I forgot for a moment that I had the rucksack on my back and when I went to sit down, my arse missed the seat completely and I fell in a heap on the slatted floor of the carriage. I suppose it must have looked funny but having said that nobody on the crowded tube laughed. They didn't even as much as smile and certainly didn't offer a helping hand. I stood for the rest of the way, my face puce, losing my balance from time to time, stray straps on the bag slashing people on the face. And still nobody said anything to me, an example of typically English behaviour, I believe.

I didn't have an address for good old Balls but even if I had I wouldn't have gone there first, not until I'd found out just who the hell he was living with and what drugs he was on. And anyway he'd be mad jealous when he found out that I called on Gaffney before him.

I found the street, Fairfield Road, and immediately stumbled and kicked the corner of an uneven flagstone. I almost broke my toe. The sole of my shoe came away from the upper. That accident left me flapping along the footpath, my foot like a sturgeon feeding, or Pac-man. That was all I needed. Can you believe that? Uneven flagstones on the footpath in a so-called civilised city? I personally find that hard to understand. Not only were they bumpy and misshapen but they were different shapes and sizes and colours too. Different materials, different qualities. Some were replaced with concrete tiles, smooth or rutted, lumps of tar, strips of pitch, even cobblestones. Now either the cobbles were left there for old times' sake or the last time the gas company was repairing a pipe they couldn't find a matching slab and threw down a few cobbles. That's just careless, in my opinion. Shoddy. I didn't know they still made cobblestones. It's lazy, disorganised. A fuckin' disgrace. I slowed down to a standstill to let a lad pass me, I don't like people walking behind me. That's one thing I can't stand.

A black girl answered the door, Jaysus, the rumours were true, he had a black girlfriend. Don't get me wrong, I have no problem with that only she was very unfriendly towards me and didn't want to let me in. I explained to her who I was and after a while she relented and I gained admittance. Ah for fuck sake, I couldn't believe my eyes, there were two black babies playing on the carpet inside. Gaffney kept that quiet, the sly bastard. Wait 'til they hear about this in Castlecock, I thought. I was in such a state of shock, I didn't know what to say.

We sat there in silence for about two hours, the children staring at me as if I were from another planet. The girl, Vanessa was her name, didn't so much as offer me a cup of tea. I only found out her name by looking at the front of a brown envelope. Vanessa Simpson, same initials as our Valerie. I tried to start up a conversation.

'Have you been in the country long?'

'What?' she snapped.

I repeated the question.

'All my life!' A dirty look with the whites of her eyes and straight back to her book. I was hoping that Fergus would come in soon and put her straight. After a while I cleared my throat and tried again.

'Ehh where are you from, originally?'

'Are you taking the piss?'

'No!'

She just shook her head, put down the book and took the kids into the bathroom to give them a bath I suppose or potty training or something. Talk about rude. I don't know what Fergus saw in her at all. Knowing him he was just trying to be different.

Fergus arrived home at about six o'clock and when he saw me he was stunned.

'Scully, you can't stay here.'

I swear to God, they were his first words. No big handshake. No words of welcome like, 'Jaysus, Scully, long time no see,' or 'That was some crack we had the last time I stayed with youse in Dublin.'

No, it was, 'I'm sorry Scully. There's four of us in the one bedroom. I can't put you up.'

'No problem at all Fergus. No problem. I understand the position. I'll stay with Balls.'

It turned out by coincidence that Fergus was meeting Balls in a pub near Piccadilly Circus that very evening.

'Jaysus Scully look at the state of you. You can't go anywhere looking like that.' And he threw the towel that he'd been using to dry his hair at me. I had a cold shower, thanks very much Fergus for using all the hot water, and a shave and I sprayed some woman's deodorant all over my body to compensate for the smell of my clothes. And I dried myself with the wet towel.

'Have you got any glue?'

'Will Sellotape do?

'It'll have to, I suppose.' And I taped up my shoe.

In fairness to Fergus, he apologised to me on the way in for his initial lack of hospitality. He was knackered after a hard day working as a carpenter on a development called Canary Wharf and wasn't thinking straight, he explained. Working six days a week, ten hours a day, and shacking up with a black bird and her two children certainly took its toll on poor Fergus. He was a changed man. I tried to get the crack going a few times but with very little feedback. For as long as I'd known him, he looked older than the rest of us, but now with his receding hairline, he might as well have belonged to a different generation. By the time we reached Piccadilly Circus, I couldn't think of a way to fill the pothole that was our embarrassed silence. And let me tell you it was with some trepidation that I entered the pub.

Shortly after we sat down, Balls and wouldn't you know it Mick King arrived with a party in tow made up of people I had never seen before – men and women, Irish, English and even Australian, work colleagues, flatmates and a crowd who shared a squat in Elephant and Castle. I hardly recognised Balls. He'd had his hair cut and dyed blond, no, practically white. I don't know what the fuck he was playing at. More folk followed in dribs and drabs as the evening took a hold of itself and before long our corner of the pub was raucous. But I stuck out like a sore thumb, with my rucksack. I felt like a stranger among friends. I'd say the groups of French students with braces on their teeth, sitting around the fountain outside, were better off than me. Sipping cans of Coke and gabbling away in French, to beat the band, they were less ill-at-ease amidst the noise and the traffic with absolutely nothing to do only wait for their chaperones to emerge from 'browsing' in sex shops, looking for kinky presents to take home to the wife. Jaysus, I wouldn't have been able to put up with that outdoor cacophony. As it was, I could barely cope with the hysterical laughter indoors and the music, mainly the J. Geils Band, thumping from the jukebox.

'Scully it's your round.'

It was practically the first thing Balls said to me all evening and he didn't say it, he shouted it across the table. I gave him the evil eye, a look which he duly ignored. Admittedly it *was* my round but I had decided to keep my hand in my pocket seeing as how I wasn't earning as much as them, and had to pay a fortune to get here.

'Scully's round! Scully's round!' he started chanting, and clapping his hands, exhorting the rest of the congregation to join in. They thought it was great fun.

There was nothing I could do except give in to their demands, thinking I'd get away with buying maybe three or four drinks in total. But no, everybody at the table ordered one. I swear to God, I had to get seventeen drinks. That is unprecedented in the history of mankind. Even people who still had a full one in front of them. I'm not making this up. Nobody and I mean nobody offered to share the expense. There was still at least a half an hour to go before closing time and plenty of other people hadn't got a round in. Some of them in fact had just joined us. It was totally unfair of Balls to pick on me like that. I was bulling. Nobody even helped me to cable-car the drink down to the table. Can you believe that?

I thought then that some of the beneficiaries of my generosity might have made more of an effort to include me in the conversation but no, it was every man for himself around here. As usual, people were only interested in gravitating towards the centre of the action and that of course was Balls O'Reilly. And I was tongue-tied. My tongue was trussed up like a bale of hay. When we were finally kicked out of the bar after trading racist insults with a Maori barman, we made our way via Leicester Square to a pizza restaurant.

Two things happened on the way. First of all, while waiting on a crowded footpath for the lights to change, the wing-mirror of a speeding black taxi struck me on the back of the hand. I yelped in pain, fearing the limb was broken for sure. Those who witnessed the accident laughed, not I'm glad to say at my misfortune but because they thought I was only messing. Maybe if I'd dived under a bus they might have warmed to me even more.

Secondly, we stumbled into a full-scale riot involving two Rastafarians and about a hundred policemen. The bobbies were charging from all directions crashing through chairs that were outside restaurants and pushing bewildered tourists aside. They all converged on a sidestreet where officers had one man pinned to the ground and another up against the wall. We followed the action. Balls annoyed a policeman by asking him in a French accent for directions to Buckingham Palace. The policeman through gritted teeth told Balls in no uncertain terms to fuck off or he'd arrest him.

Needless to say, I didn't enjoy the meal. For a start, Gaffney and a few of the more sensible ones had gone home. And when the main courses arrived, everybody who was left got theirs except me. The waiter, a wee bald man with a moustache, forgot about me completely. And when I eventually got his attention, he threw his arms into the air as if it were my fault.

At a prearranged signal from Balls, the whole party scarpered out of the door without paying. When I say signal I mean that Balls stood up suddenly and said 'Let's go!' They did a runner, the bastards, leaving me and another fella who wasn't in on the scam behind. I made the mistake of taking one last bite from my pizza margherita, the cheapest thing on the menu, which I'd covered in parmesan cheese and chilli flakes, before I realised what was going on and made haste for the exit. But the proprietor had managed to get there before me, lock the door and bar my escape. To be honest, I thought that the lads were only messing and would show their faces any minute, but no.

We were quickly surrounded by angry waiters who didn't

get the joke. I'll tell you one thing, there was no way after what happened in the pub earlier on that I was going to pay for anybody else's pizza. So I paid for exactly what I had, down to the last penny and explained to the other fella who by the way worked with Balls in an insurance company, I think it was, that I had absolutely no money left. So he had no choice but to pay the balance and try and reclaim it from the boys when we caught up with them. I wouldn't say he had much luck because, as we found out later, this was what they got up to every weekend. The rules of the game were clear, anybody who was left behind, tough luck.

We found the lads in a queue for a place called the Hippodrome, a huge nightclub just off Leicester Square. We nearly got in another scrape for bunking the queue but there were still about twelve of us at this stage so it never came to blows. About an hour later we got inside. It was fuckin' huge and I spent most of the night wandering around, up and down the different levels looking for a familiar face, getting more and more drunk all the time. At one point, I sat down beside a few girls in skin-tight jeans and white shoes to try my case. One of them, who claimed to be of Irish extraction, offered me a cigarette which I accepted. Don't get me wrong, I didn't smoke it. No, I ate it. They didn't see the funny side of me munching a fag at all. And they, absolutely appalled when I swallowed the tobacco, almost immediately moved off. A pair of oul' dryshites. Mind you, the taste was disgusting and I puked about ten times on the way to the jacks before I was collared by the bouncers and thrown out on to the street. On production of my ticket stub, they got my rucksack from the cloakroom and threw it on top of me.

I suppose I could have waited outside the entrance for Balls and the rest of them, that's of course if they hadn't already left, but I didn't bother. I didn't need them. I could look after myself. Siamese twins are the only people who aren't truly alone in this world. But the rest of us surrounded and separated from others by skin must fend for ourselves.

I didn't know London at all but that didn't seem to matter. Aimlessly, I followed the flow and ended up in Trafalgar Square at about three o'clock in the morning. The place was thronged with the haunted and the homeless, and the overspill from the tourist hostels. There were hot-dog sellers with no expressions whatsoever clogging up the footpath and big fat cockney pigeons, very tough-looking birds. I half-expected to see them wearing braces and Doctor Martens and going 'oi' instead of 'coo'. There were the jilted and the joined at the hip, the whole of London trying to get back to their graves in the suburbs on the nightbus before first light. Although I'd no idea where Balls lived except that it was somewhere in South London, I checked the noticeboards at each of the bus stops as if I'd find a clue. Streatham, Crystal Palace, Battersea, Vauxhall, Ball's House. No luck. I wasn't going to go back to Gaffney's place not after my previous reception there so I wandered around the centre of London for the night.

First thing in the morning, I rang Gaffney's house to ask him for Balls's address. Vanessa answered and didn't sound pleased. Fergus was annoyed too but gave me the details I required and hung up. Within a few hours I found the house in Clapham that I'd been looking for. The door was opened by a fella with a large bottle of Guinness in his hand who was definitely still drinking since the night before. He made no sense whatsoever. The rest of them, Balls included were dredging themselves up from the floor or wherever they had fallen in the early hours. I dropped my rucksack, and took a seat at the kitchen table, thinking that this was where I'd probably be living for the rest of the summer if not longer. I was determined to start the day on a positive note so I made tea for everybody. I estimated that there were about six or seven lads in the house, no girls. Nobody shifted last night obviously, a fact which I have to say made me feel an awful lot better.

A problem arose. There were only two cups in the kitchen, both of them chipped and stained beyond belief. If tea could do that to a cup, can you just imagine what it does to your insides? I poured tea into every available vessel, grimy glasses, a jug, a jam-jar and a small saucepan for Balls. I thought he'd appreciate that. He did too and we had a good chat in the kitchen while the others washed themselves and figured out who and where they were. I was telling him all about Geoghegan and his deranged behaviour, leaving out a certain incident in a certain park, and how I told Mr Dunn to fuck off, which of course I hadn't done but he wasn't to know that.

Balls was laughing away and genuinely engrossed in my tales until we were interrupted by Mick King holding a joint. Well that ruined everything. After a while they were all stoned except me. Balls was trying to get me hooked but I said, no way. However, despite a fierce headache and a degree of heartburn, I had a few cans of beer and half a bottle of Cinzano Bianco – don't ask me how that vile bile ended up in the fridge but it did. Then we left and got the tube to Notting Hill. Apparently there was a big carnival there, the Notting Hill Carnival as it is known.

On the tube, we sang rebel songs in harmony at the top of our voices and my heart nearly burst with pride. As the other passengers averted their eyes in horror, we held each other tightly and emptied our lungs of passion. Most of us started off on the Northern Line, singing for the crack and not wishing to offend anybody but by the time we hit Bayswater on the Central Line, we were bawling defiance and recalling centuries of pain and oppression. Jaysus, we worked ourselves into a voodoo-like frenzy, for once free from fear. We weren't afraid of making a fool of ourselves, or afraid of being caught or afraid of provoking a reaction on the part of the more assertive passengers. Only one person had the nerve to reproach us, she told us that we were a disgrace to our country, but that just made us sing all the louder. We got off the tube tingling, feeling that there was nothing we couldn't do. I was a man transformed, mightily relieved to have shared such an experience with the lads. But the feeling didn't last long.

Once overground, our spirits were drenched and dazzled by the rain and sunlight respectively. Our brief uprising was squashed by a greater force. Our songs, still reverberating around my head, were drowned out by the deafening steel bands on parade. We were outnumbered by about a million to one. I had never seen so many black faces. I thought a carnival meant bullies in bumping cars, candy floss and a rifle range but this was different. And we soon discovered that there was nothing to worry about. And then, the music sneaked up behind us, knocked us out and started to manipulate us as if we were dummies.

That night we ended up at a party back in Clapham, I punched Balls, I don't remember why and ate a tenspot of hash. At six o'clock the next morning I made my way in a daze to Liverpool Street Station to catch a train to King's Lynn. There was no way that I was going to spend any more time with those bastards and I'd heard that there was work to be had in the canning factories around that part of Norfolk.

9

To cut a long story short, I got a job on a production line canning peas. I wore earplugs to drown out the sound of the machines and the anti-Irish taunts. One fella who was only my age told me that he wanted to join the SBS who were even tougher than the SAS so that he could kill Irish people and get away with it. He was one of my best friends.

I slept on the floor of a disused barn in my overalls, got up and worked a twelve-hour shift, from six to six, six days a week, living on a type of seaweed called samphire which was plentiful in the nearby mudflats, reading the *Day of the Triffids* and being genuinely frightened. I had very little money left at this stage. At night I drank alone in the local freehouse, playing 'When Doves Cry' over and over again on the jukebox, and dreaming of Francesca. On my day off, I walked the three miles into town with a bag of laundry. After spin-drying the few items of underwear I had, I left the launderette only to walk straight into the middle of a gang of skinheads on the march. I was trapped among them as they snarled at pedestrians and broke shop windows. I kept my mouth shut, looking frantically for an outlet, me with my big bass drum encircled by a tight formation of vicious trumpeters. Luckily, while they were trying to think of something particularly nasty to do to me, the rain came in sheets. My old friend, the rain. In fact, I would safely say, it was the heaviest rainfall I'd ever seen. A bottomless reservoir had been upturned upon us and the skinheads dispersed for cover. I walked on head-down for a mile or so until I was weighed down with water and could go no further. I took refuge from the deluge in a church, a Catholic church, I'm glad to report. At once, I experienced a warming glow, my clothes miraculously dried and I shivered to a stop. I sat down on a pew at the back of what was a bare church in comparison with Irish ones.

Normally I wouldn't darken the door of a church and if I did, I'd be standing down the back, fidgeting, looking at women, messing with Balls, reading pamphlets or eating a choc-ice. But now for the first time I understood the whole point of a church. I couldn't have been happier, sitting there. I didn't want to leave. I bore no ill-will towards anybody. In fact I had nothing but love in my heart. The Virgin Mary and all the angels and saints were cooing all around me, pampering me as if I were a newborn baby. I was no longer cold, lonely or afraid. I was at peace, full of goodness, a mug of hot milk.

Hypnotised by the flickering candles, tranquilised by the organ music I imagined, I didn't notice the priest until he ordered me to leave. A very gruff man. 'What are you doing here? Did you get permission?' An Irish accent and all. 'Get out or I'll call the police. You're destroying the place.' I didn't mind. I was content and ready to go. Whatever happens, I'll always remember that hour or so I spent there, in the company of our Lord. As long as I live, nobody can take that away from me. I was suddenly reminded of another blissful time, when I was eleven and my appendix nearly burst. My father gathered me gently in his arms and drove me to the hospital in the early hours of the morning. As the anaesthetic wore off after the life-saving operation, I entered a state of profound euphoria, eternally grateful to my father, my family and the medical staff and the guy in the next bed who wasn't allowed to sit down.

On Thursday afternoon, I got paid and went for a drink with a thin bespectacled lad who wore a Chairman Mao style of hat, and was always raving on about Van Morrison. He was about twenty-five years of age I'd say and went out of his way to be nice to me, smiling pleasantly whenever he caught my eye. During the breaks, he bought me tea and listened, like a psychiatrist, to what I had to say. I poured my heart out to him in the factory canteen. I told him all about Francesca and Balls and my whole life story. It was he who hit the nail on the head and suggested that I give up the drink for a while. I'd never thought about that before. Drink of course was sending me astray in the head. At closing time, he ruined everything by asking me to go back to his flat with him. It was then I realised that he was probably a fuckin' queer all along. He even looked like that fella that was in the news, Dennis Nilsen. For all I know, he could have eaten me alive. Jaysus, I thought, you just can't trust anyone, especially anyone who's nice to you.

I decided to clear out of England as quickly as possible. I worked for one more day and hitched back to London on Saturday morning. It was the day of the FA Charity Shield match in Wembley between Manchester United and Liverpool. I got a lift with a Liverpool fan and his family who parked in a handicapped space right outside the twin towers although I could detect no sign of disability among them. That was as near as I ever got to the hallowed turf of Wembley Stadium.

Twenty-four hours later, I was back in Dublin, stewing in a gumbo of conflicting emotions.

Delighted on the one hand to be back. In fact, I'd say that the best thing about most trips abroad is coming home again. At the same time even though my journey didn't work out exactly as planned, I was glad that I had taken the plunge.

Aching with loneliness on the other hand. I was missing Francesca terribly. I'll tell you one thing for sure, she was going to see a new side of Patrick Scully on her return. I was going to meet her at the airport, smart and sober, more self-confident than ever before. I was going to show her a good time, I'd take her to the pictures twice a week and to restaurants too, and I'd more than likely ask her to marry me and settle down. What more could a girl want? I'd hear about the guards for certain within a couple of months, and you know I was beginning to get a good feeling about that too.

Yes indeed the summer was nearly over, autumn was coming, whistling down the street, and I'm an autumn person. I was born in the autumn and I'm going to die in the autumn. No more boils and runny noses for me. I was elated and I was back at work first thing Monday morning.

PART 3

Francesca's Diary

Saturday, 1 October 1983
I arrived at Dublin airport at seven in the morning my face reconfigured by jet lag and, I confess, too much recent pizza. I thought I was hallucinating with exhaustion when I saw Patrick in the arrivals hall, beaming and with a big bunch of flowers wilting in his hand. Patrick, fresh as a daisy, had been waiting for me since midnight, it seems, when the last bus to the airport dropped him off.

Gráinne's parents were there too to meet her and take her home to Killeeny. They offered me a lift which I declined for two reasons. Firstly, I wanted to go to the flat, and secondly I wasn't speaking to Gráinne. We fell out in Cape Cod. Sharing a bed and generally living in each other's hair for the summer didn't help. And considering I'd been dealing with loud, patronising people for months, I couldn't face a car journey with Gráinne's mum.

After much hugging and squealing and promising to keep in touch, the chatter subsided and we migrants went our separate ways, wiser women of the world now with our new ideas and articles of clothing. Patrick, his smile fixed and crazed, like a Mormon's, carried my bags to the bus.

2

I was actually in very high spirits the day it happened. '*Ar cipíní,*' as they say *as Gaeilge*. I had come to the conclusion that it was partly my fault that myself and Francesca hadn't been getting on so well of late. And I was going out of my way to make an effort. There was only one thing for it, I had decided, and that was marriage. And today was the day I was going to pop the question. So I sprung out of bed. It was impossible to know what sort of a day it was outside on account of the room being so dark, but I had a feeling in my bones that it was a lovely day. That was one thing about the flat, and indeed about the city in general. You know, a person can't really wake up properly unless and until the day itself touches you on the shoulder and says 'Excuse me, rise and shine'. Without sunlight and dew and, say, the crowing of a cock, your brain can't really and truly fire up in the morning. Similarly, but not the same, you can't really sleep that well in the metropolis. There's either alarms going off willy-nilly or police sirens wailing or people having rows out on the street or drunks roaring at the moon or people moving the furniture around upstairs, if you know what I mean. I read that there are some people who get very depressed during the winter months due to the lack of natural light and I'd well believe it too, so I would.

I blame my fucking bedroom for a lot of my problems.

You wouldn't even know what clothes to wear for God's sake, wondering, Is that my shirt or is it Balls's? or is it some fuckin' rag that's been there for the last hundred years? You wouldn't even know what day of the week it was without first of all seeing what the hell was going on outside, how much traffic was on the road, whether the bins were in or out and what type of expressions people were wearing. Some day, I swear to God, I'd love it if a demolition ball came crashing through this wall and let some fucking light into the room.

Anyway, I walked into the sitting room in my bare feet. I was right. It was a lovely bright sunny morning. And it was a Wednesday. The carpet had been well warmed by the dust-filled shafts of sunlight beaming in through the window. And the flat even smelled less damp than usual.

I had it all worked out to a tee. On Monday, I bought an engagement ring from the shop, admittedly with money I'd earned from my, shall we say, little nixer. I then asked Mr Dunn for Wednesday off. At first, he said 'no'. That was his automatic response to everything, although apart from my brief holiday during the summer I'd never asked him for a day off before. I explained to him, somewhat falsely, that I had to go to my auntie's funeral. He mulled that over for a while, eyebrows dancing away. He did most of his calculations and computations with his eyebrows. Finally he agreed on condition that I worked right through lunchtime every day the following week and for an extra couple of hours every evening and every Saturday for the next three weeks. Without taking into account my loss, I said 'Fair enough, boss,' delighted as I was to be able to proceed with my plan.

I would put on my best clothes, buy a bottle of Piat d'Or and be there waiting to surprise Francesca in her flat when she came home from the hospital. She'd fallen yesterday while running for the college and sprained her wrist. So today she was having it X-rayed and probably plastered. I wasn't going to beat around the bush with any smalltalk, 'How's your wrist? Will you be needing a dictaphone now?' No no, none of that nonsense. I was going to come straight out and ask her to be my wife. She'd break down in tears and say 'I thought you'd never ask,' and we'd crack open the wine. Of course there'd be no corkscrew in the flat and I'd have to push the cork down into the bottle with my thumb. We'd have a laugh and she'd ring her mother to tell her the good news while I went out for a Chinese takeaway. Then we'd go to bed and make love for the first time in our lives.

So after practising my lines and meaningful looks in the mirror, I went around to her flat at about one o'clock.

There was a large crowd of pot-bellied men in Ireland jerseys already milling around in the vicinity. Ireland were playing Holland in nearby Dalymount Park that evening in a vital European Championship qualifier. I would have loved to have gone to the game myself but had more important matters to consider.

I let myself in – I had my own key. Francesca gave me her key one night last week and asked me to be there to let the plumber in to replace a radiator. I was more surprised than anyone that she trusted me with a key but the strange thing is we are getting on much better now than ever before, now that we were just friends. She couldn't be there at the designated time herself seeing as how she had an Athletics meeting in Cork. So I took a few hours off work hoping nobody would notice my absence, to be honest not giving a shit, and met the tradesman on her behalf. On my way there that day I got a duplicate key cut in case of emergencies. And with that I was going to let myself in.

I had a feeling that Gráinne wasn't going to be there on this particular afternoon because I overheard her talking about going down to Galway for a 'cooler-booler' long weekend. Everything was 'cooler-booler' to her except me. She had no time for me at all, the bitch. And Francesca would still be queuing for treatment in the Casualty department of the Mater unless the health service in this country had dramatically improved all of a sudden.

The flat was spotless as usual I noticed on my entry, on account of the mice. Because they had a problem with mice, they kept it very clean. Personally I had no objection to mice as long as they didn't abuse a person's hospitality by multiplying and running riot all over the place. Only in extreme circumstances like, for example, a plague would I use poison or traps.

There were piles of Gráinne's medical textbooks on the floor. In my opinion, there's no way a doctor can learn all of them off by heart so it makes you wonder if they know what they're on about half the time. I fuckin' hate doctors. Apart from that there wasn't a thing out of place in the living room except for a thick black notebook, A4 hardback, lying on the table, with Francesca Kelly's name on the front in exotic script. As a matter of fact I thought her writing was atrocious, unreadable altogether, but you couldn't tell her that. People take criticism of their own handwriting very badly. I put the book back down because it was of no interest to me whatsoever. The course she was doing sounded like a load of rubbish with very little chance of a job at the end of it. I would have preferred if she worked in the post office or did something practical like that.

Getting bored, I wandered into her bedroom. Would you believe it, in all the time I was officially going out with her I had never actually stayed overnight in that room? She always had an excuse. Grainne who shared the room would object. 'I don't believe in sex before marriage.' 'I hate you.' I slept on the couch which converted into a bed once in the whole year I'd known her and that was during the big freeze last February when all traffic and all life, plant and animal, came to a complete standstill.

There was a plastic bag on the floor which upon closer inspection proved to contain a pair of tights and two or three pairs of soiled knickers. I picked up a pair and pressed them against my face, inhaling deeply.

I remember going to the hot press at home once to get a towel, it must have been when I was about fifteen when suddenly I stopped short. A pair of my mother's frillies, a light blue pair, brushed against my hand. I fingered the soft material unsure of my motivation. Blushing furiously, despite the fact that there was nobody else in the house at the time, and my legs literally trembling, I lifted them out of the press and rubbed them lightly on my face. I then rolled them into a ball and placed them inside my own underpants, my cock immediately jumping to attention as if to say 'What the hell's going on here?' I walked around the house in that state for about an hour before putting them back in the airing cupboard, vowing on my knees never to do anything like that again.

And here I was years later pulling myself off into a pair of my girlfriend's dirty knickers. Once I started, there was no way I could stop myself. My dignity was one untamed bucking horse that threw me to the ground and bolted. Of course the second it was over I felt like a sick pervert having instantly forgotten the intense satisfaction of just moments ago. Ashamed and tired of myself, I put the panties back in the bag.

Feeling a bit peckish after that, I went into the kitchen which was extremely cramped and made myself a tomato sandwich. That's all there was in the fridge, bread and bloody tomatoes. The girls' solution to the rodent invasion was to starve them out of the house, unfortunately starving themselves in the process. I put the kettle on and re-entered the living room, taking a pew at the table.

There was an ESB bill marking a page in Francesca's notebook. Honest to God, I opened it up at that page purely to inspect the bill which was for £12.67. I could see at a glance that the book was some sort of diary. I didn't know Francesca kept a diary, but I managed to restrain myself from reading the contents. Diaries are private. I wouldn't want somebody reading my diary. If I kept one. Although I have to say the thing was lying there open like an invitation. I felt obliged to read it.

About two years ago, I remember I got a postcard from France. The boys were on a school trip which I wasn't allowed to go on and Balls sent me a card with a pair of tits on the front and some terrible comments on the back about him wanting to have sex on the boat with Mrs McCabe, the science teacher, some chance, and about how much they were all drinking, Balls knowing full well that my mother would read it. She had no business reading it but she did. 'I have the right to see everything that comes into this home,' she cried. 'Youse'll all go to hell!' she added somewhat unnecessarily.

An hour later, there was still no sign of Francesca. What was keeping her at all? My fingers were getting sore with all the drumming. Ah fuck it, I'll read it, I thought, sure aren't we practically man and wife?

She had obviously been working on it that morning because the last entry was for Tuesday, 25 October, in other words, yesterday. Just as I thought, there was nothing too startling in that particular entry. No major revelations. You know, Francesca doesn't have a great imagination. It was mainly boring old nonsense about her forthcoming assessments but on account of the fact that I was breaking and entering and perusing her mind illicitly, I found it tremendously exciting all the same.

I had no choice but to move over to the couch seeing as how I was going weak at the knees. I knew it was very wrong. Very. On a par with flashing, I'd say, but I couldn't help it. Although, in some ways, I think it should be compulsory to read the innermost thoughts of your nearest and dearest. You'd learn an awful lot more about them that way. You'd understand them better. What makes them tick? What are their likes and dislikes? What are their fears and fantasies? Because they're never going to tell you out straight. 'There's no need to move in together, here's my diary for the last two years. Read it at your lesiure and get back to me if you think you can cope.'

I would say what I did then, which is a form of mental rape, is probably the worst thing I've ever done, worse than stealing from the shop, even worse than battering that fella in the park last summer with Geoghegan. I was, to put it mildly, a low-down dirty bastard, hotflushed with guilt, and me sliding around like Bambi on an adrenalin slick. It reminded me of the time Balls's mother caught me and him with porn mags above in his bedroom. We were sitting up in the twin beds, pretending to be reading football annuals but when she bent down to kiss him goodnight she caught sight of the dirty pictures concealed beneath. Ever since then I pictured guilt and shame as the pair of curly blond Dutch footballing twins, the Van der Kerkhof brothers.

I skimmed through the book at random. My first official port of call was America in August because I was curious about that time in Francesca's life. I really just flicked through it because most of the stuff was quite mundane, mostly about her working in the restaurant in Cape Cod and the people she met and the places she went. To be fair she'd told me a lot of that already. There was the bit about her appearing in the local newspaper, a full-page photo and all, but I'd seen the clipping. My suspicions about her behaviour in America were by and large put to bed. Mind you there was hardly any mention of me at all. It would have been nice to read, 'God I miss Patrick terribly.' That

I have to say was a bit disappointing but at least she didn't get off with anybody else.

I decided to go even further back in time and find out what went through her head on the first night we met. What were her first impressions of me? But unfortunately the records didn't go back that far. The details of that momentous occasion must have been entered in last year's diary. I'd have a look for it later if I had time before she arrived back. No, you see, she only started this notebook on New Year's Day 1983. Oh brilliant, I thought, her opinion of New Year's Eve, that was a fucking deadly night. The night we went down to Killeeny and drank the place dry.

3

Francesca's Diary

Thursday, 1 January 1983

I really don't know where to start. It is very very difficult for me to write this down. It's like writing an SOS with frostbitten fingers. I feel as if I'm preparing the closing speech for the defendant on the Day of Judgement. I mean, what if someone finds the diary? Mam certainly would never speak to me again. (Maybe I should photocopy it and send it to her.) As for Patrick, all I can say is, God forbid. If anybody is reading this, please stop now.

But I must persevere while the memory is still fresh. What's the point of keeping an account of your life if you leave out the juicy bits no matter how shameful or despicable they may be? Oh well, here goes.

Patrick and Xavier came down to Killeeny for the weekend. Gráinne was supposed to stay on but rang at the last minute to say she was going to a party in Dublin. If only she'd been here, none of the following would have happened. My soul would not be a lobster dangling over a boiling pot. We had been planning the weekend for ages. I think Patrick saw it as his big opportunity. Needless to say, Mam wasn't at home. She had gone to England to visit Auntie Nora in Croydon.

I met P and X at the bus stop at seven thirty p.m. Xavier ran towards me in slow-motion and swept me up off the ground. It was like a scene from a war film, me waiting chastely to welcome the returning hero. Patrick of course was furious and scowled at me as if I'd encouraged Xavier to do it just to spite him.

I had to help Jimmy in the pub until closing time. The two boys didn't mind at all. They were as happy as Larry propping up the bar. Although it was New Year's Eve it wasn't very busy. The business was going downhill rapidly and it was really just some of the older crowd who remained. I keep telling Mam to sell but she won't listen. She's convinced herself that I'll come back with some chrome and do food at lunchtimes and, with my new media skills, record wedding videos at the weekends. Unfortunately there was a brand-new disco bar down the road, Reflections, which catered for the younger people. That's where we were supposed to be going later on.

I finally ejected the stragglers at about one thirty a.m. Poor old Enda Keane who was usually the last to leave had died in November. Nobody had told me. He had been dead in his house for a week before the body was discovered by a burglar.

We didn't even ring in the New Year. It struck me that a lot of the customers weren't exactly looking forward to another year and were glad to have missed the chimes. I was looking forward to a new year but it wasn't this one.

We stayed on drinking after I locked up. It was too late for Reflections. Nobody complained. We were all quite drunk but Patrick was absolutely stocious. I had never seen him so incoherent. I shouldn't have been surprised because he had tried every single drink in the bar, every spirit, liqueur and digestif. After a while he fell asleep and slipped off the stool on to the floor. Slightly alarmed, I shook him and slapped him and shouted at him. I poured water on his face but he just would not wake up. Xavier thought it was hilarious and assured me that he'd seen him in worse states. Although he was unconscious he did have a big grin so I suppose it couldn't have been that serious.

But then he got sick all over his clothes. It was disgusting. I cleaned him up as best as I could and with a tremendous effort Xavier and I dragged him up to bed.

Neither of us were in any way tired so we retraced our steps on tiptoes to the bar and stayed up talking.

We chatted for ages and ages about absolutely everything. College, politics, religion, philosophy, life and death, nature/nurture, the concentration span of fish, *Battleship Potemkin*, everything. Our voices echoed and reechoed around the otherwise empty room. It was like as if the conversation had become an entity in itself and in a death-defying attempt to preserve itself for posterity multiplied and went forth. At least that's what I thought at the time, admittedly under the influence of drink and Aristotle O'Reilly beside me. We even talked about that i.e., where do conversations go? What a pity you can't save them and keep them like books or tapes! I cried for each moment as it passed. X came up with some amazing theories. He claimed that speech, and even thought, travels indefinitely through time and space, like light waves, affecting everyone who comes in contact with them. He explained *déjà vu* although I can't for the life of me remember what he said. And he reckoned that we would all live for ever if only we could keep our bellybuttons clean.

They say 'Sticks and stones will break your bones but words will never hurt you.' Well that's just wrong. They hurt and they heal. Language is the most offensive weapon known to man. Or at least the misuse and abuse of language is. Inarticulacy is more dangerous than a hangman's noose.

The ability to express yourself, on the other hand, to communicate with a permutation of primitive sounds is surely the greatest gift God has given us, well some of us at any rate. (I envied Mick King so much in the final of the *Irish Times* debate.) Writing is for dummies. A poor relation of spontaneity. All writing is a lie, an attempt to make sense out of chaos. It's just lies. Lies, lies, lies. Lucid, logical, lies, written ponderously in the cold light of day. Lies illuminated and illustrated in the elaborate style of the medieval monks. I thank God, profoundly and profusely, alliteratively, floridly, on bended knees for the relief writing provides for my arid tongue.

I could never imagine having such a chat with the lovely Patrick.

Silence descended on us like the Holy Spirit and blessed us both. All we could hear was the faint humming of the ice-machine. I felt blissfully happy but at the same time dizzy and disloyal.

We kissed. Well X kissed me but I didn't resist. Sitting face to face on bar stools he reached over and placed his hand on the back of my head. He told me that I'd lovely hair and kissed me tenderly on the lips. He stood up, his high chair falling backwards on to the floor with a crash, and cupped my face, like a priest with a communion host, and proceeded to drain me of all strength. After a while we separated. He apologised. I couldn't speak.

Hand on heart, I was utterly ashamed but powerless to stop it happening. X broke the ice by fetching more drink. We laughed nervously, recklessly, unable and unwilling to imagine the consequences.

Immediately we resumed our flighty discourse, startling ourselves with our newly-fired imaginations, delighting in the discovery of novel concepts as if they were rare shells. He told me about the time he put a mouse in his mouth. I tried to cover my ears as he described the scene. I was in convulsions, choking with laughter. He was jumping from one subject to the next like a comedian losing a crowd. Anything to take our minds off what had passed between us. We were like a pair of formally-dressed frogs leaping together from one water-lily to another, soaring in time to a Strauss waltz, afraid to stop for fear of being turned back into posturing fakes. My knickers were frankly wet at this stage. I felt I was going to leak or melt if I didn't go to bed then so I said 'Goodnight' and stood up to go. He put one arm behind his back, bowed stiffly, took my hand in his other hand and licked it. A current ran all the way from my fingertips to my shoulder blade.

We floated to the door in the dark, hand in hand, trying to avoid tables and laughing deliriously. In the doorway, he hugged me and stroked my hair. (He seemed to be obsessed with my hair.) We kissed again, more passionately this time, moving like, God forgive me, like tango dancers with Parkinson's, towards the seating by the wall. We half-sat half-lay on the bench, the coarse stuffing bursting up through the black leather-look lining. X opened the buttons on my shirt admitting a draught of air which momentarily cooled me down. In that instant, I forgot where I was. I was suddenly six years old on a makeshift raft in the stream behind the house. The image, however, was fleeting as X summoned me back to the present by undoing my bra and massaging my breasts. I was sprawled all over him like a set of Uillean pipes, moaning, I'm sure just like them too and bucking like the guy in *One Flew Over the Cuckoo's Nest* in electric-shock therapy. He opened the button on my jeans and unzipped me. My heart insisted on being heard. 'Let me out.' My brain expanded to accommodate immigrant sensations. Bang, bang, bang. My heart again. 'Let me out.' I acted deaf to its pleas and ripped his clothes off, leaving only his neckerchief (yes) and his socks. His chest was skinny and hairless. A washboard, I played like a Cajun novice. He peeled off my trousers and then his own and pushed me down on to the seat. My freed legs shuddered uncontrollably as X clambered on top of me. In anticipation of a stabbing pain, a prod, I shouted 'Noooooooooooooooooooo!', certain I'd wake Patrick. 'No, no, no Xavier, no we can't,' I whispered at breaking point. 'We can't.' 'I know,' he said, hovering above me, 'I know.' I glanced down to see his penis pointing at me, parallel to his body like a missile on an aircraft's undercarriage. 'What will we do?' My entire body felt as if it had been turned inside out, every square inch raw and alive to the slightest touch. My mother, the ghost of my father, Patrick and the whole class could have entered the room and I don't think I would have noticed them. Xavier's last words before we made love were, 'I've always wanted to do this with you, Francesca.'

Friday, 2 January 1983

I woke up in Mam's bed with a start after one of those dreams in which you're in a car that hurtles over a cliff. I was immediately aware that I'd fallen headlong into a huge crater where my self-respect used to lie. My head was swollen and heavy like a wet football. Vodka and crushing guilt, a combination deadlier than poitin or Parazone. It was only about eight o'clock but I had to get up and face the day.

It suddenly dawned on me that God *is* the day and the day *is* God. And the devil is none other than the night. Omnipotent and ubiquitous as God is, I could not hide from him. I was at his mercy. And I couldn't skirt around Patrick either. Although knowing the lads I guessed that they wouldn't surface until at least midday. The bus for Dublin left at six fifteen p.m. Thankfully Patrick had to be back at work for the January Sales but that would leave a period of six hours to kill.

On my way to the bathroom, I looked into my bedroom where we had put Patrick to bed. He was nowhere to be seen. Oh my God, I initially thought, gobsmacked, he must have seen myself and Xavier last night. In his state, he could have jumped into a lake or anything. I was absolutely terrified. Standing on the threshold of a nervous breakdown, I was surprised to hear the sound of the front door closing followed by footsteps on the staircase. It was unmistakably Patrick. I dashed into the bathroom to defer the inevitable and splash some rationality on my face. I looked in the mirror and gasped in horror at the sight that confronted me. Lovebites ringed my neck like a steel torque. I became quite frantic. Patrick stood outside the door and called my name.

'Francesca?' he enquired.

'Yes?' I hesitated.

'Do you want a fry up?' I couldn't believe my luck. He had gone out to get rashers and sausages and eggs. 'There were no eggs,' he slurred still drunk, 'can't have breakfast without eggs. No shops open. Stole them off the hens.'

Fuck, I breathed relieved, turning on the tap. 'What did you say?' 'Yes,' I managed weakly, 'I'd love a fry up.'

God, the lovebites were so big I thought he'd be able to see them through the frosted glass. I didn't want breakfast. In fact I didn't want to eat for at least a week. The very thought of food revolted me. My own behaviour repelled me too. I said yes just so as he'd clear off to the kitchen. Patrick was always happiest when he was eating. He wouldn't notice anything amiss as long as his mouth was full.

As soon as I heard the rashers sizzling in the pan, I sprinted back to my mother's bedroom, convinced that Patrick would poke his head out to catch a glimpse of me in my nightdress.

In haste, I put on one of my mother's Rayon polo-necks which just about covered the evidence. Though my neck was somewhat restricted I was able to breathe normally again.

It was one of the longest days of my life. I blushed and

stammered every time I opened my mouth. To make matters worse, Patrick was in unusually good humour and was very pleased with his matutinal gesture. Breaking and entering Lanigan's henhouse at approximately half seven on New Year's Day and stealing about forty eggs did wonders for his personality.

I don't know which was better/worse, losing my virginity or opening up my mind to Xavier. I mean, I regretted everything that happened, all that incredible joy, but it was right and proper at the time. Wasn't it? It was practically preordained.

Xavier didn't look at me once during the day. He sat legs crossed, smoking, listening to the radio. I wasn't expecting him to go down on his knees and ask me to marry him but some sort of acknowledgement of my presence would have sufficed. It's not as if I thought for as much as a second that we were on the cusp of something great and meaningful, but a wink, a conspiratorial nod, a reassuring smile or any signal at all that showed a bit of concern, would have been a help in the circumstances. I have no doubt that in the wan winter light, sober and in the dock of our Lord, he must have felt equally sickened by his actions. His betrayal in a way was even more profound than mine but it looked to me as if he wanted to forget the whole thing ever happened.

4

It goes without saying but if I hadn't been so fuckin' nosey and opened that fuckin' diary in the first place I wouldn't have been any the wiser about her and Balls. In fact, that story I had just read might never have been written, if you know what I mean. It could have been a figment of my imagination, that I, feeling guilty, somehow projected on to the page. It was a type of self-inflicted punishment for invading Francesca's privacy. I couldn't read on. The tears were stinging my eyes.

I felt like I'd just been informed that my whole family had died and that I was suffering from an incurable disease. The rug had been well and truly pulled from underneath me. No hostage or hermit in history knew what it was like to be so alone. No voiceless soul in the infinite void of hell knew what it was like to be so desolate. I sat numbly on the couch, veins and arteries hardening, tears backed up frozen to form needles of ice that sent jabs of pain back into my brain. I took the engagement ring out of my pocket and looked at it. I had never actually imagined it on Francesca's finger so I suppose should have known that it would never come to pass. Nothing ever happened to me that I hadn't already foreseen in vivid colour. I swallowed the ring whole. I don't know why, I just did, then I stood up and paced the room. I sat down again. I stood up. I walked. I sat. I stood. I sobbed.

There was a poster on the wall, a picture of a fuckin' monkey sitting on the toilet, a poster I always hated. It was fuckin' stupid so I ripped it down. There was steam billowing from the kitchen, the fuckin' kettle. My own blood was boiling too and thousands of thoughts were racing through my head as the full realisation of what they'd done struck me. I suppose thinking about it now I should have left the flat immediately, just fucked off and never contacted her again. I certainly didn't want to see her face. To be honest I didn't want to live, I wanted the ground to open up and swallow me. They might as well have mugged me and maimed me and left me for dead. For hours I waited, in agony. But it wasn't until just after eight o'clock that she showed up.

'Don't worry Francesca, you'll never see me again.' I was all ready with my big speech, when I heard the key in the door, like an important speaker clearing his throat. It was the wrong key. You'd think she'd know by now which key to use, the fuckin' bitch. She tried again. This time the lock opened. She closed the door behind her and came up the stairs humming, can you believe that?, humming a fucking Chris de Burgh song, 'Don't Pay the Ferryman' and I wouldn't have minded only it was one of my favourite songs. Without a care in the world. Halfway up the stairs, she stopped and went into the bathroom for what seemed like a century locking the door behind her even though as far as she knew there was nobody else in the house. She flushed the toilet, washed her hands, opened the door and climbed up the rest of the stairs and into the living room, her arm in a sling.

I was standing there in front of her ready to greet her. She jumped about four feet into the air and let out a little yelp, 'Patrick, it's you, you put my heart crossways!'

She could see behind me the steam-filled kitchen that was like a pressure cooker and hear the kettle rattling like a champion tap-dancer on the sideboard.

'Patrick, what's the matter?' She must have copped on there and then what the matter was. 'Oh!'

I couldn't remember any of the fifty million speeches I had mentally prepared. I couldn't even remember the English language or even a sound resembling human. I stared at her until it suddenly dawned on me that I never really liked her that much anyway.

'Patrick!'

Something exploded in my head at that moment, a nuclear bomb went off. Towers of common sense collapsed, a powerful wave of thick black smoke obliterated everything, words, thoughts, shapes, feelings, morals, and needless to say there were no survivors.

I lost control of the plane and went into a nose dive. I, I, I just thumped her square on the face as hard as I possibly could shattering that veneer of porcelain once and for all. Francesca with only one good arm to protect her lost her balance and fell backwards, hitting her head on the table, I swear to God. I think I killed her. I think I killed Francesca. As I hit her, a big cheer went up in the background. I thought at first that I'd imagined it but no it was a genuine cheer all right from the stadium across the road. Liam Brady, I later discovered, had just scored a second goal for Ireland to put us 2–0 up before half-time. By the way, Holland went on to win 3–2 with goals by Ruud Gullit and a young fella called Marco Van Basten.

5

'C'mon Mammy let's go home. The doctor says they're keeping him under observation for tonight and they'll let him out tomorrow.' Good thinking, Joe! He can read my mind sometimes so he can. And if she doesn't budge of her own accord, ask for assistance and have her removed forcibly. If there was a shopping trolley or something like that handy, that would be just the job. Go on Joe, whisk her away, before she gets up on top of me and gathers me into her arms. Jaysus I can smell her lipstick, and her hugging me, trying to hug the life back into me, transferring her own dwindling supply of energy into my sorry frame. Steady Joe, trusty Joe. Do as I ask!

A man who spent many years in South Africa, who now lives on his own on a small farm out in Mullahone, told me that burglars there used to strip naked and smear their entire bodies in oil so as they couldn't be caught. Well, do you know what?, lying here in the bed, greased in my own sweat, as I am, I feel like one of those fellas except in my case I'd like to be caught. I'd like to be tackled and brought to the ground. But as my mother and maybe Joe reach out to try and grab me as I fall, I keep slipping and sliding through their outstretched hands.

Like the daredevil stunt motorcyclist who put on a show in our town once, I had no safety net. I remember him well, the chancer. It was during a Chamber of Commerce festival – just after the barmen's race and before the street skittles – that he was due to perform his highwire act. We had all, young and old, been eagerly awaiting his arrival for weeks. The advance publicity led us to believe that he was as good as Evel Knievel, if not better. A thick length of wire had been strung up between a platform on one side of the street and a platform on the other side of the street, about twenty feet off the ground. And let me tell you by the way it was one of the widest streets in the world so there was plenty of room for manoeuvre.

A lot of people didn't believe he could do it, ride the bike across the wire, sceptics and begrudgers. Impromptu conferences were set up, in the preceding days, in doorways awash with spit. Like a crowd of Jesuits, the locals debated first of all whether or not the feat was physically possible and if so were the black arts involved? On the day, the whole town turned out, and lined the street ten deep, children on their fathers' shoulders. We waited for ages, growing restless, thinking like a ghost, or a UFO or an apparition of the Blessed Virgin Mary or an honest politician, he wouldn't show up at all. Anyway this fuckin' clown in a helmet eventually materialised on the platform to a great cheer. But we were all very disappointed when we saw the bike. It had no tyres, but big thick wheels with grooves that fitted perfectly over the wire, like you'd find on a pulley system, and stabilisers too, I'm not joking, a big paddle with two girls sitting on it, one either side of the rider. He rode over and back once and that was it. Everyone booed. It was like riding a fuckin' tricycle. I could have done better myself. There was a lynch mob going around for days looking for anybody in multicoloured leathers. Jaysus, he was lucky to get out of the town alive.

So I was under observation, it seems. Like some sort of insect. There was probably a giant microscope over the bed monitoring my every movement, my every thought.

Maybe with the aid of that instrument they'll be able to figure out where I went wrong. For the life of me, I can't. I'm baffled.

I wish I could list for you now in the presence of a solicitor, with a Bible in my hand and my hand on my heart a number of reasons and excuses that might go some way in explaining the damage I did.

'My mother was a bit mad, my father died when I was at a vulnerable age, I drank too much, your honour, I had a bad temper, a brick landed on my head and I haven't been the same since, I was scratched by a radioactive cat.'

If, for example, I was drunk when I hit Francesca, I'd be charged with manslaughter and serve maybe two or three years at the most. There'd be bonfires lit and bunting raised on my release and I'd be the toast of the town. You wouldn't believe the number of people around here, guilty of the most vicious assaults and brutal killings who not only avoid a lengthy prison sentence but get unbelievable sympathy and support on saying the magic words, 'I was drunk.' 'Oh well, that explains you hitting your wife seventy-five times with a bottle. If anything, I should fine you for wasting the court's time.'

But no, I wasn't drunk and to tell you the truth I don't have a single good excuse that stands out. I mean, to the best of my knowledge, I wasn't abused or beaten as a child. I wasn't held upside down like some fellas. But I will say this. I'm convinced that the incident wouldn't have occurred if my father were still alive. I would definitely be happier if he hadn't died when he did.

It's not as if we were even close in the last few years of his life. To be honest, we hardly ever spoke to each other – not I might add on account of any animosity between us. We were still on nodding terms. In fact our heads nearly fell off our shoulders with all the nodding that went on. You see, he was, number one, a very quiet and private man by nature, a chronically shy man from a family of more or less mutes and, number two, he had high blood pressure that was getting higher all the time. So the standard practice in our house towards the end was to leave Daddy alone and not bother him with idle chit-chat.

Don't get me wrong. I was not at all uncomfortable with this arrangement. As far as I was concerned he was no different to any other father in the town. They'd all important things on their minds and worried frowns to prove it. I used to think, 'I can't wait 'til I've lines on my forehead.'

When I was much younger, say up to the age of about twelve, he'd ask me about my homework and football and maybe quiz me about car number-plates. Or he might ask me to name the Donegal team, or the Louth team, which of course I'd have memorised from the sports pages of the Irish Press. *We'd have a bit of crack for about five or ten minutes a day. And I treasured those moments.*

But as time went on and I got older, his eyes would glaze over whenever I asked him a question and it didn't take long for me to realise that he wasn't listening to a word I said. Not out of malice or disinterest. No, I assure you. The poor man hardly knew I was there. I don't know if depression is contagious or not but somehow or other he contracted it. To make matters worse, he simultaneously began to adopt a type of religious mania. Some evenings, he'd spend hours on his knees, still in his uniform, head buried in the armchair, fingering rosary beads and miraculous medals and various prayers he received in the post.

Most evenings, though, he'd trudge in from work. When I say trudge, I never actually saw him trudge as such, I assume he trudged. But the strange thing is, he would just suddenly appear in the front room, like one of the lads from Star Trek, *smile vacantly at us all whether we were there or not and slump down in front of the television. He'd remain in that position and eat his tea mechanically from a tray, not really watching anything but away somewhere in his thoughts.*

By this time, he'd even stopped reading the newspapers and the detective novels he used to love. Valerie, the eldest, was the only one of us who could still ignite a spark in his eyes. She amused him no end. There was no doubt about it, she was the apple of his eye. The only time he got slightly annoyed with her was when she wrote Horslips and Thin Lizzy, her two favourite bands, all over her jeans with a pen. He hated to see a good pair of trousers destroyed. If he had been alive when she got pregnant, it would have shaken him to the core, even though every family in the town had at least one illegal child. After a couple of years of indignation and disgrace, my mother, surprisingly enough, got used to the idea of the baby. But there was always a coolness between herself and Val, a rift, and as a result we didn't see very much of my big sister in the recent past.

Daddy was the kind of man you didn't want to offend. No way. Me and Joe didn't need to be told twice not to curse or shout within earshot of the man. I'd say that he probably had a similar effect on layabouts and cornerboys up to no good on the main street. 'Garda Scully's on duty, boys,' they'd observe, lips not moving like a ventriloquist's, 'we'd better watch out.' Normally he wouldn't have to chase or collar a wrong-doer. One look from his big sad face was all it took to stop you in your tracks. You'd go down on your knees and examine your conscience, cry and apologise for things you didn't even do.

At home, he'd rarely offer advice or, say, help with the repair of fishing equipment but we didn't mind. It was good enough for us that he came home at a certain time and just sat there, taking up space, a huge reassuring presence. A bit like a statue of a Buddha. If we were in any doubt as to what to do or think or if we needed to know how to behave in any given situation, we only had to conjure up his image and concentrate.

And like I said before, he didn't have a bad word to say about anybody. What a lonely life he must have led since he arrived in Castlecock? No wonder, he had so few true friends.

Luckily for him, as he reached the end of the road, he finally mastered the art of no conversation whatsoever. No need for smalltalk or throw-away remarks. No complications or mis-understandings. And even in his darkest moods he gave us loads of pocket money, more than anybody else in the school.

I remember well the day he died. It was the day my voice broke. And the whole class was teasing me on account of the deep, bassy sound coming from my throat. I was treated like some sort of freak. I didn't know what was going on and decided that the best thing to do was to keep my trap shut.

Daddy drove back to his beloved Donegal that morning to attend the funeral of a boyhood friend. When he hadn't returned by nightfall, my mother got worried and called the guards. Of course, they loyally sprang into action.

'Right Mrs Scully, leave it to us.'

'The IRA have got him,' she repeated over and over again. It was a bit like, what you'd call, a mantra.

The guards in fairness must have contacted every garda station and RUC station between here and Donegal. Shortly after the investigation began, we heard reports all right of a car going over the end of the pier at a lonely place called Magheramore. Later, it was confirmed by a colleague and friend of the family, that the man in the driver's seat was indeed Daddy. And that he was indeed dead. The sarge said that he must have fallen asleep at the wheel. And the car must have rolled in. I have no reason to dispute that theory. For all I know the car could have had faulty brakes, it could have been swept away by a freak wave. He could have had a heart attack. He might have kept the engine running to keep warm as he dozed. His foot might have slipped on to the accelerator as he lurched forward in a dream. Either way, the man was drowned.

There was nothing he loved more than sitting in the car at an isolated spot, listening to the radio and staring out at the tempest that was more commonly known as the Atlantic Ocean. I could picture him clearly at his post on the coast like one of those huge stone figures that surround Easter Island. Believe me, I dwelled on that image for a very long time. What music was on the radio *at the time? What seannós lament accompanied his descent into the hungry, ruthless, I would have to say, implacable sea? Can somebody tell me that? For how long was he there, mesmerised by the ghostly shape of Tory Island in the distance, its people, willing subjects, under the spell of the sea? Was he afraid at all, as the wind whistled urgently at the door, trying the locks? 'Let me in, Garda Scully, I'm freezing.' 'No I don't trust you.' Of what exactly was he thinking as he drifted off to sleep for the last time? Which demonic power reeled him in? Did he calmly smile as he plunged to the seabed, unruffled by the fury of the waves, finally at peace? I don't know. Did he regret leaving us in the few moments before his lungs filled and his face bloated? I'd say he did. I know for a fact that he loved us in his own utterly, uncommunicative way.*

We were all very proud at the funeral. The whole town was out to pay their respects. A guard of honour made up of Gardai and Donegal footballers flanked both sides of the coffin as it left the church. There were plenty of dignitaries in attendance too, both local and national. Politicians pressed the flesh and prominent members of the GAA stood in semi-circles, looking important and well fed. The Tricolour as well as his cap had been placed on the coffin, as if Daddy had been a military hero or international statesman.

I'd only ever been to one funeral before. That was when I was six years old. A boy in my class died of a 'hole in the heart'. Somebody, Balls O'Reilly probably, misheard the condition and convinced the rest of us that he had in fact died of a 'hole in the head'. It all made sense. We suddenly remembered the patch of artificial skin on his forehead that covered up the hole. Somehow or other, the patch must have come loose, yeah, and some sort of poison must have seeped into his skull and killed him. We got a day off school for the boy's funeral. On the way to the graveyard I laughed at something another lad said. A big boy slapped me on the face and said 'That's no way to behave at a time like this.' I wasn't going to make the same mistake again. At my father's funeral, I wore the most solemn expression of all time.

You know in a way I think he was every bit as heroic as De Valera or General de Gaulle. If he had been French, I'm sure that he would have been a key figure in the Resistance and would have had a fondness for soft cheese. But the main difference between my father and historical figures of the twentieth century is that Daddy never got the opportunity to show what he was made of. He didn't complain of course because he was satisfied in the knowledge that he served the public and the State impartially to the best of his ability. General de Gaulle might have knocked the stuffing out of the Arabs but he never won an Ulster Championship medal against the sturdy men of Tyrone. Did he? No he did not.

Far be it from me to associate his death and my loss with my subsequent downfall. If I could have helped it, I wouldn't have done anything to offend his memory or sully his reputation. As it is, I know I've disappointed him greatly and all I can say is, 'Sorry, Daddy.'

6

Francesca's Diary

Wednesday, 26 October 1983

7

I was released from the hospital on Monday morning, a pitiful figure, my ribcage encased in plaster, and my head wrapped in bandages. I must have looked like one of those Indian swamis, frail and ancient and unintelligible. The swami or yogi or whatever the fuck you want to call him is of course a very wise man thanks to a lifetime of starvation diets, sleeplessness and all-round self-denial. And fair play to him. He's harming nobody. I would say that I was led from the hospital by my brother Joe a wiser man too as a result of a hiding, a hangover and having killed someone, namely my beautiful girlfriend Francesca. Sorry, Mrs Kelly.

Very few people of course know what it feels like to be a murderer. Most people would never want to know for that matter, and to be honest, I wouldn't recommend it. But I have to say, having blocked the whole incident out of my mind for the best part of four days, I felt surprisingly calm as I sat down in the passenger seat. I assumed that a person, after committing such a deed, would be twitching and stammering and scratching his head and gnawing his nails and headbutting the wall. Thanks to the swaddling and the sedatives, I couldn't shiver and stutter and behave erratically, even if I wanted to. You might think that your average killer would be in a blind panic by now, looking for cheap plastic surgery and false documents and a one-way ticket to New York. That didn't cross my mind at all. Although for all I knew, I could have already been given a new identity. And Miguel Donnelly could have got me a passport at short notice. But knowing him, he'd whip it from his little brother's spy kit and it wouldn't get me far. No, believe me, running away is the last thing you'd want to do.

I felt serene, a bit like the sound of a flute. That's the only way I can explain it. Hollow too, like a wind instrument. Whatever personality I had up to now had been dishonourably discharged. My flesh had fallen away. I might as well have been both disembowelled and lobotomised. Numb, I suppose. In shock. A zombie. A cool breeze gusted through the empty vessel I had become.

'What's so funny?' says Joe.

I must have been smiling. A condescending smile, I'd say it was, like you'd find on one of those Hari Krishnas you'd see from time to time banging drums on Grafton Street. I always hated them, the way they'd listen to you patiently as if you were a fool, and have an answer for everything. You couldn't beat sense into that shower. But now I had an idea of where they were coming from. I too had stepped on to a higher plane and freed myself from the concerns of lesser mortals. I felt superior to Joe, I suppose. Sorry for him almost. I was strangely ecstatic, raving.

Make no mistake, I am a murderer. I killed another human being with my own bare hands. Murderer, that's my official job description from now on. I'll be called back to the school some day to give careers advice, to discuss the pros and cons of my occupation.

Well boys, on the one hand, I have joined an exclusive band of thugs and outlaws. You could say that I am one of the elite. Nobody even knows about the accident yet as far as I can tell. Apart from me. I am the only person in the whole world who knows that Francesca Kelly is dead. I'm not exactly proud of that claim but can you just imagine how it feels to be sitting on top of such a secret, like the goose that laid the golden egg. I am as powerful as an ESB station at half-time on All-Ireland Final day when the whole nation puts the kettle on. Superhuman, now that I am personally beyond responsibility for my actions, wiser now that I never have to think for myself again. There's no turning back the clock. My fate is no longer in my hands. Oh and I eliminated a foe and there's an awful lot of shit I'll never have to deal with again.

On the other hand, boys, I have committed the ultimate crime and am damned for the rest of this life and for all eternity too which is a long time by any stretch of the imagination. The SAS train hard as do astronauts but there's absolutely no preparation available for the never-ending assault course I've signed up for. You may well ask? Do I experience remorse, grief, regret at this time? Well, of course I do. In fact they are all emotions I know well. I am a friend of the family. You may be on nodding terms with their next-door neighbour, who goes by the name of self-pity.

So I'm not looking for remission or sympathy. I don't want a reluctant friend of my late father to stand up in court and give a glowing character reference to the jury. I don't want the oul' fuddy-duddy judge to be lenient. 'You're only a young fella; you play Gaelic football; your father was a guard; she was probably asking for it; you deserve a second chance.' No, I want the works. I want to be dragged from a black maria in handcuffs with my jumper over my head, I want the family and friends of the late Francesca Kelly and bystanders with nothing better to do to jeer and spit at me and throw tomatoes. And I don't want Francesca's mother to forgive me. I want her to curse my rotting soul and burn effigies of me. I don't know what to say about my own mother. I'm afraid, I can't think of that right now. I know I'll be the talk of the town but there's nothing I can do about that. Really, I can't feel anything at the moment. My heart is a lump of shit in my trouser leg. I don't exist any more.

'Nothing!'

'What?'

'Nothing's funny!'

'Are you all right?'

I started to cry. I wished that I could tell Joe, my own brother, Joe. Not that he'd understand my predicament but he wouldn't throw me out of the car and never speak to me again. No. He'd visit me regularly in jail, shuffling self-consciously from foot to foot, to bring me news of Mammy and a cake that I'd know right well by looking at it she hadn't baked at all. We shared secrets and even a bed for years, talking confidentially of penknives and 'gutties', canvas runners with little air vents on the side that you could wear under the covers without fear of getting smelly feet. We tickled each other's backs and sang snatches of the few songs we knew over and over again into the small hours.

Joe always looked up to me. Idolised me in fact. At school, he'd seek me out during breaks with his friends to play 'chase Patrick all over the playground'. They could never catch me on account of me being so fast but would go back to class exhausted and content, their spindly legs weak and glowing after the exertion. I protected him. Well to be honest there wasn't much protecting to do because Joe was well liked and rarely got into trouble. If anything, I might as well tell you, it was the other way around. He defused situations for me. But although I was a bit of a hot-head, we hardly ever rowed among ourselves. Apart from the time I nearly strangled him for prying into my files. That was one thing I couldn't stand. Nosey people.

Some places are sacrosanct and I believe that our Joe learnt that particular lesson on that occasion.

God, I used to be able to tell Joe anything, indeed I felt obliged to tell Joe everything but as we got older and our paths diverged we had less and less to say to each other. Of course there was no easy way for me to impart the information I had to offer. I didn't want to burden a priest in the confession box or God himself, never mind my only brother, with the enormity of my crime. It would kill him too.

Would it, as they say, mitigate the circumstances if I explained to him that I only hit her once, instinctively, under extreme provocation and that it was the first time in my life that I'd ever struck a woman full in the face? Would it? I felt like hitting her and hitting her hard many many times but always managed to restrain myself at the last moment, nearly always. I mean, Joe, it was just one thump. She was off-balance, her arm was in a sling, I didn't know she was going to keel over the way she did and smash her head open. I know now better than anyone that just one thump is one too many. A split-second is all it takes to score a goal and change the course of the game. But I didn't have the words at my disposal or indeed the energy to convert Joe around to my way of thinking.

The problem, as far as I can see, is that I ran out of words a long time ago. I simply ran out of things to say. All my stories and anecdotes and funny sayings and reminiscences seemed to go stale overnight. I didn't invest in a new set in time. Up to about the Leaving Cert, I thought I knew myself. I knew Castlecock. I knew the world was round. I knew Balls was my best friend. I knew that I was going to be a guard. There was nothing I didn't know.

But as soon as you leave school and leave your home town and leave your friends, everything changes. You're suddenly stripped of your certainties. You begin to think that your personality was never anything more than a Hoover bag full of fluff. All you knew was just oul' recycled rubbish. Your brain is just one big hard mass of overchewed Wrigley's spearmint gum. And that's all there is to it. Once your friends begin to sidle away to become individuals, looking back over their shoulders for approval, like babies learning to walk, you realise that you were what they wanted you to be, you were what you thought they wanted you to be, not what you yourself thought you were. If you know what I mean. I'm getting confused myself. You spend your whole life trying to belong, to impress the right people, who usually turn out to be the wrong people.

My father's father who died before I was born left Daddy an old wireless as some sort of a memento. It was one of the first of its kind in the country yet still in reasonably good working order. I asked my father if he'd give it to me and to my surprise he did. In fact he was delighted that I took such an interest in something to which he was so sentimentally attached. But the only reason I asked him for it in the first place was because Balls told me one time that he'd love an old wireless. When my father found out that I'd given it to him, he was heartbroken. By giving away a family heirloom, just like that, I realised that I was also giving away a part of my family, a part of me. I always said that I'd never donate my organs to science in the event of my demise, not after I heard what they get up to in medical school. But having said that I find that you give much much more away during your lifetime than you do after your death.

All hell breaks loose after the exams, it's dog eat dog. Best friends become rivals for jobs and college places and above all girls. Balls thinks nothing of stealing your girlfriend. Why is that? Was it just another conquest for him, another notch on his belt, was he just drunk and horny that night, or was it to punish me? Or is he just plain evil? Was it maybe to prove he's a better man than me? Is that what he was up to? Was he just merely obeying the laws of some cosmic imperative? Because if he was, I'd nearly forgive him for that. And Francesca gives him permission to have his wicked way with her. Until the end of time, I won't understand why. Why Francesca?

You all plunge right in at the deep end of a cold and bottomless pool and only the ones with the most rubbery skin and fuckin' gills have any chance of emerging with hope. Washed up and shrivelled, the rest of you flounder on the shore. Yes indeed folks, it's yet another long and laborious birth. Like an amoeba or some other single-celled organism from a place commonly known as the primordial swamp, you discover to your cost that you are out of your depth on dry land. You must relearn everything and you've nobody to turn to. How about that? There's nobody there with torches to guide you. Your parents are old and mad or better still, for them at least, dead. And what good was your education? It only served to confuse you further. A big bully in jackboots, he kicked the shit out of his arch-rival, imagination.

One evening, when I was ten years old, each boy in the class had to write a composition for homework on the subject of a car graveyard. There were plenty of scrapyards in the area and even fields full of old wrecks from which to draw inspiration. For some strange reason, unprompted by anyone, I decided to write the story from the point of view of an old car rusting among the weeds and debris, a noble grandfatherly Toyota Crown, its spirit unquenched, reminiscing fondly on its life from assembly plant to show-room to driveway, recalling various owners and accidents, cigarette burns on its upholstery, crack with other cars on the road, and reflecting on the comings and goings in the scrapyard since its retirement. I put everything I had into that essay and was very proud of it, very. I couldn't wait to present it to the teacher the next day. I wasn't trying to be clever but Master Lynch blew a fuse when he read it and awarded me exactly no marks out of a hundred for my efforts. 'Did I think I was some sort of smartarse?' Slap. 'Who said I could write from the point of view of a car?' Slap. 'Did he say I could?' Slap. 'No he didn't.' Slap. 'Did I ever hear a car talk?' Slap. 'Why couldn't I write about a car graveyard like everyone else?' Slap. Six of the best is what I got for my trouble. He grabbed a hold of my ear and wrenched me out of my seat and ridiculed me, humiliated me in front of the class, me speechless and my ears a-glowing. I came home crying my eyes out and told my mother what had happened. She asked me to show her the story. I did. She read it and agreed with the teacher that it was useless. And she sent me to bed without my tea for letting her down in public.

'Why are we stopped?'

'Ehh I've to do my driving test at twelve o'clock. No passengers allowed. I'll be back within an hour. Is that all right?'

'What? Yeah, no problem.'

'Are you sure you'll be able to manage because I can cancel it and do it some other time? It's just that I've been waiting five months . . .'

'I'll be grand. You go on ahead.'

'Right! You might as well get something to eat and I'll see you here at one o'clock on the button. Do you need some money?'

'No, no . . . well . . . I suppose . . . thanks.'

'Take the paper with you. Okay, see you in a while. Good luck!'

Joe handed me a fiver and a local paper that had been lying in the car and dropped me off outside a chip shop. A bit embarrassed by the timing of his test and by my unexpected tears, he couldn't wait to get away. That was another thing that Joe could do that I couldn't – drive a car. He had a provisional licence and all and the use of our mother's light blue Nissan Sunny. He drove it everywhere, to and from college in Dundalk every day, to the Mirage at the weekends, and sometimes to the seaside at Blackrock with his girlfriend on a Sunday. Fair play to him. Would you believe it, he's at least two inches taller than me now? Our Joe, he's shot up in the last few years.

I went inside and ordered a plate of chips. Jaysus, they gave me a huge portion. Whether they felt sorry for me or not I don't know. An unbelievably big portion of chips and all for under a pound. I picked at them and flicked through the paper, landing as if by fate on the court reports.

The defendant, a Mr Ernie McKevitt, also known as 'Nuts' removed Mr McGoldrick's glasses and flung them on the ground. He then jumped up and down on them until they smashed into smithereens . . . later punched Mr McGoldrick and called his girlfriend 'an old sow' according to the plaintiff . . . outside O'Hanlon's pub, there was a further disturbance witnessed by Garda O'Donnell . . . defendant denied shouting 'youse better watch out when Nuts is in town' . . . McKevitt pulled the wing-mirror off the plaintiff's car and threw it at the front windscreen causing it to break . . . when approached by Garda O'Donnell, defendant ran off . . . he stole a red Hiace van and tried to ram McGoldrick's car . . . caused damage to seven vehicles including a garda patrol car . . . drove through a shrubbery prepared by the tidy town's committee . . . before finally losing control of the vehicle and crashing through the display window of Carroll's Butchers . . . defendant apologised . . . in his defence he told the court that his wife had given birth to twins that morning . . . the celebrations got out of hand . . . he was the worse for wear . . . upon further questioning, defendant admitted that he had drunk about fifteen pints of beer and about ten or twelve vodkas . . . didn't like the way the plaintiff was looking at him in the pub . . . never met Mr McGoldrick and didn't have it in for him . . . sorry for any offence or injury he had caused . . . never been in trouble before . . . came from a good home . . . had a steady job as a plasterer . . . totally out of character . . . didn't know what came over him . . . agreed that it was unprovoked . . . The Judge acknowledged that he was a good provider but due to the serious nature of the charges had no choice but to sentence him to six months in jail.

When Joe arrived back to collect me, I could tell by the look on his face that he got the licence all right but in fairness to him he hid his pleasure on account of the state I was in. Me and Joe, we were cut from the same cloth but we were very different suits, if you know what I mean. I would have waved the document in his face if the roles were reversed.

It was as usual a wet and dreary day and the car windows soon steamed up. Between the mist and my bandages I couldn't see a thing. I was finding it hard to breathe too so I rolled down my window and stuck out my nose. There was a great smell of pig slurry in the air, fresh and full, which was something of a comfort to me. I inhaled it deeply until it filled my lungs and purified my mind, I savoured it so I did as it circulated inside me. I always loved the natural smell of pigshit, you could always depend on it around Castlecock.

I'll tell you one thing, my senses, keener than ever before, appreciated the stale familiarity of home. The dull wallpaper and the faded carpets seemed duller and more faded than ever before. The house I would say was surreally dull. It was as if the nozzle of my shower had been cleaned. I could see through the walls and under the carpets, and even into mouseholes. Time, my worthy opponent, slowed down all of a sudden and into the gaps leapt household sounds, the ticking of a clock, the creaks and groans of the floorboards, a tap dripping, the cord on a window-blind brushing against the glass, each one distinct and loud and, wouldn't you just know it, ominous.

Mammy ushered me to the couch and propped me up with cushions. Within seconds I was swamped in all the cushions and pillows we ever had. She must have borrowed more from the neighbours and made some too from patterns in the RTE guide while she fretted in my absence. I was regally ensconced. Plush wasn't the word.

Almost immediately, she fetched some scissors and tried to cut whatever bits of hair weren't matted beneath the bandage. I was too weak to protest. She fussed and footered for a while. At one stage, going down on all fours, I thought she was going to offer herself up as a footrest, as if to say, 'I'll stay here for as long as you need me Patrick.'

'Can I get anything for you. Do you want ice for your head?'

'No thanks.'

'Will you have a scone?'

'No I don't feel like eating.'

'A beetroot sandwich?'

'No honest to God, I'm not hungry. I had chips.'

'Nurse McNulty said she'd have a look at you later.'

'I'm fine.'

'We thought you were a goner for sure. Were you wearing your scapulars? I bet you weren't. Didn't I tell you to wear them. How is your memory? Any memory loss? Who am I?'

'You're Mammy.'

'Nurse McNulty advised me to look out for memory loss. That's a tell-tale sign.'

I think she was about to prepare a quiz for me when she was interrupted by the sound of the phone ringing, tinny and deafening, in the hall. Although we had the instrument for over two years, she still got tremendously excited every time it rang. I was alarmed for about a second until I remembered that I didn't really care.

'Now who could that be?' She responded to its beck and scurried out into the hall.

A few moments later, she scurried back in, a little breathless.

'Patrick it's for you, it's Mr Dunn, above in Dublin.' And she straightened her skirt as if he were actually at the door.

'It might be a promotion.'

Promotion, my arse. He probably just wants to know 'where the fuck are you Scully you were supposed to be here four hours ago?' He likely as not got the number from Balls in the flat, disturbing his lie-in.

'Scully?'

'What?'

'Don't what me? You know right well what this is all about.'

'I was in hospital for the weekend. I have to rest . . .'

'Don't give me that bullshit. I don't care if you were in Timbuctoo for the weekend. There's stock missing from the shop? Ehh? Ehh? What do you have to say about that?'

He paused, barely able to control his temper, to let that accusation sink in. But my head was fuzzy and I wasn't in the right frame of mind to deal with that sort of thing

'What's that got to do with me?'

'You tell me,' he exploded. 'Ehh? You cheeky . . . fu . . . ba . . . so and so! You tell me, laddie?'

'I don't know what you're talking about?'

'Do you think I'm stupid? Do you think I came down in the last shower? Ehh? Who else could have taken the stuff, ehh? You monkey?'

'How do you know it wasn't Kevin Egan or one of them?'

'You really are some chancer. Kevin Egan, I'll have you know, has been a loyal employee of mine for many years.

He told me that he saw you with his own two eyes filling your pockets with my stock. You have some nerve, you little fu . . . twerp.'

'Mr Dunn?'

'Don't talk over me. I'm on your case, laddie. There are two detectives from Store Street here at the moment looking through security tapes. Now I'm going to give you a chance to come clean and replace what you stole from me. Ehh? Not many employers would be as fair as me in that regard. So you better play ball, or you'll be a very sorry man. You little fucking fucker, you . . . you . . . you cunt. So what's it to be?'

'Fuck you Mr Dunn!' And I slammed down the phone. Little did he know that his own son Fintan was robbing him blind too. Served him right.

'Well, Patrick, good news?'

'Yeah, he's going in to have an operation next week and he wants me to take over.'

'What sort of an operation?'

The phone rang again, its bell reverberating shrilly around the hall, as Mammy tried to pamper me back on to the couch.

'Now who could that be? Joe, will you get it, pet. It's probably one of your friends.'

Joe who was on his way out shouted. 'It's the Gardai in Dublin. They're looking for Patrick.'

'Ohh! That could be the news we've been waiting for. Stay where you are, Paddy, I'll take the call.' And she more or less pushed me, fixed her hair, and bustled out to the phone.

'Hal-lo, this is Mrs Scully, Patrick's mother, speaking.'

'Good afternoon Mrs Scully, this is Garda Doug Cutlass here in Phibsboro Garda Station. I'm looking for a Patrick Scully, I believe he may be currently at that address.'

'Yes, what is it in connection with?'

'I'm afraid I'll have to speak to the man himself. Is he there?'

'Has he got the guards?'

'I'm sorry?'

'Has he been accepted or hasn't he? You can tell me, I'm his mother.'

'No, I'm still not following you, Mrs Scully.'

'Is this not about his application to join the force?'

'No I wouldn't know anything about that. Could you put him on, please?'

I sleepwalked to the phone, and could hardly hear my own voice when I spoke. 'Hello.'

'Patrick Scully?'

'Yes.'

'My name is Garda Doug Cutlass, I'm enquiring about the whereabouts of a missing person, a . . . Francesca Kelly. Do you know her at all?'

'Yes, I do.'

'That is, let me see, Francesca Kelly of Flat 4, 33 Longford Parade, Phibsboro in Dublin 7?'

'Yes.'

'Right. Her mother reported her missing this morning and thought maybe that she might be with you. She's not with you, is she?'

'No.'

'You are her boyfriend, is that correct, Patrick?'

'No, well, I mean yeah, she was but she broke it off last week.'

'I see, sorry to hear about that. Do you have any idea where she might be?'

'No.'

'She was supposed to show up at her mother's in Wicklow on Friday but there's been sight nor sound of her since. Do you have any idea at all where she might have gone? A friend's house, maybe? A college outing?'

'No. Have you tried her flat?'

'We did. There was no reply from her flat. When was the last time you saw her, Patrick?'

'Last Wednesday, I think.'

'Right. And did Francesca say or do anything out of the ordinary?'

'Is there anything the matter?'

'What do you mean?'

'I mean, is she all right?'

'She's probably fine. Why do you ask?'

'I'm just worried, that's all.'

'Is there a reason why she shouldn't be all right?'

'I don't know. Have you checked inside her flat?'

'Not yet. Should we?'

'I suppose so.'

I hung up. And opened the front door. My mother heard the click and made her way to the hall. Before she could open her mouth, the telephone rang again, the third time in quick succession. She patted her hair, licked her lips and lifted the handset.

'Hal-lo . . . ah hallo Sergeant Donegan!' She placed her hand over the mouthpiece, barely able to contain her excitement. 'Patrick, it's the sergeant.'

'Congratulations Laura! He's in.'

My mother shrieked with joy and, I do declare, leapt up and down on the floor. 'He'll be thrilled, just thrilled, I knew he'd do it, I knew it.'

I left the house and walked slowly, like a mummy, out towards the lake.

As I approached the lake, a puddle of golden syrup at twilight, who did I meet with a fishing rod and no fish coming up through the reeds – only the silhouette of Plunkett McKenna. Slightly alarmed by the image I cut, he gave me a wide berth.

'Well Plunkett?'

'Jaysus, it's you, what happened your face boy?'

'Aw I was just playing tumble-the-wildcat with our Joe and fell headlong into a clump of nettles. No luck no?'

'No, a couple a bream boy, that was about it. I threw them back in.'

Bream, he looked like a bream, a dirty oul' scrawny good-for-nothing flatfish. If I were a fish, I'd say I'd be a pike.

Plunkett McKenna, the last person I meet, imagine that, and he'd very little to do with my story.